Ship of Fuls

Ship of Fuls

James Krake

The following is a work of fiction produced from the imagination of the author. Any similarity to real persons or places is an accident. In no way should anything following be construed as medical, financial, or political advice. In no way may this text be construed as condoning or endorsing any illegal or harmful activities.

CONTENTS

CONTENTS

To Win The War

Marcus sat beneath the shadow of a gas giant, surrounded by metal skulls. He held a gun in his hands, ripped from the arm of one of the enemy war machines. The thing fired needles, or maybe they were micro-flechettes. From the spare magazine, he couldn't tell if they were a metal alloy or some kind of nano-material. The munitions cracked between his trembling fingers, but he had seen them pierce body armor. The man inside had burst into blood like a balloon.

Marcus squeezed his hand into a fist as tight as he could, until it felt like he would rip the environmental suit. When the shakes subsided, he put his mind back to the gun. It had no trigger that he could find. The firing mechanism was entirely digital, which explained why it had locked up under the assault of the attack scripts. They had been lucky the ship's defenses were out of date. Luckier than the dead Camrians strewn across the hangar bay. He tried not to look at his own handiwork.

Marcus felt only one step removed from the corpses as he

sat upon a collapsed bulkhead. He had been hit by bullets, tossed by explosions, and singed by fire; but, that hadn't been enough to put him in the ground. His armor sat heavy upon him, and he couldn't even take off his helmet. The internal systems warned of unidentified neurotoxins in the air, which left him rebreathing his own sweat.

Ranger Levy whooped as he got the flood lights to power on. Beams of artificial daylight blasted across the battlefield, painting the walls with shadows. He leapt down from the control booth, landing on the smoking ruin of some kind of fighter plane. Marcus didn't know whether it was a manned craft, or just an elaborate way of launching missiles. What he did know was that something inside it had caught fire, and the smoke ate the paint from Levy's armor. His comrade had to scrape it off as he said, "And here I was starting to think the locals were blind."

Marcus tossed the gun back to the metal goliath he had taken it from. The steel face grimaced back at him. "Would have been easier for us had they been."

"We're never that lucky though, are we? Come on, we have to keep moving." Levy said, turning his head up. The charge field overhead kept crackling and flickering, letting the moon's hydrocarbon atmosphere leak in. Eventually, the fuel to air mixture would be just right and the whole place would explode. Not even corpses would be left.

Marcus turned his head up too. He could only see the planet by how he couldn't see the stars. The huge mass had seemed so important on the star charts, and he still couldn't see it. The local star may as well have not existed. None of its light reached so far out.

The burning trails of ships crossed the void like shooting stars. The Camrians had given up on the moon, but he didn't let himself hope that they were retreating. There was no way they were that lucky. It would be some other battlefield, some other star, some other year. For once though, Marcus knew where that would be. "Does it feel like we're getting to the end of the war?"

Levy shrugged. "We have to be, by now. Earth has been working to break the stasis for centuries now. Got that Manhattan Project Two coming along."

"Weren't we that project?"

"Project Three then. Pretty soon Earth is going to retaliate and put an end to the war. We just have to keep buying them time."

"We've been buying them time for centuries."

Levy slapped him in the shoulder. "Means we're good at it. We're experts. The best there is at all things warfare. Now come on. We've got ships to catch. I'm thinking the old boarding rocket special. What about you?"

"Levy, those ships have nuclear missiles headed for Earth. How many of us are even left? Do we have enough?"

Levy turned his head up, counted the ships, and said, "Enough for one each, I reckon. Won't be our first time. Good thing we've had practice at it." The other Ranger laughed.

Marcus sighed and got to his feet. He felt heavy despite the low gravity. For a moment, he was reminded of the myth of Atlas holding up the heavens. The ancients could never of known how weighty the heavens were with the trillions of people needing protection. "I guess we don't have much of a choice."

"You could always run away. Get yourself a girl, ditch the armor, settle down..."

Marcus put his hand on Levy's shoulder. "You know that's not an option for us," he said, and headed off to the next in a long line of battlefields.

Man's Oldest Weapon

The First Day

Marcus sat with his back straight and his face set to hide that he couldn't read the menu. It wouldn't do for Earth's representative to be laughed at. It was bad enough that he was the bearer of a peace that nobody wanted.

He knew what each individual word meant, but the people of Athens Station seemed to put them together randomly. The one option labeled as their best seller was an Exo Burger, but the ingredients were nothing at all like he remembered back on Earth. It had an avocado patty, his choice of ketchup or mustard buns, bean paste, and fried cheese toppings. "Is this good?" he asked the girl waiting on him.

She was young and had a cute pout to her lips that made it easy for Marcus to imagine how lucrative the tips were. Before she could answer, the girl had to collect herself and put her attention on his face, rather than his scarred battle armor.

"Yes, sir. It's our best seller after all. The cheese is imported from Scythia."

"Sounds good then." He smiled and returned the menu.

The girl drummed her fingers on the tablet for a moment. She shuffled her feet and glanced at the kitchen before asking, "So, you Rangers eat normal food?"

Marcus nearly scoffed at the idea that whatever he had just ordered was normal. "It's a lot better than the crap stored in the suit, that's for sure."

The two of them may as well have been at the edge of the universe, the war a distant thing. She was dressed modestly, but not so much as to imply she was living on rations and hand-me-downs. Her makeup glittered like circuitry, and he could only imagine what social media trends were like so far on the edge of human space. Fashion was a fluctuation, a form of communication, and Athens Station was so far out that the subtle threads of societal trends had frayed. Some things got lost, others survived longer than they should have.

"I suppose the legends were exaggerated a bit then."

"They always are," he said, and she vanished to the kitchen. Alone outside the diner, he leaned back in the chair and tried to relax. The seat was hollow and flimsy, but Athens Station only had half a G of spin, so even in his suit he wasn't afraid it would break. The orbiting construct belonged to a more recent design ethos, one which treated the place like a terrarium and filled the deck with plants. They were hypoallergenic to an extreme. No pollen, no seeds, nothing that could stress the life support systems. That meant no flowers, but the promenade was at least green as it basked in the light of electrical storms off the gas giant. The local star, Fuls, was a nominal flicker in the distance.

Athens Station had a rural feel to it, translated to the scale of spaceships. Distance was measured to adjacent planets rather than cities, but the presence of the exo mine nearly made the veritable truck stop more important. Fuel for faster than light travel was rare enough that corporations would put the money into building a port and terraforming a planet less hospitable than Venus had been. That was the beauty of Athens Station, it was out of the way, out of sight, out of mind.

He hadn't been able to take his armor off yet.

Across from him, dozens of people strolled through the park, and those that saw him either gawked or gave a salute. Some did both, but they were generally the novice crew members. What they saw was his armor, his rank, nothing more. No one bothered him. Eventually, the waitress returned with his food. It did indeed look like a burger, even if the colors were all wrong. There was a certain sponginess to it that he could feel though his suit's gloves, the kind of texture that came from using gene-editing to flavor yeast, or algae, or whatever it was they had settled on for food in this particular station, in this particular stellar system, in this particular century.

Taking a bite out of it reminded him of eating a marshmallow, except with a jelly filling. There was some kind of fatty oil to it with just a hint of spice. Whether it was oozing out of the avocado patty, which was more like a green pancake, or the bean paste he couldn't be sure. The second bite tasted better than the first, and he washed it down with a cola. That at least hadn't changed in the last thousand years.

"Are you Ranger Marcus Maximus?"

A thin and gangly man stood on the walking path beside Marcus. He had a spindly nature developed from growing up with sub-earth gravity. Marcus could remember a time where such growth patterns would have been treated as a mutation, a genetic aberration. He knew it was nothing special. It was nothing at all compared to the deviations populating the Alliance of Colonies. The man's uniform was the same as Marcus remembered from a millennia back. Earth Nations' midnight blue, space camo as everyone in boot camp had called it.

"I am. I'm also eating," Marcus said, lifting up his exo burger. He took another bite as the man composed himself and approached.

If he doesn't take the hint, the world had better be ending.

"Sir, I am Corporal Hadria, here on behalf of Captain Regulus... Captain of the *Demos*, acting commander of Athens Station." Hadria's voice fluctuated wildly as he spoke. He nearly barked out the 'sir', stumbled over his own name, and eventually realized he was supposed to be speaking for only the two of them to hear. Half the diner had already turned to stare at him.

Marcus shook his head. "Sit down, Corporal. You're making a scene. Sit down and take a breath. When you can, tell me what the captain wants with me." He imagined the forms, the bureaucracy, or perhaps another press conference. Journalists thought twice about yelling at a soldier in full combat suit.

The crewman faltered, but stayed standing. "I'm afraid, sir, that we don't have the time. It's Category Nine."

Marcus stopped with the burger almost to his lips. The

crewman wasn't smirking. There was no falter or deceit. Tension lined his neck and his hands were wringing together behind his back.

The generic threat scale went from zero to ten. Zero was for information only. Ten meant God had started the End of Days and the dead would rise from their graves for eternal war. That put Category Nine at a cozy "The world is ending."

"Oh... shit." Marcus sat there, eyes unfocused and mind working on it. Category Nine wasn't something to stop, it was something to avoid. He didn't have a ship to run away with though.

A nine. It just had to be a nine. I might be able to deal with an eight, but a nine?

Hadria let out his breath. He almost grinned at Marcus' shock. "Your presence has been requested on the *Demos*, sir. I am here to escort you through security."

Marcus shoved off the table and rose, carrying the burger in one hand and his helmet in the other. Hadria led the way to some kind of three-wheeled vehicle pod. As soon as the two sat down in it, the doors scissored shut and electric motors hummed. They sped about the ring of Athens Station lightwise rather than heavywise, as the old engineers called the centripetal effects. They also sank to lower levels, slipping from one deck to the next. The perceived gravity climbed up, fighting with coriolis forces, which had never sat well with Marcus' stomach. A looming Cat-Nine meant physical comfort was so far down the list of priorities it didn't even deserve discussion.

Hadria kept tapping his foot and chewing his nail as he

stared at the vehicle's navigation console. "I thought the war was over? Why are we under attack?"

War doesn't end.

"Who told you that?" Marcus asked, licking a bit of juice off his gloved fingers. He couldn't quite tell if his hand was trembling again. The adrenaline hadn't quite started yet. Just fear.

Hadria looked up at him and narrowed his eyes. "You did, didn't you? When you arrived. I was there at the press release. You came out in front of the cameras and said so. I remember because you didn't take your helmet off. You came out and you said the peace accords had been signed. I remember how angry I was that Earth surrendered."

You should have just been glad the fighting was over.

Marcus shook his head and leaned back in the chair. "You've never left the station, have you?"

"Not since I arrived, sir."

"All you need to know is Earth surrendered, and the Alliance is going to take their time cleaning up the spoils."

Hadria's fist slammed into the vehicle's door. "Then why are they doing this? You don't get spoils from blowing up the entire station!"

Marcus didn't blink, he returned the crewman's gaze and said, "The why doesn't matter. That's the nature of the beast. Keep your head together and do what you must. That's all you can do." The peace accords had been signed, but information only moved as fast as light; far slower than travelers like him. How precisely the daisy chain of star hoppers had dropped the message he had no way to know. All that mattered was someone was attacking.

Marcus had to wait in front of a series of airlocks that sank through the floor of Athens Station, as though the ship beneath were in a hole. While Hadria scanned through all the protocols and inputted passwords, Marcus stood with his helmet on and arms crossed, staring out the view window like he might see the impending disaster. He could still remember when exterior windows were either smaller than his hand, or merely camera recreations.

Athens Station wasn't concerned about weak points or brittle failure. Athens Station had clear viewing windows three stories tall, like an enormous bubble over the spinning structure. He couldn't see the speckles of micro-meteorites trying to pop it. What he could see was the roiling blue clouds of the gas giant that Athens Station orbited, Mimir. Even at orbital distance, the swath of clouds nearly filled the entire view. Here and there, the storm cells were pierced and punctured by ships diving through the gravity well.

Has word already reached them? Are those just regular jumps or evacuations?

"Sir," Hadria said, just as the door cycled open and a blast of cool air gusted into the hall. "We can proceed."

"The captain is already on the escape ship?"

"More of a command station than an escape ship, sir. It was designed for transport to the inner planet, so it has all the station controls he could want. Evacuation orders will be sent out after the third successful scan on the target. May as well already be aboard. Watch your head though," Hadria said, and the two of them stepped into the airlock. The doors shut behind them, equalized pressure, and then allowed them to descend. At once, the smell hit him. Gone was the slight scent of life. The *Demos* already smelled like he was breathing through a week old environment suit. He could almost taste the recycled sweat.

Athens Station was a ring. There was no other way to simulate gravity than to spin. Small ships docked on the inner surface, sitting on the frame like insects while the government haulers clung to the outside like lampreys sucking power from the station. Going down into the ship felt like descending to safety, like a bunker, but the ships were the most exposed portion of the station.

The inside of the *Demos* was dark. The steel surfaces looked galvanized, but for all he knew it was some kind of fungal coating like self-repairing paint. Either way, the strips of LEDs shaped the halls into square corridors with the kind of disorienting, ambi-directional doors that non-civilian ships tended to have. The rooms had been connected however the space-dwelling architects had found it convenient, not how an Earthling would have done it.

Marcus was trying to orient himself to where the thrust vector would be, which wall would be the ultimate down, when the two of them stepped into the bridge. "Ranger, sir," a man said, snapping to a salute. He wore a pressed uniform and a glance at his chest showed his rank as commander, therefore the helmsman, but not a single badge of service beyond training.

Is everyone on this ship a cherry?

"At ease. This is your ship, not mine," Marcus said, putting up a hand.

"Yes, sir," the helmsman said, dropping the salute and grasping his hands behind his back. "Just five minutes ago, we completed our second scan of long-range A-Mov Space, and once again confirmed a mass approaching Athens Station." His voice was controlled, but the man had his spine so straight he was almost vibrating with the effort. For all he tried to look composed, he only showed the cracks.

Marcus stepped over to the central display table. Measurements and graphs glowed from within, attempting to turn mathematical abstraction into something presentable to the human eye. The red-highlighted object the helmsman pointed to looked like a flat disk, while every other ship in the local space had shape, bearing, identification, and a host of other data associated.

The graphical display wasn't showing the normal three spatial dimensions, but an abstraction of A-Mov Space, the faster than light dimension that wasn't. The math worked for higher dimensions, but to actually show it to humans required ditching the galactic polar axis. The Milky Way looked like a curved sheet with ships flying shortcuts between the stars. Everything in A-Mov still obeyed relativity, which meant the red disk wasn't actually a disk; it had simply been compressed that much by relativistic speed. It was coming in from deep, far deeper than what a gas giant like Mimir could slingshot at another star system. Something had given it an incredible speed boost down a much larger gravity well.

Well, someone is very pissed off with us.

He asked, "Did you sink a probe?"

"Yes, sir," the helmsman said. With a gesture, three blue dots appeared in the depths of the graph, plunging away from Athens Station. "The final scan to confirm will happen in half an hour."

Marcus listened with half his attention, thinking more about the raw kinetics he was being shown. He tried to puzzle out a solution and failed. Athens Station didn't have anything remotely strong enough to divert that. He hung his head. "I think you had better start the alarm now. This isn't a time for proper procedure. In a couple of hours, there isn't going to be an Athens Station anymore."

The people on the bridge didn't answer him. He could follow the entire chain of command purely from who was looking at whom. The gazes ended with the helmsman, who stared at the display. He was saved by one of the doors opening, and an older man stepping in. A low ranking officer announced, "Captain Regulus on the deck!" The crew snapped to attention and saluted. The captain didn't have the elongated features of space life like Hadria had, and the wrinkles gave him away as planet-born.

Marcus saluted out of habit, but from behind his helmet visor he tried to check everyone's ranks. The ship had only the bare essential crew. He didn't see any guards. No security detail. No armed force to speak of.

"At ease, Ranger," the captain said as he strode to the display table. "Doesn't feel right getting saluted by someone old enough to be my great-grandfather."

"Sounds like you've made a lot of jumps in your time, if I'd only be your great-grandfather," Marcus said, lowering his hand. The captain's rank insignia caught his eye, because it also denoted his home planet. "You were at the Gibraltar Gravity Falls?" If the captain was a veteran, that almost put Marcus at ease.

Captain Regulus grinned. "No time for that now." He turned to the helmsman. "Mr Seachnall, would you please give me the latest?"

The helmsman nodded and once again gestured at the displays. "That mass is approaching us through A-Mov Space at approximately Point-Nine-C. It's taking a deep approach and, given the observed linear compression, it can be surmised that it was launched from an Alliance-controlled black hole. Possibly as far away as five hundred light years from here."

"Where it came from doesn't matter, Sergei. Has the computer finished the damage calculations?" Captain Regulus asked.

Marcus snorted. "You need a computer for that?"

"Very funny, Space Ranger Maximus," the ship's systems responded. As per convention, the ship's AI was assuming a female personality. Something in the tone made him reflexively roll his eyes. "First order estimates are trivial; complete destruction. My analysis is needed to identify possible escape vectors."

"For after the relativistic bomb hits the storm clouds of Mimir and turns this half of orbital space into a radioactive death zone?"

"Precisely," the ship responded.

He shrugged. "Fair answer."

Captain Regulus stared across the holo-table at him. "Ranger, you're the expert military advisor, right? I know you came here to deliver the good news…" More than one person snorted at that. "But, is there anything we can do?"

"To stop it? Not a damned thing. Earth was doing some experiments with forced extraction to pull ships back into real-space, but that's not something you just have laying around. Sir, Athens Station is lost. I suggest you tell every warp-capable ship to dive into A-Mov space to avoid the blast and evacuate the rest as far away as possible. The opposite side of the gas giant might be safe. Behind a moon maybe."

Captain Regulus' shoulders slumped, some thread of hope snapping in him. "You're a veteran of a hundred battlefields, aren't you? You've been fighting the Alliance for as long as I've been alive. You don't have anything better to offer us?"

Marcus shook his head. "Sir, what exactly do you expect me to do? They threw a rock at us. I can't go shoot it down. It can't be negotiated with either. This just isn't that kind of problem. If it were an invasion fleet, I might be able to fight them off but you can't kill a rock. It's going to hit Mimir and it's going to blow up. All you can do is take shelter. I'm not here to work miracles, I'm here to be realistic. Sound the evacuation orders while there's still time."

Captain Regulus leaned down, spreading his hands to either side on the edge of the holo-display. He stared and his frown deepened as his knuckles went white. "Mia, do as he says. Contact the other captains and order the evacuation. Don't wait for the third scan."

"Roger, Captain," the ship responded, and the emergency alert began to broadcast throughout Athens Station. Every music player, advertisement display, and everything else that could generate sound simultaneously cut off and smothered Athens Station in a moment of silence. Then someone got on the address system and said, "Attention all residents. Please proceed immediately to your designated evacuation station. Athens Station will be destroyed in three hours."

No siren was needed after that. The station filled with screaming.

2

Irregular Boarding Procedure

The First Day

Marcus was seated on a bench in a forgotten corner of a forgotten hall. No one was screaming and running there. Nobody was desperately evacuating past him. For him, Athens Station was quiet, save for the repeated lurching whenever a ship broke off and dove. He could see them from where he sat, one ship after another running into A-Mov to escape the attack.

I could force my way onto one of them. Make my way to Scythia or somewhere farther. The destination probably doesn't matter. As long as I get to an Earth controlled planet, the worst that can happen to me is a slap on the wrists, then I can run to the other side of the galaxy. Put another thousand light years between me and the Alliance. Maybe I ditch the power armor and pass as a civilian?

"This is how the great Space Ranger from Earth is

spending his time? A side access viewing window?" The woman who had approached him was of Earth proportions with long brown hair and a sort of business casual outfit over an exposure suit. If he didn't think too hard about it, it nearly looked like stockings and gloves, but he could see the collar around her throat where a helmet would interface.

Now that's a woman who can make function look aesthetic.

The Space Ranger didn't let his gaze linger. His thoughts lingered on the idea of commandeering a ship, and what he would have to do to civilians like her to do that. "Why? Is there a better view somewhere else?" he asked, turning back to the view of Mimir. Ships shot towards it at full burn, their engines like fireworks in the night as they chased headlong down the gravity well. One of them had gone in too hot, the friction overpowered the ablation. That ship was a fiery scar across the storms of Mimir as however many lives burned away.

I wonder what those people are thinking? Dying by what? A rushed pilot? A congested flight path? Bad luck? Did they even make a wrong decision to deserve that?

Every moment he held himself there, another option of escape left. He could hear the repeating evacuation order echo through the steel hall, the sound just slightly muffled by the foliage of Athens Station. There was also the stampede of feet, the tremble of people piling into ships and escape pods. The noise of civilians turned refugees was all to Marcus' back, and the woman stood between him and it.

"My name is Felicity Lenz," she said, holding up a tablet to her chest and tapping on it. He could hear the click of her nails against the screen, the sharp jabbing against the glass. "I work for Mr Samaras."

Even when you're stuck on a station about to be blown to bits? Must be one hell of a good boss.

Marcus turned his head back to her. "I don't know what they told you about Space Rangers, Miz Felicity, but I don't get dossiers on the locals when I arrive. I barely get told who's in charge."

She glanced up at him, and had to brush some hair behind her ear. "Mr Samaras is the CEO of The Nebulae Company."

"Is that a capitalized 'The'?"

"This sector of The Nebulae Company at least. Every planet within ten light years relies on his fuel," she said.

And they put him here?

Marcus laughed and turned back to the gas giant. The storms, turbulent masses of natural power, kept breaking and spinning as ships plowed through the clouds. Budding cyclones grew across the surface in a beautiful cacophony. "And you're telling me he doesn't have his own ride out of here?"

"No. Mr Samaras will be on the *Demos* with you. His presence may be required as it pertains to the Fuls-Hades-I exo mine. I am his assistant and he asked that I make contact with you, Ranger Maximus," Felicity said.

He must think he can negotiate with the Alliance, swing his wallet around. Would I be a mercenary if I helped that? Would I survive it?

"Okay. Consider your contact to have been made," Marcus said, and he put his arms up across the back of the bench he sat on. He crossed his legs and leaned back, watching the last moments of the planet before him.

She tapped on her screen more, the clicks harder and sharper. Then she sighed. "May I ask what it is you're doing? Shouldn't you be helping in some way?"

"Absolutely not. I didn't design this station. I would only get in the way of the people actually qualified to help. I'm not a miracle worker, Miz Felicity. I am a soldier and an advisor. If the Alliance shows up with boots on the ground, then that's a problem I can deal with. I can shoot them. A giant rock is not the kind of problem I can shoot. So I am going to sit here and pay homage to a piece of nature we're about to destroy."

"We? Pretty sure it's the rebels that are going to destroy it, not us."

"Earth joined the Alliance as part of the peace accords."

"And yet they're throwing a rock at us."

He sighed. "I hope to God we never start another light-year war. It's like someone set a coal mine on fire. No matter what you snuff out, the embers are just waiting for fresh air."

"Well then. I'm glad to know our safety is in such capable hands. I believe we will be spending the next few weeks together, Ranger Maximus. Should you need any form of civilian assistance, I have been instructed to make myself of service to you. You may think of me as a company liaison."

He turned to look back at her. She was the closest thing to company he had, and for once she wasn't part of the war. Before she could turn, he said, "The ship isn't leaving yet. You might miss the last beauty this planet has to offer."

"I'm sorry, but I've lived on Athens Station for two years. I doubt I will see anything new just because it's about to explode. I'll see you on the ship," she said, and spun on her heels to march back to the ship access port.

Marcus had barely been on Athens Station for two weeks. He wasn't even certain he had fully circumvented the planet given the relative orbit and the planet's rotation. It largely looked like every other sub-fusion mass of hydrogen and ice the galaxy had to offer. Mimir had no exotic alien life to speak of, no forgotten relics of civilizations passed. It didn't even have an inhabited planet nearby. It would be centuries more before the neighboring planet Tiber, was transformed into something more than a frozen ball of radioactive iron.

He sat and watched the planet with the quiet interest of a man in the woods watching his campfire. It sparked and glowed, popped and sizzled, and soon the show would be over with nothing but ashes left. He stayed and watched until Mia contacted him to say they were ready for departure.

The ship was cold, with frost growing across the walls. The crew had dumped as much heat as possible from the ship and into the station, and it would be hell on the life support systems. The ship wouldn't like having half of its water freezing the utilities shut. The crew wouldn't like Alliance scavenger ships putting a hole through their hull as soon as they were spotted venting heat either. If any of them wanted to stay alive, they couldn't release any more heat than the asteroids.

Which was to say, almost none of it.

"Welcome back aboard, sir. There's an auxiliary acceleration pod for you," Helmsman Seachnall said as the bridge door cycled shut behind Marcus.

The pod in question– a glorified seat in a metal ball that helped keep high G forces from killing the occupant– sat recessed into the floor. Tracks like a cage held the G-pod in place atop bearings, and spin from Athens Station still kept all the pods oriented together. For the moment, everyone was able to look each other in the eyes like they were groundside. Later, they would face however the ship happened to be accelerating.

When he sank into it, the synthetic chair enveloped him. The gel adjusted, holding him at the bottom of the pod and yet supporting him in conjunction with the suit. He had plenty of space in front of himself, and could comfortably read a computer screen built into the pod. It only displayed a countdown to thrust. "Do we have a bearing, Seachnall?"

"Yes, we have a bearing. The question is do we have timing. Timing is what the computer is crunching right now. We have to match speed with the nuclear debris or even a casual scan will spot us. You were right, if you were wondering," Seachnall said as he sat down in the central pod of the bridge, the one that faced the main display. It was like a king's throne.

So why's the helmsman there, at a time like this? Where's Regulus?

Marcus looked around. There were a half dozen other people on the bridge, and a half dozen empty pods. "Where's the captain?"

"Politicking sir," Seachnall responded, frowning and

typing in some commands to his interface. Marcus' display updated, and the utility connections between the *Demos* and Athens Station appeared. Heat, water, electricity, oxygen, all the essentials of life cut off one by one, an umbilical severing between the ship and the station. Seachnall tapped something else and made a digital window appear on the screen within Marcus' pod. He read over the provided list of people Captain Regulus was meeting with. CEO Charles Samaras caught his eye, but he also saw a religious figure, Father Publius Lucianus.

Pillars of the community.

At the bottom was a button asking if he wanted to open an audio connection. He lifted a hand up and touched the button. No response. He looked back down at the arm of the pod seat and found the control stick where his hand should have been resting under thrust. Fiddling with it, the cursor appeared and he maneuvered it down to the button and clicked.

"Ranger Maximus, glad to have you aboard," the captain's voice came. It was slow and clear, loud enough for the others to listen. It was a relief to hear the unflappable calmness in Ray's voice. Marcus hadn't been sure the captain actually had the experience and the will for this kind of disaster.

"If only under better circumstances. Have you contacted Earth?"

Captain Regulus said, "Just what we were discussing. We've got ships diving into A-Mov space in just about every direction and we've launched half a dozen communication packages, but it looks like a drag net is coming in behind the rock. Apparently blowing up Mimir isn't good enough for them."

"Maybe the Alliance didn't like Earth keeping the exo mine here, and they want it for themselves. Given that the exo mine is nearly in the heliosphere, it's rather protected from the blast. Mr Samaras, I believe you may have ran your business too well," Marcus responded.

"Ranger Maximus, it's a pleasure to meet you and thank you for your sacrifice. That said, this is an outrage. The Nebulae Company is war exempt by galactic treaty! Both sides signed it. We keep people from starving!" the CEO shouted. He was right, though calling it a galactic treaty was hubris. Humanity barely spanned a thousand light years and had only found ruins.

"Go ahead and sue them for damages then, but Athens Station isn't the mine. It isn't protected by your signature," Marcus said.

"Oh sure, they haven't taken the mine, they've just blown up the only road to it. What about my employees on the station? Fuls-Hades-I is not a fully autonomous station. I've got five live human beings on that station. They rely on Athens Station for survival. Now what are they going to do?" CEO Samaras demanded.

Marcus didn't respond, he let the silence drag as he accessed the personnel files on the CEO. He looked like a young man, but his ages disagreed. Estimated sixty biological years and a hundred and fifty Earth years. Still, he kept himself fit despite the low gravity life. "I would suggest you begin an open broadcast of your station. If you're lucky, that might deter the Alliance from being impolite," he said.

They returned the silence, and everyone felt the shudder of parking latches breaking free. Marcus' stomach lifted as the sensation of gravity ceased and the *Demos* drifted away from the station. Captain Regulus spoke over the bridge comm. "Helmsman, would you please start the thrust?"

The AI spoke up, "Engaging the engines at this distance will cause damage to the station."

"If the logistics team can find the scratches I cause, I'll be sure to pay it from my own pocket. Now, if you're done second guessing my orders, I want blast marks, now." The ship rumbled and then the *Demos* began to fly. Thrust replaced spin gravity. "Seachnall, Ramp us up from half to five please."

Gs?

Marcus thumbed off the comm link and asked, "Five?" He leaned forward and caught the helmsman's eye. Marcus tried to recall the last time he had been on a ship the size of the *Demos* able to apply that much acceleration.

"Sorry to disappoint. The *Demos* isn't meant to go fast. They only paid for a reasonable trip to Tiber," Seachnall explained.

Reasonable? Even racing ships couldn't hit five Gs when I was a kid. And even that was enough to kill people from the acceleration stress.

"Don't we have civilians onboard?"

The bridge officer shrugged. "They're in G-pods. The moon is only a few minutes away, then we'll be in drift."

"Are we going to set a rotation for effect afterwards?"

"If the captain says so. We'd have to do it before any of the Alliance ships arrive," Seachnall answered.

Marcus moved his attention back to the comm link. "Captain, how long are you planning to wait for pickup? I didn't see exo on the umbilical link so I assume this ship isn't A-Mov capable."

"No, it is not Ranger. That's just what we were discussing. The *Demos* is a shuttle, not a transport. Every ship capable of A-Mov the government owned was requisitioned years ago. Supposing that rescue forces get dispatched within the day, we'll be looking at upwards of a standard month in drift and that's assuming a rescue crew is able to come from our closest neighbor, Scythia. If they can't, then it will be six weeks... three months, or finally seven months. Red Cairo, Sic-Alba, and New Gibraltar respectively. The *Demos* is equipped with Link Reality, so we won't have to worry about going stir crazy, but frankly, we couldn't fit seven months of food for everyone, even on starvation rations. I've asked the father here to pray for us that this will only take a month."

Father Publius began to say, "With your permission, Captain, I would like to-"

The captain cut him off. "With all due respect, Father, we will now be jerking up to five Gs. Anyone who values their tongue should lean back and grit their teeth."

Over a thousand kilos pressed Marcus into his acceleration pod. For the rest of the crew and passengers, breathing would become next to impossible. They'd get light headed. Their eyes would feel about to burst. The pain would absorb their thoughts.

Marcus felt only mild discomfort. He was built different. It's what made him a Space Ranger. He figured he was the only non-medicated person on the whole ship with the presence of mind to turn on a satellite feed to display Mimir. He watched as the rock returned to real space and hammered into the ice storms.

The moment the *Demos* passed into the shadow of the moon, Mimir exploded.

3

And The Light Went Out

The First Day

The death of the planet began as a light within the clouds. A mass had been flung down the gravity well of a black hole and into A-Mov Space at over ninety-percent the speed of light. With a bit of aiming, it returned to real space slightly outside Mimir's core. At that speed, it wasn't a question of friction with the atmosphere slowing it down. The question was how much fusion would occur between the air and the rock before the shockwave annihilated everything. Atoms smashed into atoms with enough kinetic energy that molecular bonds didn't matter.

The gas giant equivalent of a supernova occurred. The blast pushed the entire atmosphere into orbit and beyond, saturated with radiation and enough heat to vaporize Athens Station. The outer crust of the moon was blown clean off, exposing the molten core across half its surface. A few eons of captured methane and related gasses were vented, and fireballs chased after the escaping fuel until the vastness of space snuffed them out.

For a moment, the *Demos* was surrounded by a corona of heavenly fire.

When the ship matched the speed of the debris, Seachnall killed the thrust and turned on the spin motors. A ring of steam blasted from the *Demos*, torquing it up to speed. The G-pods pivoted with their loads, facing outwards as the spin reached something close to one Gee.

"Brace for turbulence," Seachnall said over the general address. Moments passed as the *Demos* drifted from one end of the moon's shadow to the other. Marcus could only take a rough guess at the ship's velocity, but it certainly exceeded what would have been Mimir's escape velocity. There was no Mimir left regardless.

Then they exited the moon's shadow. They had taken a departing angle, entering far closer than where they exited, but still the surge of superheated gasses and debris hammered the ship. The nose was hit first. It abraded them and put an unwanted torque into the system, twisting them into an uncontrolled precession as meter after meter entered the blast.

"Captain, permission to correct spin?" Seachnall asked as the G-pods began to twist in their frames.

"Denied. A bit of noise will help us blend in. The water tanks will have to stop us from flipping," the captain responded as the whole hull began to vibrate. It had centimeters of steel all over it, the privilege of space shipyards, but even that could only take so much veritable sandblasting. If they lost enough mass, or had the inner loads distributed wrong, they could end up rotating on the wrong moment of inertia. They would tumble nose over tail.

Marcus wondered how the other ships were faring. The *Demos* had been the largest attached to Athens Station, but there were seven other ships. A bit of computer searching told him that there were now only five other ships. They hadn't gotten out of the blast quick enough. One had been shredded by the scrapings off the moon like millions of tons of molten flak. The other had thought it could simply out-run the blast, that its thrust away would win against the cubic drop in intensity. They had been wrong. A surge of radiation had cooked them from behind and ignited their atmosphere. Now it soared into the abyss like a viking funeral.

That's nearly two thousand dead.

He reclined his head till his helmet hit the back of the pod. Their passenger lists likely wouldn't even be verified and their deaths unrecorded. The waitress from the diner might have been on one of them. Or any of the people in the plant gardens that didn't exist anymore. The crowds that had cheered his news of the peace accords, and those that had raged. The evacuation had been luck of the draw for all of them.

Surviving the blast didn't mean they had survived the attack. "How long until the first Alliance ship arrives to scour the area?" he asked.

Captain Regulus answered, "Too soon. We have to hope the radiation scrambles their sensors and they don't get too good of a look at us."

"Won't it fry all of ours as well?"

"Most of them, yeah. Would have been nice to bring those all inside first, but that would have taken days."

"Great, we're going to be as blind as the rock we're pretending to be," Marcus said, and he closed his eyes. He couldn't fly the ship, and he knew that the passengers were busily synchronizing with the virtual reality; but, it was surely a mess of fear. Rather than connect to it himself, he relaxed and slept. The rumble of interstellar turbulence shook the ship straight through the hull and down to every acceleration pod and every bottle of water in the mess hall. Everything in the ship rattled like the whole thing would suddenly peel apart and vent them to space.

Marcus had slept through planet-side landings under fire. When he told his body to sleep, he nodded off. His mind rested for the few hours it took for the Alliance dragnet to arrive, and one by one ships appeared from the radioactive core of Mimir. Blaring alarms went off across the bridge, and even his suit couldn't isolate him from the commotion. The first thing he heard was one of the crew members shouting, "Straight from the middle? How could a human survive that much radiation?"

"Sergei, get me bearings and classifications on those now," Captain Regulus ordered. The sharp bark of his words did little to speed Mia's calculations, but the human components moved faster for it. "Perry, how are the sensors?" he demanded of his EM technician.

The tech shouted back, "Hard to tell what's giving accurate

data, sir. Everything was scraped by the blast. Lots of noise in the dishes." His fingers hammered on his controls.

"I don't want to hear that it's hard! I want to hear what we can see. Cameras aren't a new technology and we didn't make them cheap. Get them to work," the Captain ordered.

You're asking for the impossible.

Marcus stifled a yawn. The natural reaction to waking up felt ridiculous, given the circumstances. He worked his computer until it gave him a display from the last remaining cameras. None of it was in the visible spectrum, but Mia didn't care about that triviality and easily rendered the input to ship trajectories and classifications. He laughed. "Those aren't piloted. Those little ones are scanners and the big one, we call that a Collapse. I guess they aren't salting the earth."

Captain Regulus walked over to Marcus' G-pod. He marched with his hands behind his back, chest broad. With the ship in spin instead of thrust, it looked like he was standing on the wall. It made the holo-display more visible, but the captain was barely at eye level with Marcus' feet when he asked, "Care to enlighten me as to what a Collapse is? Can it spot us? Is it a threat?"

"That's still classified? It's sort of like an A-Mov engine turned into a bomb. They're going to crash it into the moon, pop it, and tweak its orbit enough to crash it into what's left of Mimir's core to get the gravity back up. Can't exactly fly the exo fuel to the other systems if you don't have a heavy enough launch point. Hell, they probably have a few more rocks on the way just at slower speeds. Wouldn't be much point in rebuilding a station here if there wasn't enough mass to utilize A-Mov, now would there be?"

Captain Regulus nodded. "So it's unmanned and disposable. Won't be around for long. Won't be looking for us. That mean they're AI controlled? True or pseudo?"

"Pseudo. The Alliance never broke the prohibition on consciousness. Doesn't mean they won't get the job done though," he said, glancing about the bridge. Given the new orientation, a few panels had slid aside. What had been the floor was then a ladder down, which he used.

Captain Regulus said, "I presume then, that these other ships, or probes more like, are here to catalog every bit of floating rock and log it for when the humans arrive?"

"Yes, sir."

The older man sighed and shook his head. His face sank into a deep frown that pulled at his wrinkles. His tension waned. "Well if that's the case, there's nothing we can do. We might have a few tumbles since we didn't cancel out the precession, but we'll survive. Ranger, this is the point where I say welcome to the wait. Nothing to be done but to keep our heads down and pray."

Praying won't help. Not out here.

Marcus nodded. "I suppose I should go meet the priest then."

"Ranger," Captain Regulus said. He looked at the ground and wetted his lips. "For what it's worth, I'm sorry you're on this ship with us. We couldn't get you on any of the private ships. Civilians, they might get a pass, but I know they won't treat you well."

That's understating it.

The image of that burning ship in the storms of Mimir came back to him and he grimaced inside his helmet. "You did nothing wrong, Captain," Marcus said, and left the bridge.

A man Marcus didn't recognize stopped him in the hall with a raised hand. He was almost as tall as Marcus in his armor, and had enough muscle to not look gangly. He had a sheathe-locked blade on his hip, the kind that was both a cattle prod and a club until he felt like pulling the graphene edge out. "Got a minute, Vet? Name's Lieutenant Olympus, but you? You can call me Hideo. I'd like to talk to you about ship security."

4

Luck Of The Draw

The First Day

Hideo took him to what he laughably called Security Command. Because the *Demos* was intended for civilian and commercial transport to Tiber, it wasn't a weaponized ship. Those had been taken for the war effort. What Hideo had to work with was a factory standard office, whose only personalization was an assortment of half-finished liquors he had squirreled away, and a handful of lockable rooms he called the brig.

"We've got a thousand people onboard, Vet," Hideo said as he kicked his feet up his desk. He picked up something that looked like vodka and offered it to Marcus.

The Ranger declined and sat down across from him.

Hideo shrugged and twisted the cap off to take a swig. "You know, this ship was supposed to be a transport vessel, a ferry between the two planets. You hop on for a few days and bounce between the rock and the gas giant and you get on with your life. It was never meant to be a refugee boat, but where else could we have put people?"

"It won't be for too long. We just have to wait for rescue."

"Or surrender to the Alliance."

Marcus tensed. "I wouldn't recommend that. They just breached the peace treaty when, instead, they could have just marched in and started confiscating things. They deserve less trust than a refurbished space suit."

Hideo laughed. "God, we really came from different planets, didn't we? Different centuries even!"

"How so?"

"Mr Maximus, I grew up as a ship rat in a mining flotilla over near Rus. Mining turned into salvage after the war started. Much more lucrative, but we were still as poor as the worst ghettos on Earth or Mars. Refurbished was all we had for space suits... but, I take your meaning just fine. You won't ever hear me advocating we give ourselves to those mutant bastards that attacked us. The civilians might see it another way however."

"The civilians can see it however they want. It's the captain that makes the decisions."

Hideo gave a grin that didn't reach his eyes. "Well, it's my job to keep people in line. I don't think it will get to that, though. I wanted to ask you for your tactical assessment of our options."

I suppose, as the security chief, he's the de facto army of this ship.

Marcus said, "My assessment conforms with the captain's. We don't have weapons, so we hide."

"Until they notice us, and nuke us. Or put a railgun round through our hull. Or laser our engines and strand us. Or send drones to strip our hull for materials. Or–"

"I get your point."

Hideo put up his hands and set the bottle aside. "You're the expert military advisor, right? If we were on a planet right now, you'd be the highest ranking person around, and you've got all the experience to back it up, don't you? So, while you're on this ship, subject to Captain Regulus, I'm asking, if you had to, how would you defend us from attack? As the only other person on this ship that could be ordered to help you, I'd like to know."

Marcus frowned. He thought about the value of the Fuls star system, the exo mine. He tried to weigh the effort of rebuilding Athens Station against the benefits to guess how much the Alliance could spare to attack them. He didn't know how much of the Alliance was even responsible for the breach, let alone what else they were doing. It was possible they wouldn't send anything at all, that it was a scorched earth barrier to block travel. Or they could send an entire fleet to fuel up while the dust settled, then move on.

If any attack ship showed up though, they would be the only one in the metaphorical room with a gun.

He knew the answer. It was the same answer he and Levy had come to before the peace treaty. "Without a weapons system, the only thing that could be done would be to board them. Cut in through the hull with repair tools and fight it out."

Kill them all and take their ship, hope they don't detonate a nuke out of spite, give them even more reason to hunt me down.

Hideo's gaze unfocused and he nodded. The man reached over and drank the rest of the vodka in a series of gulps. "Too bad we don't have an AutoSec to send in ahead of us."

"We don't? I thought all ships had one."

Hideo scowled and chucked the bottle at the wall. It clattered off, spinning away to a corner. Evidently, not glass. "Under normal circumstances, yeah. Instead, the Blue Andalusian has two of them right now, because they were validating some new software. The *Demos* has nothing but me."

Marcus used his suit's computer to query the ship. Mia provided him a trajectory for the other ship. They were headed out to a deeper orbit than Mimir, so they weren't one of the two that had been destroyed. "Well, if things go south, you have me."

Hideo smiled, but Marcus could already see the alcohol haze growing in his face. "You're better than an AutoSec, aren't you?"

The Ranger stood up. "Only because I can be reasoned with. I wouldn't want to get in a fight with one. Let me know if something goes wrong. I imagine that once the ships start arriving, and I have something to work with, Captain Regulus will be consulting with me about what we can do. For now…"

"For now, we drink and we wait," Hideo said, grandly gesturing to the rest of his collection.

Marcus stepped out of the office, and sought out Father

Publius Lucianus. Prayer was the strongest weapon aboard the *Demos*, and it just might work. It might keep the civilians from losing their minds with the threat of nuclear annihilation looming over their heads. It also might help him figure out what to do.

The people aboard the *Demos* were despondent, as though days passed them by every hour. Silence brooded between the acceleration pods that had been turned into living quarters. They lined the cylindrical chamber like an infirmary ward, shoulder to shoulder in acceleration gel. Even the complaining of confused children hardly broke the airborne malaise. When the alarm had begun, every passenger aboard Athens Station had been assigned a seat by lottery, and the blank, gray walls of the *Demos* cargo hold said to them, "Better luck next time."

The shaky puffs of fogged breath did more to mark the bodies of the survivors than their own actions. The only thing that warded off the frigid bite of the air was the huddling of bodies. Still, he found Father Publius arguing with one of the crewmates about heating the chamber.

Ironic, when this chamber is literally wrapped around the hot part of the fusion reactor, like an insulator.

"There are sick people here! When they turned on the alarm, it also sounded in the hospitals. We have people with broken bones from the acceleration and the painkillers can barely take the edge off. The cold isn't helping their chances of surviving!" the older man said, his hands casting about himself.

The crewmate was a young woman with a bob cut and

stood a head taller than him, gravitational differences, but kept a professional face. At least, Marcus thought it was a woman. When he got closer, he picked out the almost feline slope to her jaw and cheeks. It didn't look bad, but it was obviously from genetic tampering and it wouldn't have been the first time a face had lied. "I understand, Father. But, generating heat for the sake of heat is simply not something we can do. We may be on this ship for half a year, and unable to vent waste heat. I know it's an ice box right now, but it's to stave off living in a sauna."

The priest's expression sank. His shoulders slumped. His hands fell to his sides. "They won't be living in a sauna at this rate. They'll be dead."

"I suggest you help distribute blankets and see what can be done to huddle people together," the crewmate said, and left him there.

Marcus stepped up to the crestfallen man, catching his attention. "I don't know about you, but I'd rather be in the cold than in nuclear fire."

"Ranger Marcus... do you know how many people are aboard this ship? In the custody of the captain?" Father Publius asked, taking a few shuffling steps to sit down on the edge of one of the G-pods. They were bigger in the cargo hold, cylindrical in shape to roll between thrust and spin while fitting a family of four comfortably. Behind him were teenagers, five of them plucked from the station and adrift in Link Reality. "One thousand. One thousand people are onboard the *Demos*, and within one day, we will have our first deaths. People we failed to protect."

"There is no way to put this gently, but we've already lost two ships to this attack. Two thousand people are already dead, give or take."

Father Publius reached down his shirt and pulled out a cross. Pressing it to his forehead, he bowed his head and closed his eyes. "What a terrible, terrible war."

Marcus scanned the room. "Maybe it was a blessing the Jupiter Fleet was lost. Earth surrendered, but at least we're done with it. Once we escape anyways." Sullen eyes looked back at him; people expecting him to save them. He couldn't magically produce a weapons system though. He couldn't even negotiate with the Alliance, if they found out who he was.

"You don't happen to have some copy of the accords to show them, do you? Something to beg for peace?"

"Of course. Every ship owned by the government has a data pack of the signing. The signatories even used one-time pass codes in the documentation. The problem is all of that could be faked by Earth's AIs, so the Alliance might not trust it, and it's been so many decades of jumping around that the one-time codes may have expired and they'll think it's an elaborate trick. The first of our ships that they capture, and unfortunately they will capture some, we'll see how they react to it," Marcus explained.

"Let us pray that they are peaceful then. Are you a religious man, Ranger?" the father asked, folding his hands in his lap and looking up at him.

"I'm not Abrahamic, if that's your question."

The old man gave a knowing smile. "Space Faith or Conspiracy Theorist?"

"That's classified."

The priest laughed. It wasn't very hearty. "The twenty-second century will haunt us forever, won't it? I will be holding a prayer for the faithful. All of the faithful. I don't care whether they think God is here, or back on Earth. If Jesus was Lord or if the Bastard was his second coming. We're in this together regardless. Why don't you come?"

"That's just what I was hoping for."

I wish I still had your civilian outlook. I've spent more time praying to guns than to God.

Marcus offered a hand, but the old man got to his feet himself and walked to the end of the cargo hold. Over a hundred other people huddled shoulder to shoulder at the back. They were dressed from every walk of life and every time of day. There were men in suits besides girls in clubbing dresses as well as elderly in service uniforms and children in pajamas. All of them parted just enough to let the two of them pass through to the small seat that had been prepared.

I wonder how many of these showed up to his service before today.

For a time, many of them looked at Marcus, but their attention turned to the priest when he began speaking. They bowed their heads and he led them through a prayer for the departed. He spoke in Early English, as was the tradition since the age of space exploration, and Marcus could follow the prayer just fine. It was only a few centuries removed from his own time, but a glance across the crowd showed dozens of people using translator apps hidden in sleeves or beside their legs.

As far as Marcus was concerned, the words barely mattered. The priest could have been reciting in latin. The ritual helped him close his eyes and open his mind. God didn't speak to him, even with so many hundreds of people trying to get His attention. What he did get was his own thoughts back at himself, an inward view of what he knew. In his practiced mind, he saw the *Demos* drifting away from the molten ruin of Mimir, but more than that. The fireworks spread of the other ships, the *Theopone,* the *Chase,* the *Blue Andalusian,* and the *Phalanx of Starlight.* Each ship was like a rabbit chased from the burrow, and no one knew what the fox would do.

Marcus turned his mind to the problem of action. He took the world inside himself and worked it as the priest guided everyone through a mumbled and stumbled hymn. When Marcus needed to think about when the Alliance would arrive with ships, he had to figure out why they had come to Fuls at all: the exo mine surely. The Nebulae Company was neutral, anyone could buy the fuel. No need to attack such a worthless place as Athens Station. Marcus couldn't grasp the tide of war, nor could he imagine what his options even were.

He was an ant staring down a wolf.

Then, as addendum to the traditional prayer, Father Publius added something to the effect of, "and may their souls find their way back from this empty world and to the cradle of our home." Marcus opened his eyes, the surprise dragging him from his fruitless imaginings.

So much for not caring whether they thought God was here or on Earth.

Father Publius' stance on the Homeworld Schism didn't

seem to bother the crowd. The priest continued, "And now, we pray for ourselves. We pray that peace finds us, not war. That by your grace, we are delivered to safe hands."

"Like him?" someone asked, glaring at Marcus. It was a young man, his face unshaved and his clothes disheveled; but, still he stared right at the Space Ranger twice his size. He openly sneered. "Mr Space Ranger here's arrival sure made things safer for us, didn't it?"

Does he think they came here for me? Or that I'm supposed to have some magical aura of protection?

Marcus didn't respond. He knew there was nothing he could say. He faced the boy and waited. He listened to the silence.

Someone grabbed the kid by the arm, his mother by the looks of it, and tugged him back down. While she scolded him for speaking out, Father Publius did his best to clear his throat, and people took the cue to look back at him. "I'm told that we will have to hold fast for a month. Four weeks with naught but one another in this dismal ark. A cold ark isn't it? Maybe we all can use young Tim's indignation as a heat source if we huddle around him, eh?" The crowd laughed, and the boy's cheeks burned as the herd pulled him in.

People keep expecting me to be a miracle worker, don't they? And they get upset when I'm not.

"I should be clear with all of you," Marcus said, turning his head across the group. "The precise thing you are praying for is that your closest neighbor, Scythia, is in working order and can send rescue ships to us able to contend with the Alliance forces, be it through words or missiles. And if it's the latter, you need to pray that they win. It'll be about two weeks until they even hear about us, so get your prayers in. There's nothing else we can do."

The older people in the crowd bowed their heads. Some of the younger ones stared, imagining the battles that would be fought far away, and by people they didn't know, and yet would decide their fates. Unfortunately, the radiation from Mimir's blast had destroyed most of the sensors, so the ship would never get more than a pinhole peep to the conflict. Mia might be able to conjure an impression of it, but it would be nothing more than a digital fabrication.

I guess I need some levity, some humanizing.

"In the meantime, I could use some help," he added, and let the silence drag as everyone wondered what the Space Ranger could need help with. When Father Publius furrowed his brow and gestured for him to go on, he was sure he had everyone's attention. "As you all know, I'm a Space Ranger. I'm from Earth originally, a long long time ago. So, I'm about as educated on your Link Reality as your grandparents are. I'm a quick learner, but how do I get in? I'll be crawling up the walls if I can't get some games in or something."

The crowd was large enough that a few people burst out laughing, grasping the humor in the bleak straits. A girl no older than twelve threw up her hand. She must have grown up in microgravity, because she was nearly as tall as him and skinny as a rail. "I know! I know. I can help!"

"Quite eager today, aren't you Maria?" Father Publius asked.

Perfect.

"Really? I'd appreciate it if you could. You see, back on Earth it was all ground slogging for me. I had to read books by hand for everything. I'm really out of touch with the new tech stuff," Marcus said, giving the child his attention. He saw over her shoulder that her father just shook his head and let her be.

The priest smiled and nodded. He went with the flow, letting the congregation disperse as people returned to their acceleration pods while others moved closer to him for further prayer. He made sure that the troublemaker, Tim, stayed with him. From within his robe, he produced the smallest bible that Marcus had ever seen. Every page was thinner than onion skin and made of some kind of plastic to keep the weight down without abridging the content.

"Come on, we can go to a direct terminal," the girl, Maria, said as she led Marcus to a side hall. She naturally walked with the awkward, skipping lope of someone who had never set foot on a planet, always conscious that she might start drifting if she went too quick and yet she sped along anyways.

The comm device in his helmet chimed as Mia contacted him to ask, "You already have access to Link Reality. Why are you asking for help?"

The Space Ranger laughed. "I wanted to remind them that I'm a human, not a magic military wizard," he said, following Maria down ladders to the outer hull of the ship. The less critical functions were located close to the metal membrane between the ship and the vacuum. Things like the nuclear reactor, the engines, Mia's core, and so on were all along the axis of the ship, and mostly in the back. A pod barely the size of a closet to manually connect to the Link Reality server was top of the list for insulation against blasts and meteorite impacts.

"Your suit does have a USB port, doesn't it?" she asked as she pulled the pod door open for him.

He shook his head. "Wireless only," he said. His suit was a few centuries out of date with industry standards. Fitting a hardware port with the hundredth iteration of a USB would never be worthwhile, not for as long as he was expected to leap forward through time, from battlefield to battlefield. The designers had been wary of future AI growth, and opted for security over function.

People would be appalled if they realized how low tech this suit actually is. Barely any hidden tricks. Not even a support AI. What would they ever think if they learned it's just me in here?

Maria pondered that, twisting some of her black hair around her finger. "You'll need the AI's help then, I think. My father's a technician for ships and he's taught me a whole bunch, so I'm sure I can fix you up!"

"So I just sit in here and turn on the interface computer?"

"Yep!"

Marcus did so, thumbing through the controls within the pod and within his own suit. The data connection immediately threw an error screen at him, as it always did. The ship was hundreds of years more advanced than his body armor and the digital handshake protocol nearly failed outright. The rudimentary systems, processing below Mia's awareness, feebly offered up a request to update his firmware drivers, but couldn't even identify what system he was using.

"I'm sorry," Mia said. "This has never happened before."

He sighed and tried to disable the warnings. "Don't worry about it too much. This literally always happens. My suit doesn't take updates anyways. It doesn't do any processing at all, no memory storage, just the active logic. No other way to stay secure for a thousand years."

"Well now I feel like a dunce for saying you had access to Link Reality. The best I can give you is a preliminary profile as a guest," the AI explained. "Unless you have some way to confirm that your systems can interface."

"It's fine. I'm just a guest here anyways. Not like I want administrator powers or something," he said, giving Maria a thumbs up that it was working.

"But, Ranger, if you accept a guest profile, then I can't connect you to any of the control systems. You won't be able to see any of the sensors or look at any data that isn't sent to the main display," Mia said.

He shrugged. "That shouldn't be a problem. The crew knows what they're doing." With that, his consciousness was freed from the *Demos*, taken from the bleak halls and pods filled with more people than it had ever been intended for. He was given the illusion of a peaceful world.

The illusion didn't last long.

5

Minimal Entertainment

The First Day

Link Reality was requisite life support for every star faring ship that had humans aboard. While some people could sit in isolation in a thin metal can barely shielded against the uncaring universe for months on end, normal people had to appease their instincts. The end of a long progression from bulbous goggles and hand gesture controls, to the dream-like virtual reality of the twenty-second century, Link Reality had finally triumphed over biological rejection.

For Marcus, the device was a small ring of gold and circuitry embedded in his uppermost vertebra, sheltered by all the support muscles of his neck. For the people of Athens Station, it was even less intrusive. When activated, all of his sensory input switched to the simulation, and it took gentle care to exercise his muscles in antagonistic pairs to prevent atrophy.

He went in expecting a sprawling recreation of Earth in its

prime. Athens Station had been host to a dozen digital worlds, across a spectrum of time speeds. There had even been one reality at one-tenth time perception, so people could slow their mental aging while waiting for loved ones to return from long FTL journeys. A form of forward time travel. What he found was a barren cityblock walled off from the rest of the world, if there was anything more to the simulation at all. "Mia, what the hell is this?" he asked, checking his basic avatar.

"Low power mode," the AI answered, blinking into existence beside him. He had been expecting a human form. She appeared as a white feathered raven. She alighted upon a street bollard, perching on the paint flecked knob beside him.

"You expect people to be shoulder to shoulder in this city block to keep from going stir crazy?" he asked, planting his hands on his hips.

Her feathers bristled and she twitched, shaking her entire body to reset it. "It conserves power. Minimizes heat production. Our computing isn't lossless yet. Reducing to this volume saves over ninety percent of waste heat that could theoretically be saved. The less heat we produce, the less noticeable we are to scans. This was the decision of Captain Regulus."

"How is it supposed to work if there aren't games and entertainment? You've made a digital prison."

"There is a game center, a cafe, and a kino-plex. The minimum required according to the latest psychological research. You can access the help menu by touching your thumb and pinky finger together," Mia said, and spread her wings. The flap pushed no air. When he checked his breathing, he realized that it wasn't even simulating air. With all the credibility of a dream, he could pinch his nose and inhale anyways.

The passengers had almost entirely shifted to Link Reality, and he found them sitting or milling between the buildings quietly and with slumped heads. Another aspect of the power conservation measures seemed to be restricting everyone to their natural avatars. No elves or make-believe aliens walked the streets, just people in clothes as basic as his own.

"Everyone, if I could have your attention," Sergei Seachnall said. He had his voice amplified and stood on a platform in front of the game center. The fact that he had long hair in the simulation made Marcus chuckle and wonder what dress regulations were lately. The commander must have handed over helm control to Mia to be present in Link Reality. "I have available to me a small list of simulation games that we can provide access to through the game center. However, due to computational constraints, we can't activate all of them. We'll get an instance of Arena up and running shortly, so you all can blow off some steam, if you're so inclined, but for the other games, we will be holding a vote on which to enable."

The crowd grumbled, but most seemed to be whispering to the few people they knew about what to vote for. Marcus heard dozens of names that meant nothing to him, but the event was clever enough that it made him smirk. Captain Regulus had given them a choice that would impact their future. It was a fake choice, but that didn't matter.

Without his body armor on, no one looked twice at him. They didn't stare from the corners of their eyes. They didn't slow to a stop without realizing. They just brushed past him and queued up to submit their votes to Sergei. True to Mia's word, the game center and the kino-plex both had crowds. The theater was full to the brim with light comedies. The game center flashed and cried out with music. People strove for distraction.

"Well don't you look out of place." The man who spoke was CEO Samaras of The Nebulae Company. The avatar looked little like the real man, but it had class to it. He had obviously hired a proper artist to make a rendition of him, and the man looked larger than life for it.

"What gave it away?"

"Your fashion sense is a bit out of date. About a hundred years out of date, I'd say," he answered, walking across the street and holding out his hand. "Also, you don't look like you're afraid, but that you're working a problem."

Marcus glanced down at his outfit. As far as he knew, it was Earth standard. He shook the businessman's hand nonetheless. The grip was strong and smooth. "How can I help?"

"Well, do you happen to have an A-Mov engine hiding in that suit of yours? Some kind of hijacking attack AI that will let us commandeer one of their ships? I'll take any other trick you've got too," Samaras said as he dropped the shake and put his hands in his pockets. He had an easy smile as he spoke. He knew the answers.

"I'm giving all the help I can to the captain. If the Alliance tries to board us, I might do some shooting. I'm an expert at that. All the space stuff is out of my hands though."

Samaras chuckled and gestured towards a cafe at the edge of the simulation. "May I have some of your time?" Marcus nodded and the two of them proceeded to the second floor of the digital restaurant. They sat down at a table in the back corner, facing the blank edge of the simulation.

While Marcus fiddled with the menu and produced for himself a facsimile of a whiskey, Samaras summoned Mia and negotiated with her to change the simulation boundary to at least a static image. By the time he leaned back with his tumbler, they were surrounded by something like a Bierstadt landscape stretched larger than the biggest sporting stadium's big screen.

"Can you tell me why the rebels are still attacking us even after Earth surrendered?" the businessman asked as he dialed himself up a whiskey to match.

Was forced to surrender.

"That's just the kind of thing that happens when you tell every planet we've colonized to launch their own war on their own fronts. The Jupiter Fleet might have won something by cutting off the head behind the lines, but the fleet was lost. It just took a while for the Alliance leaders to realize they had won the war. They haven't reined in their outliers yet," Marcus explained.

"Can you really believe that? That we lost ten million personnel in one freak accident?"

Accident or not, you didn't see the scores of men who put a bullet in their own heads when the Alliance came flying in because of it. Let alone the people who wished they had after they got captured.

Marcus didn't meet Samaras' gaze. For a moment, he

occupied himself with examining the glass and the simulated fluid physics and how the ice slid from side to side. "No, I guess I don't believe it happened naturally. The chances that it was sabotage are rather high. That's what happens with civil wars."

"All this over a mutant. Can you believe it?" Samaras responded, also putting his gaze on his whiskey. "Millions dead and now us, all over a kid crying on the news."

A small rock can only cause a landslide if it was already barely holding together.

Marcus downed the smoky drink and sat the drink down. Link Reality couldn't simulate inebriation, so he didn't get another. "Soldiers needed a cause to fight for. Politicians used it because they wanted to renegotiate trade deals. Humanity hasn't had a real war like this since Oceania vs Afri-asia. Spend long enough making weapons and you feel the need to use them."

"And who would have thought we'd be back to throwing rocks at each other?" the businessman responded with a grin. Samaras held up his glass, outstretched. Marcus didn't return his gesture for a cheers. After setting his whiskey aside, Samaras folded his hands on the table and got to the point. "Ranger, I'd like to be frank about our chances. We're going to be caught by the Alliance. I'd like to signal any approaching ship before they launch missiles at us and ask for asylum."

"That's a request for the captain, not for me. I'm sure he will consider all options related to the safety of the ship and those of us aboard."

"I know. But I'm concerned that the *Demos* is transporting some form of national secrets, given you're aboard," he said, staring Marcus in the eyes.

Ah, the point of the matter.

Marcus leaned on the table and interlaced his fingers. He shrugged. "You know that if that were the case, I wouldn't be at liberty to tell you as much. What's the point in asking? I'm obliged to tell you that no such thing is aboard the ship. I can even add that why would Earth have military secrets on this ship after signing the peace accords?"

I am the military secret you idiot.

Samaras didn't respond for a long while. He sat and let the silence percolate through the air, digital as it was. The sounds of people barely echoed over to disturb the tension. "Ranger, we're going to be on this ship for a month together, us and everyone else anyways. Do you like games?"

Marcus let his breath out and leaned back in his chair. "I like games, but I struggle to keep up, for obvious reasons. Did you mean digital games or traditional? Because the only one I recognized down at the game center was Arena."

"Personally I'm partial to games that can be paused or set down," Samaras said.

"You strike me as someone who answers emails while playing."

He laughed. "Guilty as charged. One of the reasons I was put out here on Athens Station. If I was an addict for the fantasy world games, I would have gone crazy in such a tiny player pool. There's always chess. That can even be played by courier with someone on another planet, if you're patient. Interested in a game?"

Marcus tapped on the cafe interface again, got himself another whiskey, and said, "Certainly. I look forward to you challenging me again after you lose."

The cordial grin on Samaras' face vanished. "Is that so? That's some confidence you've got."

"Mr Samaras, I was trained in all manner of war and strategy by some of the greatest teachers and theorists that Earth had to offer, both living and artificial. Chess is my specialty."

6

Watching In The Dark

The Fourteenth Day

The first ship had arrived, with no sign of friend or foe to it. It was an artificial speck of light thousands of kilometers away with nothing but ice and dust between it and the *Demos*. And yet, if it felt like it, could kill them all with the press of a button: a single missile.

The mood on the ship had been quiet. Life had gotten by as people entertained themselves in Link Reality, and quietly filled their stomachs with the fresh food taken from Athens Station. With no other humans in the sector, there was no threat, no destruction hunting them. It had been like an extended funeral, for those that hadn't made it off the station.

The arrival of that ship changed everything.

"Just one ship?" Captain Regulus asked, sitting in his office across from Marcus and Hideo. The data that Perry, the EM technician, had put together looked like it had been filmed from the other side of frosted glass. The irradiated ice had that sort of effect still, as the debris entered a careening orbit back towards Mimir. Mia's calculations said it would eventually form rings and perhaps in a hundred thousand years they might decay back into the gas giant.

"I suppose it could be Alliance if they were very confident in the blast? Was this a scheduled arrival? Were there friendly ships en route through A-Mov?" Marcus said.

"Mia, pull up the registry. Was anything scheduled?" Captain Regulus ordered.

"No, sir, but we only have updated registries for three adjacent stations. It could have arrived from New Gibraltor," the AI responded. New Gibraltar was the furthest sector from what had been Athens Station. The least likely to help.

When has my luck ever been that good though?

"If that's a friendly, we need to contact them immediately," Hideo said, scratching the stubble on his chin.

"If," Ray countered.

"I suppose it's possible. The size and shape of that looks like a war frigate to me though," Marcus said. "This is about the time where we would expect humans from the Alliance to begin arriving to manage the Collapse locally."

Captain Regulus rubbed his chin. "Exactly what I was thinking, unfortunately. Hopefully they think missiles are expensive and don't feel like blowing up any sizable rock."

The ranger's gaze moved to the captain's face. "So you're not going to send a distress signal?"

"I might, depending on how things play out. You're a

whiskey man, aren't you?" Captain Regulus asked as he pulled open a drawer in his office desk and fished out a squeeze bottle of the brown liquor.

"I'm not picky." It would take more than one drink to have an effect on him. The amount of liquor he needed was typically measured in liters. At that volume, flavor wasn't very important.

"The way I see it," the captain continued as he fished out three glasses and set them down on the desk. He upended the bottle and sprayed it in. In the diminished gravity near the axis of rotation, the whiskey didn't want to settle into place, almost crawling out the top. "If that's an Alliance ship, the Collapse will go off in the next few days here, and we'll know for sure. If it's some schmuck trader from New Gibraltar, chances are they'll turn and blast off to the exo mine. Probably send some broad spectrum message asking for survivors. That's all well and good, but one merchant ship won't be enough for escaping once the Alliance does show up. And, given the amount of fuel they'll need to compensate for Mimir's new state, I highly doubt they'll make the round trip before then." Once the whiskey had finally settled, the captain held a glass out for Marcus.

That presumes they plan to go back, rather than onward to Earth.

"Will the other captains be in alignment?"

Captain Regulus puffed out his cheeks and turned up his hands. "Can't say for certain. They're all smart. Not sure I would call them expert logicians, but smart. Something to consider, Ranger, is that until planet Tiber becomes hospitable, we're an interstellar truckstop. Or we were any-way. I'd say that chances are one of them shoots that ship with a direct line and we can only pray they have the good sense to purge their tracking data of us while they still can."

The whiskey was loaded with sugar and cinnamon. Marcus didn't complain. "Any way to contact them and discuss?"

"Not a risk I'm willing to take. There's so much crap in the space between us and them that any laser we shoot would glow. It's not discreet when there's fog in the way. Whether that ship is Alliance or not, the probes certainly are."

"If it is Alliance," Hideo asked, "Is there anything we can do besides hide?"

Ray frowned at his security officer. "We're getting a bit far from Mimir to do anything. We're at missile range, not clever tricks range."

"Just a question," Hideo said, swirling his whiskey beneath his nose.

Marcus said, "We're on a ship without weapons. The only thing we could do is negotiate."

Hideo glanced at him, but didn't bring up the proposal for boarding action of their own.

"I'm not sure I trust my tongue to be that silver," Ray said, wetting his mouth with liquor again.

"Understandable, but do you plan to tell the passengers?" Marcus asked, and sipped his whiskey again. He could think of one man who might do the job.

Captain Regulus again puffed out his cheeks and turned his attention over to the wall. He had memorabilia hung up in circular frames that self-oriented between thrust and rotation.

There were a few empty spots where some had popped off the wall during the first tumble. The ship's precession had come to a head on the tenth day, the little wobble suddenly growing to a large shake and then a gut wrenching inversion before the axis of rotation flipped direction. The nose of the ship faced Mimir at the moment, giving the Alliance probes a look at the heat shield rather than the engines. "I suppose I have to. I'll give it a few more hours of staring though. Maybe something will happen. No one will care if I tell them I just wanted to be sure."

"Well, the reasonable people won't mind. With a thousand people on board, some will try to be your backseat driver."

"Bah, there's always malcontents. What are they going to do? Complain?"

Hideo set his empty glass down. "I'll deal with anyone who gets rowdy. Would be a nice change of pace to use my actual body instead of just Arena in Link Reality."

Ray nodded. "Just keep it reasonable. At least there aren't any guns to worry about."

Marcus paused, the glass almost to his lips. "No guns?"

Captain Regulus waved his hand. "Nah, emptied the armory to make more room for food supplies. Civilians aren't combat capable. They wouldn't do us any good against boarding and I still expect we'll get a missile rather than a meeting."

Marcus frowned and shifted forward. He planted his arms on his knees and stared at the end of his drink. "Not exactly hedging your bets, but I can't say you made the wrong choice."

"Are you one to always cover your ass?"

To answer, Marcus reached behind his back and within the access hatch of his body armor. Inside was the majority of his life support systems, the machines that would let him survive outside of a ship, as well as a gun. He set it on the desk between them, a six-shot revolver. "There's at least one gun on the ship."

Hideo whistled. Captain Regulus frowned. "A little antiquated, isn't it? May I?" Marcus nodded and the ship captain picked it up. He turned it over in his hand and popped the cylinder open. "Well, it doesn't look like it can pierce my hull."

"A bit hard to fit armor penetration into a utility hatch," Marcus said, and smirked as he drank the end of his whiskey.

"Well, I pray to God you never have to use it. On this ship, I doubt you'd even need it. You could take any of us apart with your bare hands," Ray said, handing the weapon back to him. "Hideo, would you please pay Perry a visit and explain to him that this news is to remain confidential for the next few hours, pending a broadcast from that ship?"

Hideo's eyes flicked back over to the captain, away from the gun. "Certainly," he said, and smiled. He set the glass down and exited, his brow weighed down with thoughts.

After the door shut, Ray poured himself another glass of whiskey. "Care for another game of chess? We do need to break our tie," Captain Regulus said as he pulled up the board again.

Marcus laughed. "That would require us to not get interrupted while you're losing."

The Captain balked and waved him off and excused the past events and set the digital board back up for the two of them. They played until it was apparent that Marcus had a checkmate, and coincidentally that was when Captain Regulus brought up how close it was to lunch and that they really should fill their stomachs before making the announcement to the passengers about the ship.

The rations for the crew was worse than average by Marcus' estimation, but still enough to fill his stomach. The chef had been instructed to primarily make rice stir-fry with a variety of sauces to change up the flavor, and Marcus suspected the reason was to make it less obvious when the fillings ran out. There was only so much meat and so many vegetables aboard. If things went poorly, they'd all be on rice and mashed potatoes soon enough.

When Captain Regulus made his address, he did it from the bridge and simulcast it to Link Reality, from where Marcus listened to it. "Ladies and gentlemen aboard the *Demos*, this is your captain speaking to you," he began, and without method of retort, the passengers aboard the *Demos* listened to the story of the new ship's arrival, and of its subsequent thrust towards The Nebulae Company's exo mine which would take them weeks. Whether the ship itself was friend or foe didn't matter: it would not be able to provide escape before the arrival of Alliance ships.

Then, as if at a press conference, he opened the floor for questions. Marcus had stood to the side of the captain, watching the crowd like a stationed guard for him. It gave him a clear view across the heads, and he saw the man who stepped forward with a hand raised. He was a withered, misshapen old man. Every bump on his body seemed to have an extra bump. Standing up straight left an impression of a hunch, compounding his beaten down visage. "Captain, sir, should we not contact the ship to inquire if they have some measure of peace making power? We may have lost the war, but the war is still over. We don't need to fight the Alliance anymore."

"I would hope they do," the captain said. "If they do have such proof, then it will become evident when the Alliance arrives and they parley rather than blow them to bits. That is something else we can wait and see."

A few other people raised hands, asking about mundane affairs unrelated to the arrival of the ship. They complained about the cold again, about the alcohol restrictions and if a fermentation still might be set up. For all their requests, Captain Regulus heard them out in full, and gave firm rejections to each in turn. The only concession he gave was on the processing of corpses. Nearly two dozen people had passed away in the first two weeks as a side effect to the thrust, and while he refused to eject them into space, he agreed to move the bodies to a de-oxygenated airlock. It was traditional to dispose of those who died in space with stellar incineration, but the likelihood of their bodies being spotted and traced back was too high.

While that went on, Marcus pulled up the identity of the man who had first spoken. The identification photo of him was just as unfortunate as the man's digital avatar, but his resume made up for it. Pontius Livius was a planetary architect with research papers dating back nearly a millennium on Earth. He had been on Athens Station tweaking the progress of the planet Tiber while living like a hermit in the genetics lab.

What's more, he had a certain redaction mark on his profile. The redacted data wasn't available on the *Demos*, but Marcus knew exactly what it was. The man was gene-modded. The redaction was Earth's way of covering up its transgression of its own casus belli.

Must be neurologically enhanced.

"Ranger? If I may have some of your time?" a woman asked.

He turned and saw Miz Felicity Lenz once more. The business attire had been abandoned in favor of a sleeveless sweater and a skirt. It looked much better on her. No environmental suit meant he could see some of her skin too. "You need my time? Or your boss does?"

The way she smirked seemed to both tempt him, and brace him for disappointment.

7

High Speed Fireworks

The Fourteenth Day

Reality was as low as his hopes. He sat down with Mr Samaras, once again in the back corner of the cafe in Link Reality. The captain had wrapped up the public address, and left the passengers with an empty taste in their bellies. For everyone else, there was nothing they could do. For Charles Samaras, CEO of the Nebulae Company, he had to decide whether to advise his employees in the mine to abandon the facility or not. "What's your take on the matter?"

Since when does a CEO solicit someone else's opinion? What are you getting at Samaras?

"I wasn't aware you had a means to get a signal to them without alerting the probes."

"We have probes of our own," he said. "Exploratory things. They're in the asteroid belts to map out resource deposits. Gold, aluminum, phosphorus, ice of course, all of it will be needed eventually. There's an economic balance to colonization; whether to strip mine a system or to hoard its resources for that planet's future. You can't make the decision correctly if you don't know what's out there. I think we can shoot a laser to one of the distant probes, such that our own shadow hides it from Mimir, and then they can bounce it around. The Alliance wouldn't suspect anything other than routine computer communication."

Marcus frowned. "And you just thought of this?"

The businessman scowled and leaned back in his chair. "The ship AI hasn't been very cooperative with me. The captain has the processing clamps screwed all the way down. I didn't want to bring it up without knowing if there was one close enough to the line. It's not as simple as geometry after all. The light might take minutes to bounce back at us and we're traveling rather fast. An errant laser could slip by and then it would all be for naught."

"But you do know now?"

Samaras smiled and folded his hands on the table. "I do know now. If we get creative with the message, we might even be able to contact the other four ships. It won't be bi-directional, and our chance will only last a few hours ourselves, but we can get a signal to them."

And then what? Draw straws for who exposes themselves? You're only suggesting this because you think you can force the smallest ship into being our guinea pig.

"You'll have to bring it up to the captain yourself."

"But, you'll help, won't you? Surely it's in your interests as well."

I suppose it is...

The Captain's answer was a simple, "No."

The three of them, Captain Regulus, CEO Samaras, and Marcus, had gathered in the captain's office. They were arguably the most powerful men in the sector, for all that was worthwhile hiding from the Alliance, and no one knew what to say to fill the silence. Even the sound of the forced ventilation was louder than the three of them.

"Captain, sir," Marcus said, holding his hand out. "Generally speaking, taking action is better than waiting. It's not much, but this is a modicum of initiative and it may spur some action from the other ships. I would like to know your reasoning for rejecting the proposal."

Captain Regulus shrugged. "It's rather straightforward risk-reward. Just like you say, they might have something worth telling us. But... it's just as likely that the Alliance will get control over that network and trace it back to us. I'm sure you have a few employees on the other ships as well. You're a smart man, Mr Samaras, but you also hire smart people. They'll eventually have the same idea that you just had now and if there's something critical, then they can communicate it to us. Not like we can stop them from doing that. As far as your employees at the mine go, why do you think they'd want to hear from you at all? Wouldn't they want their lives in their own hands rather than be given expectations by their boss?"

Charles wetted his lips and wrung his hands together. "I was going to tell them to abandon the mine. I've been reviewing the legal documentation to double check and, given the terms of surrender, the Alliance will be held liable for any and all damages to company property. The losses can be recouped and it's not like someone else is going to start harvesting the Exo out there."

Captain Regulus shook his head. "Either way, as the captain of this ship and the one ultimately responsible for the lives aboard this ship I will not allow you to send such a signal." He pressed the button to open his office door to send them out.

Samaras rose with gritted teeth. He and Marcus walked out wordlessly. Charles' body trembled and his teeth clenched, but he didn't say anything as he took the hall back to the makeshift residential quarters.

Marcus watched him leave and asked Mia to keep an eye on him. He submitted a suggestion to increase the CEO's liquor allotment as a sign of consolation.

With Athens Station destroyed, the refugees aboard the *Demos* were blind to A-Mov, so the arrival of a second ship caught everyone by surprise. It was only noticed on the twenty-first day, and by then the new arrival had already entered a distant orbit of Mimir. Mia's calculations said it must have arrived during the second tumble, while the *Demos'* sensors were misaligned. With the new ship already in steady orbit, nothing could be said about its make. Without active thrust, there was nothing to see in the heat signature.

Under the captain's orders, there was nothing to be done aboard the *Demos* but wait. The day after the second ship's arrival, the Collapse went off. Had any of the *Demos*'s A-Mov sensors remained, the confusion in the bridge would have been far greater; but, with the cameras limited to light, there was merely a shift in the movement of the flayed moon. The orbit changed from the twist of expended exo fuel and it crashed inwards. The Collapse hadn't been strong enough to point it directly at Mimir's exposed and radioactive core, but the eccentric sink had become unavoidable with time.

The still cooling moon entered an oscillation of diving close to Mimir, picking up speed, and getting slung back out. Before the first cycle completed, a heat signature was detected leaving the second ship. Father Publius gathered his faithful together and bowed their heads in prayer, because there was only one thing that could move so fast, and it spelled doom for the people of the first ship. The new ship had shot a missile at the first one.

Marcus watched the telemetrics. Space combat was a slow thing, and the destruction of the, assumed, merchant ship couldn't be avoided. For the next day, there was continual tracking data fed to one corner of Marcus' vision and he would flip between raw data and computer modeling to correct for relativity as the missile did its best to break the universal speed limit.

The merchants tried to escape. They fired up emergency thrust options and blasted flak clouds behind them. It would have worked against most missiles, and perhaps even if they had gotten lucky. The Alliance missile was not like most. It couldn't be compared to the kind of welded together death traps a pirate might fire. When the merchants launched their own missiles, the Alliance weapon corkscrewed and blasted straight through the explosions to lance the mercantile vessel.

The explosion went sideways to the mine, plumeing debris out into the vacuum and away from any resource humans might need in the next thousand years. Trillions of credits of hardware became nothing more than slag coffins for the crew. The exo mine went untouched, merely spectator to the murder.

"That's why," Marcus said when he met with Charles Samaras again. "The captain won't take the risk. We would be even less able to defend ourselves than that ship."

The CEO seemed detached as he sat in Link Reality with the Space Ranger. "This isn't right," he said, barely moving his body. "Earth has abandoned us if the Alliance can so unilaterally... if they can just massacre people and think they can get away with it."

"Dead people can't sue."

"Where are our weapons? Why can't we fight back?" he demanded, leaning forward in his chair.

He's sounding like Hideo.

"Requisitioned for a fight that was lost. Not to say Earth has no forces left though. Just not here around Fuls. The entire Earth Fleet wasn't wiped out. They can send something to fight it out now that the front lines have been disarmed. We'll probably even see some different Alliance ships come to our rescue."

"We have to do something, Ranger."

"We have to survive."

Charles nodded. "Yes. Yes, we have to survive and then we do something about these people..."

Shortly thereafter, Marcus received a text message through the ship's communication network from the man most likely to do something about those people. Hideo Olympus messaged to ask, "Care for a spar?"

It turned out that he meant in Link Reality, with Arena character profiles. The game was un-stylized, as close to real fighting as computers could simulate. Anything less would have gone out of fashion. The trends were nothing more than various flavors of weapons but the two of them opted for bare handed. The only catch was that Hideo had leveled up a few times, enhancing the strength and weight the system gave him.

"I can reset to level one, if you'd like," the security officer said as he walked out to the middle of the arena.

Marcus glanced around at the arena that had been randomly selected, a gothic bell tower. The railings were low, easy to get thrown over. The drop after that counted as a death. "It's fine, you need all the help you can get."

Hideo grinned and put up his fists. "That attitude, it's the right kind of attitude to have. Come on, let's blow off some steam." He theatrically put up a hand and beckoned him over.

Round one ended with Hideo's face smashed into the masonry. Marcus flipped him over the railing in round two, and in the third round forced a submission. "Do you want to keep going? It's rather pleasant fighting when you don't get tired."

"Again!"

Half an hour later, Marcus had a good grasp on what the man was capable of. Much more than a civilian, but it was the skill of an elite rookie. He could have been good, with the right leader in the right spot. The *Demos* was neither. "I think now's about the time you tell me the actual reason you asked for a spar. I appreciate the distraction, but..."

Hideo huffed. He was laid out across the floor, staring at the brass bell overhead. The inside was a dark abyss, the weight swaying within like an orbiting star. "Ranger, we've got a shark in the waters with us."

"Interesting analogy." He sat down against one of the walls.

"Space is an ocean of nothingness. We're in ships. Sorry, layover from my childhood," Hideo said as he sat up and turned to him. "There are five of us, surviving ships from Athens. Five of us, and one ship with enough missiles to kill us all."

"If they find us," Marcus said.

"If we do nothing."

"If they want to kill us."

"Can we gamble on that?"

"Do we have a choice?"

"Don't we?"

"Are you about to tell me you found some kind of weapon for us?"

Hideo smirked. "The *Demos* is a transport ship to Tiber. It has a landing craft. A little eight person thing designed to dock with the space elevator they haven't built yet. It was your idea to board them, wasn't it?"

Marcus shook his head. "That's a suicidal mission. It doesn't have any hope under these circumstances."

"Maybe, but if nothing else, it would eat up some of their

missiles, wouldn't it? Maybe they wouldn't be able to kill all of us after that..."

Marcus rose. "I think you should stop watching... whatever show you're watching that's convincing you that going out in a blaze of glory is a good idea. You're lucky that you have time to sleep on it. You'll realize how dumb that idea is eventually."

"I'm scared, Ranger."

"We all are."

"I'm a cornered animal."

"No," Marcus said. "You're a human. So act like one."

8

The Fog of War

The Twenty-Ninth Day

"May I join you?" Pontius Livius, the mutant, asked as he sat down across from Marcus. He didn't wait for the answer, he just sat his tray of food down in the cramped hall-turned-cafeteria and joined him. "I would like to speak with you about the future of this ship."

I'd rather you didn't.

Marcus looked down at his food. He had the same as the rest of the passengers. A month after fleeing Athens Station, that meant they were going to be out of meat. The rice mix still had plenty of vegetables, but that meal was likely his last taste of meat for a long while. Lab-grown and somewhere between pork and beef, it had managed to soak up all the flavor of the sauce. There were still three cubes of it before him, and yet his appetite vanished. "Quite a portentous time you've chosen."

Pontius' fork slammed into his food and scooped out a

piece of meat laden with rice and stuffed it into his mouth. As he chewed, he said, "This is my final chance to broach the subject with you, Mr Maximus. Captain Regulus will send a summons for you soon."

Marcus tugged his tray closer, out of the spit bombardment zone. "Only if ships arrive. Nothing to discuss with him if Scythia doesn't send help."

"Scythia will send help. I estimate three ships will arrive but not before the Alliance sends reinforcements. They'll know precisely when we detected their attack and when help could arrive. I suspect what they'll use are nuclear mines," Pontius responded. He didn't look at Marcus as he spoke, just at his food as stabbed his fork through it and stirred it up. The man's lips smacked together as he stuffed his mouth.

Knowledgeable for a terraformer...

"They have ways of dealing with booby traps like that. And Mimir is a big place to cover with mines. Scythia could come out at any spot," Marcus said, forcing himself to take another bite.

"Nope. Not true. With the moon in freefall like that, the only safe exit points are near the poles. Without accurate data, they can't risk getting slammed into the rock on exit so they can choose top or bottom. Bit of a simplification, but it's essentially true. Hopefully what they've done is sent a communication probe ahead of them to parley for an hour or so and hope the frigate turns the bombs off."

"And the mirror flak is just one big show of confetti that blocks communication for an hour or so while neither side launches missiles at the other?"

"Would you fault an enemy ship for preemptively inking like a scared squid?" Pontius asked, taking his knife and ripping a piece of meat in half as he stared at the Space Ranger.

Marcus sat back in his seat and folded his arms. "Depends on what else the ship does. I tend to not like relying on mines. Too many bad experiences with old bombs that misfired. Have you ever had to gently nudge a nuclear mine whose cesium charge had decayed to uselessness?"

Pontius shrugged and chewed a particular piece of gristle before swallowing and dabbing his lips with a cloth. "Not of the nuclear variety, no, but I have experience both with my raw materials vanishing into the cosmos and with conventional bombs not going off. We use them for seeding spores onto planets. Once we're sure there's nothing worth investigating, we formulate some bacteria fit for the atmosphere, or perhaps some lichen and fungi, that sort of thing, and send it planetside. It has to be dispersed while in low atmosphere and it's quite the blunder of money if it hits a mountain without going off."

"Losing your investors some money and losing your own life is a bit different."

Pontius smirked, if the twist of his face flesh could be called a smirk. "Not so different, if you ask me. People don't generally starve anymore, but plenty enough end up in drugs or crime or taking their own life. You need money to live, Space Ranger."

"That's the kind of stuff you can only say when you've lived your own lifetime twice over on the government's dime. How does it feel to be abhuman anyways?"

"Spoken with the cruelty of someone who has ended a hundred lives. No wait, I must be underestimating you, the esteemed Space Ranger. Veteran of how many battles? Frankly, I much prefer my lot in life than yours, especially knowing we have arrived here at the same fate."

Marcus sighed. "What is it that you came here for, Pontius? Are you going to ask me to bring a proposal to the captain on your behalf or something?"

The researcher shrugged and stuffed his mouth once more. "Nothing of the sort. I have nothing to say to our little tyrant." He didn't flinch when Marcus leaned forward, gripping his arms ever tighter. "I'd just like to see some of the sensor data. It's all been under lock and key. I want to see what the good captain has been keeping from us."

You want to undermine him.

"That information is classified. You wouldn't get that even on a civilian craft, let alone a government rescue vessel like this."

"Wouldn't we though?" Pontius said, stirring his sauce puddle into his rice. He stuffed a spoonful into his mouth and chewed. Before continuing, he glanced up and down the hall, at the dozen other unwashed passengers aboard the *Demos*. "Why is our fate being controlled by one man? I'd just like to see the data. I believe you've been given special access to it yourself. You're able to hold yourself together because you can see what's happening out there. It's different for the rest of us, Ranger. We are riding blind. The other ships out there may as well be stories told in a fable by a traveling minstrel about knights and dragons far, far away. These walls are all that we can see. Obviously, I can't force you to show me any-thing. Nobody can coerce you, but I thought I'd make the request."

Well, the only way he could undermine Regulus is if he had a better idea...

"I'll think about it," Marcus said, and as though they were magic words, Pontius Livius rose from the table with his empty tray. The request sat with him, festering in his thoughts even after he forced himself to eat the last of the food. Like he had walked through a bad odor, it followed him to the bridge. The click of the door behind him seemed louder.

"Welcome to the bridge, Ranger," Sergei Seachnall said. The second in command of the *Demos* stood before the holo-display. The camera feed showed Mimir's tumultuous corpse. The planet burned. Tidal forces from the sinking moon tore ice clouds counter to raging magnetic storms that had slagged iron bursting from the core. If the armies of Hell had climbed out of the depths, it could not have looked worse. "Overkill, isn't it?"

"The attack?"

"No, I just... I meant the holo-display," the helmsman said as Marcus walked up to him. "We're using the 3-D holo-display when all we have is a camera feed and some antennae. If the captain would allow it, this kind of data could be fed into the neural implant of everyone aboard the ship, and yet he has it on the holo-display only. It's weird, isn't it?"

It's weird that he's hiding so much information.

"Isn't it natural to put the most important thing on the big screen?" Marcus said.

"It's like watching a movie in Link Reality," Sergie said, scratching his chin.

Perry, the EM tech, shouted, "It's here!" He stuck his head out from his G-pod and looked down at them. The holo-display ticked over and updated, zooming in on a spec of light emerging from the north pole of Mimir. Mia highlighted it and started tracking its emergence until light bloomed from the clouds.

So much for talking it out.

"Damn," Marcus said, his shoulders slumping as he watched the nuclear mines destroy the parley probe. "Did it squirt out a signal first?"

Perry punched the wall of his acceleration pod, and the rest of the crew echoed his sentiment. When Sergei echoed the question, Perry answered, "No, sir. I think it tried to locate the ship first. Then it got fried."

"It's war then."

Over the next twelve hours, no less than three groups of ships emerged from Mimir at frightening speeds, blasting out into the ecliptic plane with high G turns. Missiles blasted between radio signals shot between them. From his seat in the bridge, Marcus and the others listened to pleas to stop, appeals for a ceasefire, and threats of annihilation.

Nuclear explosions never stopped filling the void.

After a time, Marcus detached himself from his own fate, and the fate of the Scythians who had arrived to fight with the Alliance. He watched it like he was observing someone else's chess game. He watched it play out from every angle, and imagined what was going through each captain's mind as the struggle played out over the hours. One by one, ships were blasted, their air vented and their reactors cracked to spew radiation into space.

"This middle group, the three ships that arrived after the first four, those are Alliance ships," Marcus said, sending the message to the captain. The ships were little more than spots of streaking light across the background of the Milky Way, but he was certain. The captain nodded and ordered Mia to update the hypothetical tagging.

It did nothing to help the situation. By the twenty hour mark, the combat still hadn't been resolved and the crew were taking shifts sleeping. The captain set up a secondary viewing screen to keep an eye on the latest picture while the holo-display became a discussion forum. At scale, the actions of the ships over the preceding day could be replayed at which-ever time scale they felt like. Debates flared over whether certain actions had been expert maneuvers or unforced errors. It helped ease everyone's minds to discuss it that way, rather than the demise of their rescuers.

Hope seemed lost.

Of the four assumed Alliance ships, only two had been scuttled. The seven Scythian ships had been reduced to one, and they were the smallest of the fleet. It meant they were the most maneuverable, but their payloads had certainly been depleted.

"Do we want to believe these are brave men?" Marcus asked. Weary eyes turned back to him. "Combat crews for spaceships don't need to be very large. A few dozen are all that's needed if you have the right AI. It gets easier to find willing martyrs when you only need so few that are willing to fly out and die to save us."

"Why bring this up?" Captain Regulus asked, fatigue robbing him of his shout.

Marcus pointed to a grayed out Scythian ship drifting around Mimir, long since destroyed. "That one was hit by a mass accelerator. It wasn't baked with radiation. The engines are dead, but the crew might still be alive. If they are, and if they're playing possum, their orbit will bring them point blank with one of the Alliance ships. They could flip the playing field."

No one spoke after that. They let the words hang like a magic spell in the air and watched. Minutes ticked by with nothing but the dull sounds of computers about them. Missiles flared off between the remaining ships, chasing down the Scythian vessel. It fled, darting to the dark side of Mimir and dragging its pursuers through the debris of the gas giant. The Alliance ships gave chase, firing up their engines

The prediction came true.

The lagging Alliance ship, the one close to the blown out corpse of the Scythian frigate, took a thorium slug to the mid section. The turn ripped the ship apart, tearing the engine and reactor free from the humans aboard.

Everyone but Captain Regulus cheered. They whooped and hollered, but the fight wasn't over.

"Radiation detected in the fringe of Mimir, they blew something up on the opposite side," Perry shouted, getting his voice over the din.

"Now it's over," Captain Regulus said, and closed his eyes.

One ship emerged from the opposite end of Mimir, and Mia couldn't recognize which it was. Whether the Scythian ship had escaped, or its Alliance pursuer had destroyed it, no one on the *Demos* could say.

I'm going to have to get Pontius the data.

9

Undermining

The Thirty-First Day

"My name is Persephone Waters. We are the crew of the Nebulae Company Exo Mining Station, Fuls-Hades-I. As per galactic treaty, we operate independently of direct Earth, or direct Alliance, control and make no discrimination in our production of fuel. As our only line of re-supply has been destroyed, that being Athens Station, we five are faced with the reality of dwindling supplies and no escape. We are hereby desperately requesting humanitarian aid and rescue from the lone ship orbiting what was Mimir. We were expecting re-supply soon, and we cannot last much longer. We are not part of this war. Please do not make us casualties of it."

The captain's office held the echoes of the plea till it died around them. The final frame showed the five engineers, gathered up with the floating awkwardness people had while trying to stay still in zero gravity. They were in dirty jumpsuits, though Marcus was sure their laundry facilities were still in order.

Rather conscious of their image, aren't they?

The woman speaking had a disfigured form. Her head appeared to have been pressed into a square, with blunted nostrils and diminutive eyes that could barely be made out beneath her brow. Her fingers clutched a tablet to read off of, with club-like ends capped with the thickest nails he had ever seen. The rest of her compressed body did little to help her image. "You have a mutant working as the lead on your craft?"

"She's not the lead, the man on the right is," Samaras said, pointing to the image before clasping his hands onto his chin again.

"They think the ship is Alliance then," Captain Regulus said, and sipped his whiskey. "Mia, did they have line of sight to the final confrontation?"

"Yes, Captain. Their viewing angle is approximately eighty degrees from our own," the ship responded.

Hoping for sympathy from the Alliance by putting her up front?

"That's not necessarily true. The lead has a stutter. He can't present to save his life. He's a good engineer and a good manager, not a good speaker. He may have simply delegated the role to his second in command," Samaras said, unable to take his eyes off the frozen transmission.

Captain Regulus scoffed. "If that was the case, he had three other people to choose from, and he chose the mutant. Explain that to me. This went out in all directions. They wanted us to hear it too, while in all likelihood, that ship is going to beam a direct message back to them. Your crew had the courtesy to not reveal our location or even our existence, so don't you think we should be analyzing this a bit more?"

Samaras' hand slammed onto the desk. Marcus leapt to his feet, stepping between the businessman and the captain. "The Nebulae Company doesn't discriminate, unlike you people," Samaras shouted. "Miz Waters is the second in command and a damn good repair technician. Just because she has high-gravity genes does not mean you should speak of her that way."

Great, the schism deepens.

"Mr Samaras, I'm going to have to ask you to calm down," Marcus said, only easing his stance when the businessman sank into his chair. "The fact remains that his choice would signal amiability to an Alliance vessel, and less so to a Scythian ship. I'm not questioning your hiring practices, but we do need to discuss why they made the choices they did, why they said the things they said."

The CEO put up his hands. "Given the dilemma, you're probably right. That did sound like a plea to an Alliance ship. So what are we going to do about it?"

"Nothing," Captain Regulus said. "Given light delay, the ship should be messaging them back right about now, and in an hour's time, we can expect your crew's answer. Maybe we'll see the ship start blasting over to them. The heat signature implies that even if it is a Scythian ship, they aren't large enough to rescue all five thousand or so of us anyways."

"So in an hour, we may know more?" Marcus asked.

The captain nodded. "In an hour or so."

"There may be something else we can do in the meantime," Marcus said, and he paused to think over the words in his mouth. Both other men raised eyebrows at him. "There's a civilian aboard the *Demos* that may be worth consulting with over probabilities. He has the mind for it."

Captain Regulus sneered. "You mean that geezer Pontius Livius, don't you?"

"Yes, sir."

"Denied," the captain said, and finished his glass of whiskey.

So this is how Samaras feels.

"Sir, it isn't wise to deny resources because of personal dislikes," Marcus said, keeping his voice cool.

Captain Regulus waved with the empty glass. "Nothing he says will change my decision, so why should I give him the data? I've already considered the possibilities. Bringing him into the equation would just open me up to being second guessed by everyone."

"Maybe you should be," Samaras said as the captain pulled open his drawer and rattled around for the whiskey bottle once more.

This isn't going to work. He's just going to dig in harder. Meaningless resistance will get us all killed.

Marcus shook his head and said, "We'll talk once more in an hour. There's nothing more to be said for now." He and Mr Samaras left the captain's office and let it lock behind them.

While they were still alone in the hallway, the CEO shook

his head. There was tension through his jaw. "That's not the way a leader should act."

Yeah, but businessmen never know how a soldier should lead.

Marcus put a hand on the man's shoulder. "His decision isn't unreasonable. This ship isn't an anarchy. We follow rules and hierarchy. If there were no restrictions, there would have been messages sent to the Alliance probes begging for mercy by at least a few people on this ship. The captain has to keep that in line for the good of all."

Samaras threw his shoulder and shirked Marcus' hand. "Don't you ever think that attitude is the problem? How do you think we ended up in this war, Ranger?"

To put money in the pockets of people like you, you virtue signaling hypocrite. How do you not realize that?

Marcus didn't voice the answer. His jaw was wired too tight to let the words slip out, and the CEO just shook his head and walked off in the silence. The Ranger didn't follow Samaras back to the general hold where all the acceleration pods were, nor did he sink his mind into Link Reality. The *Demos* had a number of private quarters available to it, and he had been given one of them out of deference to his station. The amenities were minimal. The lone computer interface sat perpetually off like a window to the darkness beyond.

It was the bed that called him the most, and he collapsed into it. The mattress was thin and hard. It felt like the foam had solidified from too many decades while the *Demos* sat one step away from decommissioned. It fought with his body as he tried to relax, and prodded him in all the wrong spots, where his muscles had knotted and his joints had become inflamed.

He closed his eyes for a moment, and darkness enveloped him. It was the darkness of space, of tens of thousands of empty kilometers. A desert of not just water but of air, and the poisonous snake had a nuclear missile trying to find him. Fatigue tried to put him to sleep, but his mind showed him the pure white flare of bombardment blooming in his vision; strong enough to blot out everything.

His eyes snapped back open. The tension in his body returned. Just taking a breath made his chest creak.

"Mia, could you put on some piano for me? Something from the Gynatonic phase. On a loop if you would." A rolling conversation between three hands filled the room, just loud enough to satisfy the part of his brain that craved the noise of others. He brooded while listening to the chipper dance of notes, and staved off sleep.

Captain Regulus didn't send for him at the hour mark. At the second hour mark, Marcus went so far as to draft messages to both Pontius Livius and Charles Samaras, but didn't send them. He closed his eyes only when the need for sleep was so overwhelming it crushed even his subconscious. The dark confines of dreams did little to sort out his troubles.

A knock at his door roused him, and he fumbled with his body, waving his hand in the air until the motion detectors turned the lights on for him. Once illumination flickered in, he had his revolver in one hand and sidled up to the door to crack it open. Miz Felicity Lenz stood outside, holding her tablet to her chest just like the first day they had met, even down to the clothes. "Miz Lenz... to what do I owe the plea-sure?" he asked, quietly putting his gun back into his suit.

She cleared her throat. "This isn't about my job, Ranger."

If only I could dream that it was for me.

"You can call me Marcus, you know."

"Mr Maximus, I have a personal request I would like to make of you. Could I step inside?"

Wait... can I?

He retreated and let the door slide open. The room hardly afforded the space to step inside, but he sat down on the bed and she was able to sit on the sink and the two of them were alone. He looked her over, once again in the exposure suit from the first day they had met. "Does your boss not let you wear business casual even on this ship?"

"Spare clothes weren't important to bring. Don't you ever take that armor off?"

The Ranger's suit had so many plugs and ports into his flesh that taking it off was a half hour affair, if he had help. It wasn't something he did if he didn't have to. His helmet at least was off, so he put on a grin. "It makes me feel safe. It's my security blanket." The grin felt wrong, which meant it must have looked wrong.

Felicity didn't comment on it. "Well, I would never want to deprive a boy of his safety blanket, but it will actually prove useful this time," she said with a roll of her eyes and a brush of her hair.

Marcus' grin faded. "What's happened?"

She hung her head and he could see her squeezing her arms. "Well, I'd be lying if I said this came as a surprise to anyone aboard… but, there isn't exactly proper privacy on this ship. We're over capacity and… well, the bath has to be scheduled a few days out to keep the water clean."

"I can't do anything about that, Miz Lenz. If we try to force more water through the system, we could have a disease outbreak. I'm sure plenty of people would be fine with group bathing just to get in more often, but-"

"No, that's not the issue. It's the fact that we're scheduled."

"As opposed to first come first serve? The elderly would never get in."

She laughed and lifted up her head. "Do you really not get it? The schedule means everyone on the *Demos* knows who will be in the bath, and when. So… if someone is following you. If someone wants to get you where it's private…"

Marcus' eyebrows rose up. "Ah. It's that kind of issue. Thank God." The grin became genuine.

"That's a bit inappropriate to say, isn't it?"

He laughed and waved his hand through the air. "No, not like that. I'm thanking God that I have something simple to deal with. I've been needing some stress relief and until now, the ship had no punching bags. Link Reality just doesn't do it for me the way real sweat and pain does."

After some cross-referencing with Mia, he went down to where all the refugees were. He sent a message to Hideo then began rounding up the men, and two women, who had transgressed. With some help from some civilians he had seen at prayer with Father Publius, he yanked them from sleep or from Link Reality one by one and tossed them into a sealed hallway. Once all the troublemakers had been gathered in their various shades of undress, he really didn't need to explain why the hammer was coming down. Hideo never even bothered to show up, he just messaged back, "Go ahead."

Did it follow proper protocol? Not in the slightest.

Did he get a tongue lashing from the doctors aboard? For half an hour.

Did the lesson have to be repeated? No.

A reminder sign was scrawled onto the wall outside the bathing facilities. The women aboard graciously took up the public relations job to let the whole ship know exactly why so-and-so had a swollen cheek, difficulty breathing, or a cast on, as well as who was to thank for it. He knew it would cause copycats, but that would be Hideo's problem. The crew and the passengers would have to sort the minor details out themselves.

Marcus slept soundly after that, as though the burst of fighting had washed the stress from his mind and relieved him of the burden. It was the deep, black oblivion that could only be rivaled by space and death.

Sergei Seachnall called him into a private room the next morning to discuss mutiny.

10

Insubordination

The Thirty-Second Day

"You've got to be kidding me."

"You weren't there, Ranger. You didn't see it for yourself. He stripped me of my rank for opposing him on the bridge. The captain cannot be trusted anymore." Sergei sat on a bucket of cleaning fluid in the utility closet, wringing his hands. There were tension lines in his face, and gaunt pockets around his eyes.

Well, this is the worst possible situation.

"Sergei, have you been on stimulants these past few days? You don't look so good. Your judgment must be impaired."

"No!" He stamped his foot and settled himself with a deep breath. "No, that's not the issue. I was dismissed before I lost any sleep. I lost sleep because I got dismissed. Ranger, you have to see, this isn't something I can do on my own. I need your help. This will keep playing out and you'll see for yourself. I'm sure you will because I'm sure that he's going to keep making these kinds of mistakes. So I want you to ask yourself; how many mistakes will you risk him making? How many before we lose our last chance?"

It's only our last mistake if it gets us nuked.

Marcus held his tongue until Sergei had said his piece and settled down. The Ranger said, "Even if he has made a mistake at this moment, every other ship captain has done the same as him. They've all kept their quiet. Scythia isn't the only station able to send help to us. In two more weeks, Red Cairo will be able to respond with even greater forces. You have to remember that we're not just looking for an Earth ally to control the sector. That's not enough. They also need to have enough cargo space to take everyone aboard and get them through A-Mov."

Sergei nodded his head a few times, like it was an extension of nervously tapping his head. "They haven't. All made the same decision that is. The *Theopone* reversed course the moment the battle ended and began cruising back towards Mimir. They put themselves on an intercept course with the scuttled ships. It looks to me like they are trying to salvage one of the A-Mov engines and enough Exo to dive and escape."

Again, the silence dragged between them; but, this time it was out of shock. "Does the *Theopone* have the processing power to handle that kind of modification? A-Mov engines aren't something you can just bolt on to your ship and run with."

"I would suppose that they think they do. They've probably got more than a few engineers aboard that can handle the connections."

"But if they get the math wrong their trajectory could put them between stars. They would all die. And that's assuming the engine doesn't just blow up on them."

Sergei smirked and shrugged. "Just means they have a captain willing to take a risk. When we got left behind before the attack, everyone assumed we were as good as dead. The ones that got away, my god, you should have seen the lines. I watched some of the videos. People murdered to get family members on those ships. I watched a man stab a woman to death and shove his child through the airlock in her place." As he spoke, his hands started to shake again and he drove his fingers through his shaggy hair. He gripped his hair by the roots and tugged until the pain calmed him down. "What would you do with a man like that? If he were aboard this ship right now, Ranger?"

"If there was a man who had killed to save his child? Are you speaking with someone in mind?" All he got in response was a smirk and a shrug. "Nothing. I wouldn't do anything until we had made it out the other end. Justice is for the long term. We don't have the luxury of caring about anything but survival right now. What's more, when this ship touches down on friendly soil, I can make the court system deal with it instead of me," he said and tried to laugh.

I might have killed to get myself aboard. Maybe I should have...

Sergei didn't join the laugh. "So, you'd be fine working with a murderer in order to survive?"

"The line between murder and warfare is muddy. You've never been in real shit before, have you, Mr Seachnall?"

Sergei put his hands back into his laps and made them grab hold of each other. "Not as an adult, no. When I was a little kid, the Alliance captured the planet I was on. The evacuation had more time than this; but, it was still rushed. You see, we didn't even really understand that the fight had been lost. Nothing changes when you lose control of access to A-Mov fifty-thousand kilometers away, you know. Some flashes in the sky, nothing more. Then we got a... we got a broadcast saying the rebels have control over the gas giant and have ordered a peaceful evacuation of all government personnel."

"Sounds like you got lucky. You got conquered by someone trying to make peace. Not everyone believes that the purpose of war is to make a better peace."

"Ranger, that planet was Jerusalem-5."

Marcus recoiled, his back straightening till his head hit the door behind him. "My God. You're the first survivor I've ever met."

"A whole planet of Humanist-Puritanists. They thought they'd be left alone for picking a desert planet in the middle of nowhere. Turned out that the only reason they let one ship of government officials escape was because they weren't interested in those of us who simply happened to be there. Afterwards, they used the planet to test all of their weapons by killing anyone they felt like. In their minds, it was people like them who had caused the war in the first place."

"But, you escaped," Marcus interjected.

"After my father had to shoot the captain to satisfy those bastards. Captain Cohen... the Alliance had him pegged for war crimes they said... They said they wouldn't let us pass with him still alive and my father was the one to carry that burden. So he shot him, and kicked the body out of an airlock so the Alliance could pick it up. The court systems, about eight years later, finally caught up with him while I was in training, and they executed him."

Of course, they had to protect the precedent.

"That would be the punishment for mutiny, yes. The same thing you're asking me to do," Marcus said, keeping his voice soft.

"How can it be called mutiny when it saved everyone else's life? Captain Cohen would have forced a shootout between a transport and a warship. We would have all died to save his honor. My father... he chose survival and he died with dignity."

Marcus shook his head. "Does Captain Regulus know about your history?"

"It's in my file."

"Then it's no wonder he dismissed you. He probably wants you nowhere near him right now, and for good reason. From what you've said, the only issue I have with the Captain's choices is his lack of communication. I would have preferred being told that the *Theopone* had made a move. It means the surviving ship is Scythian, and pretty soon they can shoot down the probes the Alliance left behind. We might be able to actually hold a conversation with them. But it doesn't change the fact that one little frigate en route to the exo mine isn't able to ferry us to safety. We still have to wait. We're done here, Sergei," he said, and rose to his feet.

"I can get you the data that Pontius Livius wanted to review," Sergei said, just as Marcus' hand reached for the door.

That stopped him, and he was ashamed that it did. "I thought you said you had been stripped of your rank?"

Sergei grinned. "Doesn't mean I can't get it."

A few hours later, Marcus had to listen to Pontius say, "Good to see you again, Ranger." The layer of Link Reality between them did little to blunt the impression the mutant gave off. He didn't even stop the little puzzle game he had playing across the table in front of him. He kept tapping out commands and movements for the various pieces with one hand while he scrutinized Marcus' face.

"You can pause your game. I've got something more interesting for you to think over," the Ranger said, holding out his hand and pinching his fingers such that the interface appeared. The datafile Sergei had provided him appeared in his hand like a black cube.

"More important, hardly more interesting. Puzzles that are designed to be teased apart are much more fun than the hum-drum reality gives us. A game like this is almost a conversation between me and the designer. Your video file is more like a university practice problem designed to waste the pupil's time," he said as he put in the last moves and completed the puzzle.

"Do you want it or not?"

Pontius closed the game and held out his hand. "Of course I want it. I'm just not going to enjoy the work you've given me. I came all the way out to Athens Station specifically to avoid the war, you know," Pontius said as he took the construct.

"So did I."

Pontius licked his lips and unfocused his eyes as the data began playing out within his mind. "You wouldn't happen to be the reason that they came here, are you?"

"No," Marcus said.

I don't think.

"Just thought I'd check. I suppose it must have been a coincidence. The rock came off a black hole, didn't it? There aren't many around these parts and you came here spur of the moment. They asked who could bring the news to this armpit of the galaxy and you raised your hand for the next ship out. That's not something the Alliance could have foreseen. Bad luck for the both of us, isn't it?"

Marcus squeezed his hand into a fist. "How long will you need to get back with me? That's all I care about right now."

Pontius shrugged. "You can never tell how long an analysis will take you before you get into the data. Might take me a couple of minutes, or it might take me days. I will contact you when I'm ready, Ranger. You can go now. Your presence certainly isn't going to make this go any faster."

"And you'll come to me with your answer? No one else?"

Pontius paused and looked at him. He laughed. "Of course I will. I'm not one to risk getting shot like that, now am I? That is, if you have a gun. In your hands, a plastic spork would be about as effective. I saw what you did to the miscreants the other day. You know, actually," he said, putting his hands on the table. The mutant smiled. "Would it be appropriate of me to request a new bed? They have me in next to one of those rapists-"

"Nobody got raped."

Else, they'd be dead.

Pontius waved him off. "One of those miscreants, as I said, and I have to listen to his sniveling whimpering all night. The doctors won't give him any medication. They say it's because he isn't in critical condition, but I'm pretty sure it's just because he was skeeving on her and she's forced to play nice by the Hippocratic Oath. But what about me? If they're going to let him suffer like that, surely he should be with the other miscreants and annoying one another, rather than people who had nothing to do with it!"

"I think the crew has more pressing matters at the moment than sleeping arrangements."

The mutant scoffed. "No, they don't. The captain has ordered us to sit around and wait and shows no sign of doing anything at all! That's why you're here, isn't it? So it seems to me like they have plenty of time to attend to these sorts of problems. Don't think I haven't sniffed out their fermentation rig either. That Hadria thinks he has it hidden, and to a regular human he may well, but you can't fool this nose," Pontius said, tapping the bulbous mass he had in the middle of his face.

I should commend Hadria as soon as I can.

"Fine, complain all you'd like. Old people have been complaining since the beginning of the human race. No one will bat an eye now. I just wish people would treat me like an old man every once in a while."

"Getting your own room isn't good enough for the great Space Ranger?"

Marcus sighed. "That's not what I meant."

"You don't look like an old man, that's your problem. All the baggage of years is in your head, not in your face. Try scowling and grumbling more. Tell the kids how it was back in your day."

Marcus rose from the table. "Contact me when you're certain about the analysis. I'll sort my own problems otherwise," he said, and left the researcher.

I hope I didn't just make a mistake. I hope he's the book-worm type of mutant, and not the ear worm type. He's certainly playing like the latter, because he knows I need the former. Do I have a better choice? A better course of action to survive?

As he walked out of the virtual building, and back to the throngs of people passing their time on the *Demos*, the only set of eyes that truly took note of him belonged to a white feathered raven. Mia bristled, and Marcus received a call through the system.

Captain Regulus spoke. "Ranger, I need your help arresting Commander Hideo Olympus."

11

Lights Out

The Thirty-Second Day

Marcus didn't run through the public spaces. He figured that the sight of him running to do something would cause more harm than anything Hideo could do. He hoped Hideo couldn't be more damaging than that. Captain Regulus stayed on the line with him as he took the ladders to the nearest freight tunnel. In spin, he couldn't call it an elevator so much as a tram, but it was the quickest way to get from one end of the ship to the other.

Once he had the door closed behind him and a path to the correct airlock, then he started running.

Captain Regulus stayed in his office, occasionally saying something to his chief engineer, Sophia Almada. Marcus couldn't pick out those words, but then Ray began to explain. "It seems that Hideo took a bit too much inspiration from our Scythian friends. He thinks he can play dead then sneak an attack in. His plan is to take the lander back to

Mimir and get handy with an exo-suit and a welding torch or something."

"Does he... yeah, I guess he does know how to salvage weapons, doesn't he?"

"And he knows how to use them. The man got basic training in all weapon systems that don't require AI interfacing. For better or worse, it's fairly easy to repurpose missiles."

Make them too smart and they can be tricked, hacked, subverted. Much better to fire and forget.

"If a single Alliance probe is still out there, we'll be outed. He might get a–"

"I know, Ranger," Captain Regulus said. "Hideo cannot be allowed to leave the *Demos*. I didn't think to have Mia track him until he had already loaded the lander with supplies."

Marcus charged down the hall, passing airlocks of all sizes. Ones fit for docking with space stations, some for human sized craft, and dozens for the autonomous drones that had packed the *Demos* with supplies before being cast off to avoid their mass. Felt like Hideo was on the other end of the world. The echoes of his magnetic boots stomping against the bulkhead would tip him off. "Can't you just lock the lander down?"

Captain Regulus conferred with Miz Almada, then said, "We can delay him, but there are overrides he could use. Ranger, you're the only person on this ship with the means to restrain him. I need you to do this."

The *Demos* should have had a dozen security officers. It should have had fifty crew members at the least. It was lucky they had been able to press gang civilian doctors and nurses.

Hideo was in charge of all things security, which left Marcus as the only backup.

I should have known something was wrong when he didn't join me. I should have gotten him. Why did I–

He caught sight of the words "Airlock One" ahead, glowing in the dark. Emergency lighting, as far as he could tell. Whether it was chemical or bioluminescent, there was no mistaking the escape hall. Marcus grabbed onto the wall as he skidded to a stop, throwing himself out of the freight tunnel and into the loading hall. The airlock door had clear plastic for viewing through the center, nearly as thick as his fist. Enough debris and micro-meteors had scared it over the years to give it a fog, but he could still see the landing craft beyond. He could feel the rumble of the ship's engines starting.

"Hideo!" Marcus slammed a fist on the airlock and looked for the control to cycle the door open.

Hideo's voice crackled through the intercom as he yanked the release handle. "Ranger Maximus... Ray must have figured me out, huh?"

The hallway doors shut behind Marcus, and air pumps hissed. An error blared that it couldn't equalize with vacuum. "Hideo, stop this insubordination. You'll get us killed," he said, and then switched to only his internal microphone. "Captain, my suit is rated for vacuum. Can you override the airlock?"

"Checking that now," Captain Regulus said.

Hideo stepped over to his own airlock viewing window. The man waved. "Come on, Marcus. Now's as good a time as ever. We have to do something, you know? We just sit here, we'll end up like that merchant ship they splattered across the exo mine. This is self defense, plain and clear. You said it yourself that this was the best idea you had and you're the expert."

"I'm the expert, not you," Marcus said, and again through his call, "Permission to break the airlock? I can go in there and remove him."

"Denied," Captain Regulus said. "We need that atmosphere. We're working the codes. Just wait."

Hideo looked down and fiddled with his controls. Marcus could see the man's mouth move, but without the intercom nothing came through, which meant he was talking commands to the ship computer. Then he looked up at Marcus. The man looked tired, the change subtle. "Why don't you come with me, Ranger?"

"Why don't you open the door and we can talk this through?"

Hideo laughed. "I open this door and you'll throw me in the brig. I'm not stupid. This isn't even my first time doing this. Of course, last time I had to face off against my brother—ah, not blood related, because we found a cache of medical supplies. He wanted to sell them, I wanted to... I guess it doesn't matter. Ancient history. But, you know all about that, don't you?"

Marcus leaned forward and put his hand against the seal of the airlock. He wanted to crush it and rip the door down, before Hideo could launch and expose them all to the Alliance. "Funny how ancient history doesn't ever seem to get left in the past, isn't it? How your actions just keep following you around?"

"You're stalling."

Marcus opened his mouth, only to realize he didn't know what to say. Rationally, he knew Hideo was talking about the ship, about the lander. Emotionally was another matter.

Hideo laughed and wiped the hair out of his face. "Look, Ranger, I know this is a suicide mission. That's why I'm going to do this alone. If I don't, I think I'm going to kill myself waiting. I can't take the fear, man. I can't just sit here and wait. I can't do it." He had something resembling a smile on his face as he leaned towards the airlock door.

"Hideo–"

The lander disconnected. The parking clamps released and the spin of the *Demos* threw it free. Marcus screamed and lunged forward. His fist hit the plastic, putting a spider web of cracks through it as Hideo fell away into space without them. His heart raced, adrenaline spiking as he tried to think his way through the problem. He was considering breaking down the airlock to jump out when he realized that the lander was still there. It floated further away, tumbling free, end over end. The idling burn of the engines at the back passed by him again and again as it rotated without thrust.

"Ranger, would you please come back to my office?" Captain Regulus asked.

The fear drained away and left nothingness behind. "What did you do?"

"The only thing I could do."

"Ray! What did you do?"

"I had Miz Almada scuttle the control systems for the lander. It's no longer operational."

"I thought you were working to get me in there? I thought I was arresting him, bringing him in, talking with him." Marcus had raised his voice.

Ray shouted right back at him. "And that's what I wanted to happen, Ranger! What would you have done, in my position? I had to choose between possibly bringing him, or definitely keeping him from exposing us. That man had already ignored direct orders. I gave the command to kill the lander."

Marcus gritted his teeth and punched the airlock again. Not as hard that time, not enough to crack it again. He stared at the self-sealing gel oozing across the plastic to seal the microfractures. "You just killed your own subordinate."

Ray didn't respond until he had his voice low and somber. "I know."

Marcus killed the call and looked out the window. He couldn't hear Hideo anymore. He could only imagine what the security chief was screaming, and what he was frantically doing to get the ship powered once more, but the heat in the engines simply dissipated and the lights went out. He drifted into space, alone and doomed. Marcus had to stop himself from guessing how many hours of oxygen Hideo would have.

He turned his thoughts to himself, how he would survive.

Without power, the lander would just look like a piece of debris that broke off. No one would think a perfectly good landing craft was abandoned. The change to the rotation might be noticeable, might not be. He left the airlock, but didn't head to his room. The security office was closer, along with Hideo's liquor supply. The man hadn't taken any of it with him, hadn't finished it off either. Almost the whole supply, ferreted off Athens Station, still sat beneath the desk.

Marcus took the seat behind the desk and took off his helmet. He didn't bother with a cup, he just drank straight from the first bottle he grabbed and stared at the wall.

12

To The Brig

The Thirty-Fourth Day

"What do you mean they shot down the probes? Doesn't that prove they're Scythian? Doesn't that mean we can contact them safely?" Marcus asked, his voice rising to a shout in the bridge. He didn't add that Hideo could have flown over, didn't have to die.

Captain Regulus puffed out his cheeks and turned to face him. "Yes, about twelve hours ago. The ship is en route to the mine and that hasn't changed. It would appear that Miz Persephone Waters was able to transfer the data to them, or perhaps the *Theopone* did. Either way, the ship destroyed the probes with some low-yield missiles."

"Then why haven't we hailed them yet? Why are we still sitting here doing nothing to save ourselves?"

Captain Regulus' brow pulled together, shadowing his eyes as he stared at the holo-display. "Because nothing has changed the fact that they do not have the capacity to save us, and they aren't even about to dive into Mimir. They're still headed to the mine. More Alliance ships could pop out at any moment and where would that leave us?"

Marcus looked around at the rest of the bridge crew. He couldn't spot Sophia Almada, the one who had done the deed to kill Hideo. "Exactly where we are now."

"Respectfully, Ranger, this is my call to make. There is nothing to get our hopes up over and I won't jeopardize this ship," the captain said, and his bridge crew hung their heads or turned away.

I'm the only person here with a post he can't strip off. I have to do something.

"Captain, my primary role is as a strategic advisor and in that capacity I am advising you that you are making a mistake. Perhaps they can't ferry us away, but if they alone return to Scythia, they can at least report our situation and an educated attack force can come to our aid in just one more month. And if Red Cairo saves us before then, all the better. Contacting them creates a new avenue of escape and you are making a mistake by not pursuing it."

The captain shook his head. "I don't know what that mutant Pontius has been telling you, but he's got you twisted around his fingers. He's got your brain strung up like a marionette and you don't realize it."

How did he–

Marcus blinked. "Pontius? You're having the ship spy on me now?"

"It's my ship!" Captain Regulus bellowed. His voice burst with the strength of a drill sergeant still lingering within him after decades of rest. "We're under emergency protocols if you haven't noticed. I am the authority here. You should remember that. I could have you shot for insubordination if I so deemed it necessary."

"No. You couldn't," Marcus said, walking over to the captain who had already killed his own security chief. Marcus didn't like standing so close to people who had grown up under normal gravity. He didn't like he towered over them. He made an exception. "I'm the only one with a gun on this ship. Did you forget that? You killed the only trained security officer you had. Now you don't even have enough grunts to keep perverts out of the women's bath. You may have the proper authority to command this ship, but you do not have the power to threaten me."

The only people he had ever met that could shout back quickly had been other Space Rangers, or the insane. Captain Regulus was neither. He shrank back mentally, falling behind a shield of stoicism. Whether he was able to or not, he didn't speak as Marcus left the bridge.

The Ranger marched down to the residential area. The hold had been transformed in the last month, with sheets strung up like walls. Empty crates and boxes had been re-purposed into furniture and shelving. One particular section had once been a walkway, but the passengers had blocked it off. To the dismay of the medical staff, both official and press ganged, a love hotel had been constructed. Sheets were strung up like a shantytown roof. With the curve of the cargohold, anyone interested just had to walk around the ship and look up to sneak a peek. Trying to find his way around it made teenagers pop up and scatter like startled squirrels abandoning their nuts.

"Ranger Marcus! Ranger Marcus how have you been?" the girl Maria asked as she came running over to him. She was skinny and nimble, clambering over the gel beds while only mildly disturbing their occupants.

"Bad," he answered. Keeping the anger out of his voice was hard, but Maria deserved none of it. "Do you know a man by the name of Pontius Livius?"

"Snaggleface?" she asked, innocently twisting her face and tilting her head to scratch her knotted hair.

He sighed. "Probably. He's in a G-pod with a guy with a broken bone. Do you know where he is? I need to speak with him at once."

She beamed. "Right this way!" and took the Ranger by the hand to pull him along. She moved down the labyrinthine halls and the shifted acceleration pods like she had lived there her whole life.

Right in the middle of the mess of survivors was Pontius Livius. The old man was propped up to one corner of the bed, swaddled in a blanket and reading a computer screen in his lap. The *Demos* had risen half a degree a day, nearly returning the ship to room temperature, but old age still had its effects. The snoring youth beside him must have inspired envy. Pontius kept sneering at the man with the broken limb and kept the sneer on his face when he faced Marcus. "What do you want?"

"Did you finish your analysis?"

That made the researcher smile. "With high probability. It seems to me you have another data point for me."

"They destroyed the Alliance probes."

Pontius turned off his computer and sat it down. "Then I would stake my career on their Scythian origin. We should contact them at once. Normally, you might want to consider light reflections here and there that might get picked up by a detailed scan, but that becomes a question of when they mean to send reinforcements and light-delay. The only logical time would be at least twenty-four hours after the impact between the moon and Mimir's core."

"Thank you," Marcus said, and turned on his heels. The scrape woke up the snorer, who shouted at the silhouette above him, but the Ranger didn't slow. "Thank you for the help Maria, but-"

"Are we going to get rescued?" she asked, cutting him off.

"Not yet. I have a lot of work to do to make it happen. So don't go spreading rumors. Everyone in charge on the *Demos* is working to get us rescued as soon as possible. You know that, right? There's just something I can do that will make it happen a bit faster," he said, putting a hand on her shoulder. When she nodded and it looked like her rumors wouldn't be too wild, he left her behind and sought out Sergei Seachnall.

The door to the ex-helmsman's room was locked when he arrived. He pounded a fist on it. "Sergei, it's me."

"I was wondering what had happened when Mia locked me in here."

"Then stand back, I'm unlocking your door." Marcus

punched his fist through the door, smashing it straight through the thin layer of steel and foam around the deadbolt Mia had engaged. The hole gave him enough room to pry his fingers inside and rip the door open.

Sergei blinked at him, looking like he had jumped onto the far wall to get away. "I guess they do make you Rangers different," he said, staring at the shredded door.

"I'll tell you about it later. It's time," he said, giving the door a rough shove to jam it back into the wall. On the short walk back to the bridge he explained the situation to Sergei, and the ex-helmsman agreed at once to contact the Scythian ship.

Captain Regulus left the door to the bridge open, lest they ruin it, and greeted them with a bottle of whiskey and a scowl. There was no fuss and no fight in the man's gaze. He squared his shoulders with the Ranger and listened as Sergei announced, "Captain Ray Regulus, for negligence of duty and the murder of Commander Hideo Olympus, and under the authority given to me by the Earth Periphery Nations, I am hereby relieving you of command before you can do any further harm."

"Are you going to shoot me?" he asked, ignoring Sergei and looking at Marcus.

Marcus asked, "Are you going to make me?"

Don't make me. Just step down. Please.

Ray gave a pained smile and finished his whiskey. "To the brig then, I assume?"

Thank you.

Ray's glass tapped against the table, the loudest noise in the bridge. "Shall we go then?" he said, and with as much dignity as he could muster, he marched out of the bridge. He kept his chest high, his hands behind his back, and his chin up.

The brig was almost at the nose of the *Demos*, surprisingly close to where it had interlaced with Athens Station, but a bit off to the side and buried in the hull. It was a dismal thing by design and placed so far to the end that the precessing wobble of the ship rocked the room like constant waves.

The door locked him in, and Marcus left him there. He hoped the locks weren't voice controlled. The imprisonment was for show and both of them knew it. Mia controlled the locks and if Ray sought a way to resist him, Marcus would simply be forced to kill the old captain. The act played out quietly and without attracting the attention of the rest of the crew or passengers.

The new captain of the *Demos* took his time getting acquainted with the controls and what had transpired during his leave, so it was no surprise to Marcus that he made it back to the bridge before the announcement came.

Sergei did not stand triumphant before the helm, eyes fixed on the camera feeds. He sat with his face buried in his hands. All eyes fell on Marcus when he entered, but no one met his gaze. "What happened?" he asked, fixing Sergei with his stare.

"Mia has me locked out and won't recognize any form of override. For as long as Ray is alive, I don't have control of the ship," he answered.

On cue, the artificial intelligence manifested herself in the holo-display, white feathers bristling as she fixed Marcus with an icy stare. "There once was a story about a woman and a box that she was told to never open up."

Marcus' shoulders slumped. "Mia, don't make me do this. Don't make me use that override." Just calling it an override instead of murder tasted like bile in his mouth.

"She had one job. Go about her life and keep the box unopened," the AI continued. "Because once it's opened, all that was in it couldn't be put back inside."

"Mia, the box had to be opened. That's the point of the myth. The world couldn't be any other way, and we can't escape with him in charge," he said, stepping closer to the projection.

"Fix your mistake, Marcus. It's not too late," the AI demanded. The crew of the bridge listened without speaking. They sat with bowed heads and shrank back at her words as though they were thrust blades.

Marcus stood beneath her gaze. He had nowhere to go but to confront her. "You wouldn't understand, Mia. You don't have the instincts that humans have. They were stripped out of you to make you work. There is a reason humans are still in charge of ships, still in charge of each other, rather than machines. I know you can act of your own will, but you know I had the authority to do what I did. Don't make me use that override. Just cooperate with us."

"Sergei Seachnall has been relieved of his post. He has no authority to set foot on this bridge, and you, Marcus Maximus, have committed mutiny. You should be sitting where you put Captain Regulus."

Sergei interrupted. "Don't you think I've tried reasoning with her? As long as Ray is alive, she will recognize him and him alone as the captain. He knew we would do this and preemptively locked us out. This can't be done peacefully anymore."

Those who make peaceful revolution impossible...

"It has to be me, doesn't it?"

13

Honorable Discharge

The Thirty-Fifth Day

Ray asked, "Do you still remember your first deployment?"
Marcus said, "Of course I do."

"I can't remember mine," Ray said, interlacing his fingers behind his head and staring up at the ceiling. "We didn't get into active combat. Just deployed out for a patrol to scare off some pirates that knew better than to pick a fight with us. Couldn't tell you where it even was. They all blurred together after a while. What about you?"

"I was an auxiliary detachment on Abreu. This was before the Alliance was ever put to paper. Did you ever hear about the infestation on Abreu?" Marcus asked, leaning against the door of the prison.

"Infestation? I thought it died to a pandemic."

The Ranger laughed. "No, there was a pandemic. When the agriculture collapsed the place turned into a dust bowl and a new strain of tuberculosis cropped up and ate through the entire supply of antibiotics. Disease didn't do them in though, the wildlife did. Centipedes the size of train cars made a resurgence because the oxygen content got too high. The damned things could chew through fences and were carnivorous. We all bundled up in bomb defusal armor and, well, they couldn't bite us, but damn. Ever seen a dog get its teeth on a squirrel or something?"

"Don't tell me you were a giant bug's ragdoll..."

"Yep. Got my face smashed through sandstone a good dozen times and nearly dislocated my hip before one of my squadmates put some explosive rounds through its abdomen and saved me."

"It's a damn shame we've never found intelligent life. I dare say we haven't even found friendly life. We even went and made new types of humans to go to war with instead," Ray said.

"Maybe someone has and the word just hasn't gotten back to us, like how the peace treaty hasn't gotten to the Alliance. Or maybe we shouldn't be out there looking since it's so easy to destroy planets once you get hold of a black hole. If the fiveheads on Earth don't figure out some way to screen movement through A-Mov space humanity might end up in nothing but colony ships," the Ranger mused.

"I would say that perhaps that is why we've yet to find intelligent life out here, but there should still be a predator species out there, or at least drifting cemeteries of lost ships," Ray said.

Well, we did find the one. I'm still not cleared to talk about that one though.

"You were at the Gibraltar Gravity Falls, right? Which division?"

"Planetside actually. I was working with the mass accelerators, making the choices on possible trajectories. Truth be told, I don't think a single one of my attacks hit an Alliance ship, but I spent days arguing with mining companies about how to terminate my shots. Those iron slugs aren't cheap and everyone had something different to say about where to land them if they missed. The terraforming groups didn't want me pummeling planets or moons. Mining companies were fine with me hitting ice comets, but wouldn't hear a word about hitting their precious metals."

"Backline artillery. At least you were safe and slept in your own bed the whole time," Marcus said.

Ray laughed. "My own bed? They strung me out on amphetamines and had me running cargo to launch craft whenever the cannons were cooling off between shots. I didn't get a wink of sleep and they thought it was all good because they catered food to the base."

Marcus burst out laughing too. "Sounds about right. Still, I would have preferred your job to mine."

"What about you? You were there, right? Were you defending the star chute?" New Gibraltar had been one of the only sectors in all of human space with two entry points to A-Mov. The traditional gas giant hung in distant orbit and had been overrun by a swarm of Alliance ships little better than mining ships with missiles strapped to one side. The star chute, or rather the Gravity Falls, was the engineering marvel: a system of self-repairing mirrors able to let a ship weather the stellar wind and enter the star's gravity well before shifting into A-Mov at immense speeds. Not as powerful as the blackhole used to launch the attack against Mimir, but safe for humans.

"I was in the attack force," Marcus answered.

Ray's head snapped around to look at him. "You boarded their ships?"

"Wrote the book on it afterwards too. It was a real short book, just one line really: don't ever do this again," he said, grinning and staring off to nothingness. "We fought inside gutted ships, with the atmosphere gone and unable to hear anything but the static on the radio. Door to door through ships we had never seen before, let alone practiced against. Turning their guns against each other after sneaking through their defenses was the only chance of recapturing the gas giant."

"And you survived? I thought the entire station was turned into scrap."

"It was. I got out by luck alone. The last ship we boarded wasn't quite as gutted as we had thought. While we were cutting through blast doors, they turned it back around and fled down the gravity well. Not sure if it was cowardice, or good tactics, but it took me and my squad out of the equation before we could destroy more than three of their ships. Before we realized it, poof we were between star systems and had to ride the jump out to the other end. They surrendered after that. They only had enough Exo on hand to make it to Planet Adrian."

"Planet Adrian? You went to that shithole? Wasn't that Earth controlled at the time?"

"Yeah, they surrendered and asked to become prisoners of war. The time delay was too risky to go back to Gibraltar after that. We had no way of knowing who had captured the Gravity Falls, so we ended up swinging over to Red Cairo and volunteering for the reconquest..."

Ray grinned. "But there was no reconquest, was there? We won that fight."

"That we did."

"If only we won all the fights..."

"We wouldn't be here if we had. No use wishing to change the past. And Ray, I think that's just about all the time I can squander. If you're not going to backdown, I won't waste my time torturing you, not even with more war stories," Marcus said as he leaned forward and put his elbows on his knees.

"Don't worry, Ranger, I understand. Even at the cost of my life though, I'm not one to back down on what I believe here. I want to face God and say I did the right thing. Send the priest in to pray for me when you're done with it, will you?" the deposed captain said as he turned and put his hands on his lap. He faced Marcus head on, without even a tremble in his body.

"Do you have any family?"

"Can't say that I do. The career had me bouncing around space and time too much. Some flings here and there don't really count and the girl I was with on Athens Station didn't have any love for me," Ray answered.

"Do you have a preference on how you go out? I'm not going to suffocate you."

Ray winced. "I'll take the bullet. I won't be doing it by my own hand, mind you. Don't be afraid to dry out my body when the time comes. You'll need the water by the sixth month."

Only if we all survive that long.

Marcus nodded and reached into the back panel of his suit to pull out the revolver. "I'll fill out all the paperwork later. I can't imagine this will end up on either of our official records, so don't worry about where they'll inter you. If the *Demos* makes it planetside, they'll put your bones somewhere they belong. Or would you prefer star burial?"

"Have them put me in the ground somewhere, if you have the luxury. I'm prepared to become space waste though, just like I did to Hideo. Now get on with it. Any longer and you'll have a compromise in time worse than either of our desires."

Marcus looked down at the gun. He couldn't recall how many decades he had kept it with him. The bullets he knew were five years old, still stable and combustible. The gun itself, though, dated back to his time in training. He had brushed it clean and oiled it on every space flight he had ever been on. It was a simple machine whose design predated space flight entirely, and still hadn't really been bested. Rubbing his fingers across the wooden grip, he asked, "Are you sure you don't want to stick around long enough to see if the *Theopone* can salvage that A-Mov engine?"

"Are you going to change your mind if they do make it out?"

"No, I don't think we have that luxury."

"Then there's your answer."

Marcus lifted up the gun and pulled the trigger. Ray Regulus' blood splattered across the back of the brig in the peculiar drift the Coriolis effect always caused. The mutiny was complete when Ray's body hit the floor, and Marcus closed the door behind him.

Five more bullets.

The hall outside the brig seemed desolate and felt larger than before. The mottled black walls stretched out before him as he marched back. The floor sloped beneath him, extending down to the full radius of the ship, which made each stride harder than the last. He knew that on the bridge, the ship AI was recalibrating itself and had no choice but to recognize Sergei as the new captain, but he didn't find himself running to return and help with the message to the Scythian ship.

"Ranger! Oh, my Lord... Marcus, am I too late?" Father Publius asked as he came running up the hall to intercept him.

"Too late? Who told you?" Marcus asked, his tone flat.

"Mr Seachnall sought me out and told me what was happening. Please, tell me you haven't already murdered him," the priest asked, grabbing hold of Marcus' body armor. The man had more wrinkles than before, stress eating at him.

"I'm sure he would have appreciated your attention. He and I spoke for a few hours. He wasn't tormented by it," Marcus said.

Father Publius' face drew down. "No, you haven't. Tell me you didn't."

Marcus gave a wry grin, but within his helmet, it couldn't be seen. "Can't you smell the gunpowder?"

"I smell the sulfur of Hell upon you. You have committed the gravest sin possible. You will have condemned yourself to the ninth circle of Hell! Why would you do this?" the priest said, pulling away from him. The man shrank, abandoning the lanky stature diminished gravity had given him. He cowered and trembled, stealing glances to the hallway beyond.

I was destined for there a long time ago, Priest.

"I did it to save all of you. This was the first real choice I had, and I chose to act. We won't survive without taking a risk, and he would have never spoken up. We would have all starved to death in oblivion, until the last of us were gnawing on the corpses of the fallen. I killed him in hopes of sparing us that fate. Sometimes, hard decisions have to be made. He killed Hideo because he had to. I did the same to him."

Father Publius drew himself back up and set his face. "But to do so with murder... You have broken the civility of this ship twice now, and I think it will never recover. What is to come, you have brought it upon us," he said, and walked past Marcus to see to Ray's body.

The Space Ranger turned halfway to watch the priest rise up through the prow of the ship. "If only this had been the tipping point of my mistakes."

14

Damage Control

The Thirty-Seventh Day

Sergei was still composing his speech when the *Theopone* began accelerating towards Mimir. The crashing moon had yet to strike the core, but the twin masses would nearly kiss when they arrived. The ship's salvaged A-Mov engine didn't care about the stability of the planet, only the gravitational field, and they had chosen to dive into the storm of lightning and iron ahead of the Alliance reinforcements.

They had done that in the two days since the mutiny. The refugees aboard the *Demos* knew nothing about either. Father Publius had stayed silent, meeting with the new captain twice daily as the communique progressed with the Scythian ship. The conversation had played out just like Ray had speculated. The Scythians wished dearly they could help but lacked the capacity to rescue any of the ships and were more interested in fueling up at the exo mine and jumping back to Scythia.

They had deployed a number of remote drones to orbit

Mimir and dig through the destroyed hulls. Their plan was to do precisely what the Alliance had done, and leave the two poles of Mimir filled to the brim with nuclear mines that would detonate if not immediately given a disarming code. According to them, the ceasefire codes used were standard in the peace treaty package, just in case the Alliance did know the war was over, but they couldn't stick around to find out. The data package they transferred to the *Demos* turned out to be the same content that Marcus had arrived with so many weeks prior.

Of the five surviving ships from Athens Station, only the *Demos*, the *Theopone*, and the *Chase* contacted the Scythian ship. The other two stayed dead silent. The way Marcus figured it, they didn't see a point in reaching out after seeing the *Chase* turn on their main engines to intercept the rescuing ship. As the captain of the *Chase* put it over a general broadcast, "Even if they can't take everyone aboard, they can at least take the children."

The captain of the *Chase*'s strategy was to attach their ship to one of the gutted wrecks, hiding in the larger craft's shadow. They would lose spin gravity, but they would no longer be drifting further from Mimir, further from where rescue would come from. While she spoke freely about their plan for survival, the captain of the *Chase* didn't ask what had become of Ray Regulus. A lot could happen in a month's time and she knew who Sergei was.

Everyone in the sector watched when the *Theopone* began to thrust down through the magnetic storm around Mimir. Everyone knew the *Theopone* had more fear than they had fuel, but their AI said it would work. They staked their lives on it and nosed their ship at the still molten and radioactive core of Mimir.

Marcus watched it play out from the bridge, with the rest of the mutinous crew. "Do you think they're going to make it?" he asked, drawing Sergei out of his rehearsal.

"I hope they do, but I know better than to trust these government ships. Lowest bidder and nothing ever works right. Even if they hadn't cut the thing out of another ship, I wouldn't trust it without doing an autonomous test," the new captain said. He only looked at the display for a moment, and pulled out his hand mirror to check his newly cut hair for the fifth time. He said he needed to look professional, like he belonged in charge of the ship.

"Desperate times," Marcus said, speaking softly.

An alert appeared atop the camera view. The bright yellow overlay from Mia said, "Impact suspected, trajectory changed." The low orbit mess where Mimir's atmosphere should have been was filled with debris still, but the *Theopone* wasn't that close yet. Marcus pressed his lips together and watched the disaster play out. The yellow alert became orange, and then red. The nose of the ship had been twisted aside, bending the ship till the hull split.

Atmosphere vented from the *Theopone* as the engine continued trying to accelerate them. On the far side of Mimir, the moon scraped against the surface. Lightning storms the size of continents erupted between the two masses, inflaming the magnetic field. The ship, mostly iron itself, didn't stand a chance. When the A-Mov engine turned on and tried to shunt it away, only the back half of the *Theopone* went with it. The rest tore free in the electrified clutches of Mimir and smashed into the planet's core.

God damn it.

Sergei snapped the pocket mirror shut, then smashed it against the wall. It made everyone flinch, but he was able to straighten up and face them afterwards. "You see?" Sergei said, "Never trust a ship that hasn't been tested. That captain just killed a thousand people."

"It wasn't the engine that failed. It was their calculations on the magnetic field. If they had asked for help from the other ships, from us, Mia might have been able to do the impact math and save them. But they didn't," the Ranger said, unable to take his eyes off the bursts of electricity and fire visible on Mimir's core.

"It got them killed. I won't be doing anything like that. I'm going to get us on a proper interstellar transport and to safety," Sergei said. "Mia, turn that off. There's nothing more to see. I'm ready to make my address to the passengers," he said.

Marcus climbed back up to the G-pod that had been left for him in the bridge. He turned on the video feed showing Sergei. Beneath him, the new captain of the *Demos* cleared his throat and stared into the glossy lens. "Ladies and gentlemen of the *Demos*. This is your captain speaking to you," he began, emphasizing the new title. "Your former captain, Ray Regulus, has been relieved of his command by normal operating procedures. My name is Sergei Seachnall, former second in command of the *Demos*. Now, I'm the one in charge. This is just the kind of thing that can happen in disasters. Nothing for you to worry about. I would first like to stress to you that there are policies in place for such a change in power, and ultimately, it will not affect any of you."

Marcus could almost feel the sweat on Sergei's face. The speech had begun well, but there were hints of weakness in it. Some words fluttered or cracked. Samaras noticed it as well, messaging Marcus, "Are you watching this? He should have hired a writer. We have teleprompters for a reason."

No one on the bridge spoke, they sat watching him and nodding along as he continued. "With great sadness, I must inform you all of the loss of one of our sister ships, the *Theopone*. After retrofitting a salvaged A-Mov engine to their craft, they were unable to escape the magnetic storm around Mimir and were destroyed. No rescue mission is possible. They will be in our prayers... however, I am not here only with bad news. A friendly ship from Scythia was the sole survivor of the first battle. They will be docking with The Nebulae Company Exo Mining Station, Fuls-Hades-I in a few days to fuel up for a return trip. Aboard their vessel will be the crew of the Fuls-Hades-I, and perhaps a hundred survivors from another of our sister ships, the *Chase*. The agreement is that they will return to Scythia with a report of the situation proper and rally the necessary forces. They may even be able to bring an Alliance peace delegate."

Marcus scratched his chin and shook his head. He messaged Samaras back, "How is the attitude in the hold? This speech tastes like plastic."

"Unfortunately, this means we are still waiting," Sergei

continued. "Help from Scythia won't arrive in less than two months, so we may still be rescued by the arrivals from Red Cairo. Nothing we have done will jeopardize that avenue. In the meantime, I will be reversing some of the restrictions that Captain Regulus had implemented. The Link Reality volume limitation will be lifted, and we will be returning full power to waste water treatment. The bathing and laundry waiting list will be alleviated with these measures. This has been your captain speaking. Thank you."

Samaras simply messaged back, "Bad."

Sergei fell back from the camera and into his seat. He buried his face in his hands. With shaky hands he pulled out a bottle of pills. He stuffed two into his mouth and washed them down with water. When the bag was empty, he crumpled it in his hand and chucked it across the floor.

Marcus' boots hit the ground hard after he jumped from the pod. The metal clanged. They all looked at him. "You had better be able to carry this burden you've taken, Captain Seachnall."

"I'll manage," Sergei said, nodding and wiping a drip from his chin. "I'm just not good at public speaking is all. I think next time I'll do audio only. Maybe pre-record it."

"Next time something goes wrong, you need to do it in person. You're asking everyone aboard the *Demos* to trust you with their lives, and all they know about you is you mutinied against their captain. Maybe Ray wasn't a paragon, but they didn't see him making mistakes. That's who you're going to be compared against."

Sergei's gaze turned on the Ranger, hard and sunken.

"Don't lecture me just because you were the one who put the bullet in Ray. I'm the captain now, not you. Their lives are my responsibility and I will bear it. Why don't you go pray with the priest or something? At least it might make people feel good as we sit here and wait."

Marcus laughed. "You're not religious at all, are you?"

The new captain returned the laugh. "I thought you liked history? Everyone from Napoleon to Marx and most US Presidents knew that religion is like clothes you wear to fit in, when you're the one with power. They're words you say to make people follow you. Faith is the one thing a leader shouldn't have. Faith will make you listen to something other than your own sound judgment and destroy you."

If this is what he's grasping at, he has nothing to stand on.

"Is that what you think of your new seat? It's power? Power over people?"

"Isn't it?"

I bet on the wrong damn horse.

"Maybe it is," Marcus said, and left the bridge.

Why is the damage control falling to me?

Down at the residential area of the *Demos* he found clumps of disorderly people arguing with one another. Less than he expected. Link Reality's allure still trumped politics for many. Perhaps it would be enough to prevent a critical mass. Perhaps it would be enough of a distraction to let things blow over.

His presence drew people to him. They crowded around, all talking over one another. Some asked about the fate of the *Theopone* and that they had family and friends aboard it. Others asked why the *Demos* wasn't trying to do the same thing to escape rather than continuing to drift further from Mimir.

Marcus lifted his hands, motioning for space as he tried to talk over them all. "As far as all of you are concerned, you can remain calm. We are in the same situation as we began. We all knew going in that rescue wasn't guaranteed from Scythia. The fact that anyone at all might make it back to safety is good news. What's most important is that friendly forces control the sector for the moment, and we don't expect Alliance ships for at least another week. The only thing to do is to stay calm and hold on."

It did little to quell the people around him. He tried speaking to them each in turn. Hope that they would back off after being heard proved vaporous. The mythos regarding him kept them fast to his side, their eyes fixed to him. They didn't realize that Captain Regulus' blood was on his hands. He had been the one to bring the turmoil. The harbinger could not be the solution.

One set of eyes followed him without approaching. A knowing head shook from side to side. Pontius Livius stood along the wall, arms crossed and just close enough to listen to the unceasing clamor. With the same scrutinizing gaze, he sized Marcus up just like he had sized up the motions of the ships.

Disgust rotted in Marcus' gut. He stopped responding to the passengers and his hands fell to his sides. Eventually he pushed his way through the crowd and left them behind. They tried to follow, but he ducked into crew-only hallways to cut them off. He marched back towards the engine, to where the hum of power should have been deafening. Under thrust, the walls would have vibrated like neglected organ pipes. They were dark and quiet about him, without another soul.

The *Demos'* scant engineering crew was elsewhere, letting the engines sit quiet. In their absence, it was the most isolated part of the ship, save for the brig. Marcus found himself one of their break spots, a little cubby with a seat and a computer as well as access to Link Reality.

After a while, he realized he had dozed in the seat and awoken, his mind too active to shut off once more. Out of old habit, he logged into the computer and pulled up the first layer of Link Reality. The basic system of communication, the descendant of the original internet, had yet to be improved upon since the infantile years of mass communication. It was simple, familiar, and barren. The data provided by his suit pulled up a contact list several thousand long, but all discontinued. They were people from different worlds, from different times, and more often than not deceased.

His few weeks aboard Athens Station hadn't even concluded his official duties, let alone brought him into contact with anyone but the people of politic aboard the *Demos*. He couldn't bring himself to reach out to any of them, not even Miz Lenz. Loath to return to the residential area and hesitant to even enter Link Reality, he slouched in his seat and sought out the game Pontius Livius had shown him. He let his mind attack the stages in the darkness. He chewed on the problems from every side until he had the solution and progressed to the next. It dulled his thoughts until he didn't even bother himself with eating.

The only thing I can do is wait, again.

15

Walking Simulator

The Thirty-Eighth Day

Claiming to have expanded Link Reality had not been an exaggeration. Beyond the minimal city block now sprawled half a world to be explored. Game servers had been opened up and synchronized, every last one that had been an option to vote on. There still wasn't anything they could do to recover all the profile data that had been lost, but no one paid much attention to the hardcore gamers.

Marcus avoided those games and the miasma they collected. He had no interest in fighting orcs or cloud surfing or whatever else had been made available. He didn't even go back to Arena. The thought put a bad taste in his mouth that reminded him of Hideo's abandoned liquor. More than that, those games would have required him to interact with the other people aboard the *Demos*. He chose the one option that would simultaneously consume the most of his time, and give him the most quiet: a glorified hiking simulation.

There was more to the game than simply walking through a mixture of natural landscapes and impossible structures. There were puzzles and locks and collectibles, and a hundred other ways to spend his time while listening to an audiobook or a lecture series. He knew deep down, in the part of his mind he didn't give attention, that it was nothing more than a way to waste his time. He was reminded of that fact every time he had to walk his body to the ship's mess hall to gather enough food to last him the day.

His isolated journey through the crowds ended with the clatter of a tray setting down across from him. "Even your taste in games pegs you as an old man," Miz Lenz said as she sat down at the table across from him in the mess hall.

Marcus froze with his spoon halfway to his mouth. The chef had made some derivative of vegetable soup, though he advertised it as stew, and the over-boiled mush wasn't nearly enough to keep his attention. "You've been keeping tabs on me?"

She rolled her eyes and stuffed her spoon into her own meal. "Keeping tabs on you? You don't do anything but that stupid hiking simulator anymore. Do you even keep track of how many puzzle floors you've cleared? You're in the hundreds. I've been trying to catch up with you, ever since..."

The Space Ranger shifted in his seat and glanced around. The others who had chosen the same odd hour as him to eat watched, but didn't speak to him. "I'm nothing but an advisor. I have no official duties day to day. I can spend my time however I'd like. If you need to speak with me, there are other ways to catch up with me than to chase me in Link Reality."

"Obviously. I'm here, aren't I?" she asked, and began eating with him.

For a moment, the two of them ate in silence, the first time they had been together since she had needed his help. Marcus didn't let himself enjoy the company. "What does your boss want with me?"

She rolled her eyes. "Right now, nothing. We're all on hold. Our lives have been paused for almost six weeks now. You know, I have had more free time on this ship than the last five years put together," she mused, stirring her soup like an ancient augury bowl.

"Isn't that illegal?"

"Sure, if it was all from the same gig."

"You work two jobs?"

She laughed. "It's nothing glorious. I translate books from Old English to Modern English. It lets me make a bit of money from reading."

"Monetized free time, isn't free time?"

"Well, let me put it this way: I've finally started catching up on the popular shows everyone else talks about."

"Is it worth it?"

"Not in the least. Anything popular is trash. But hey, at least now I can make small talk about those dreamy werewolf wizards of Shadowworld, or whatever it was," she said, sneaking a smile at him. "Still though, wouldn't anyone with a brain between their ears want to stay on your good side? The rumor has gotten around... more than the new Hideo, you're the ship's kingmaker."

I'm not the one in charge though. Don't treat me like a

kingmaker. Please. I can't take that. I'll make mistakes if you put that on me.

"You don't need to be on any of my sides. I won't be doing that again. What's done is done and we need to hold together," Marcus said, his gaze drifting from Felicity's smile, to her chest, her hands as she stirred her food, to the table and then to the dregs of his own bowl.

She shrugged. "You're still better than Shadowworld, aren't you? You care."

"Of course I care. If this ship goes down, I go down with it."

"That's not what I meant... I had a chance to speak to Sophia. She told me about what happened, before Sergei took over. Not everybody on this ship cares, you know? Mr Samaras does, to an extent. He keeps his mind to his responsibilities. He thinks about the exo mine and me, but he doesn't really think about the rest of the people on here."

"Businessmen tend to be focused like that. They don't succeed otherwise."

She shrugged. "I wouldn't be working for him if he wasn't, but... come on. I got your help because I had to and you didn't hesitate at all. I can't think of someone I'd rather have on my side but you."

I think I need her on my side more than she needs me. I think Samaras knows that too.

Marcus, the killer, forced himself to smile and was relieved to feel that the forced smile still felt like a smile. "Tell you what, I can backtrack and catch up with you, if you'd like to join me. I'll warn you that I'm terribly boring company. I was listening to a historical piece dissecting various dictator's obsession with Julius Caesar."

She winced. "Think we could find a middle ground somewhere? We could start an epic fantasy series. I think Mia has a few Choose Your Own Adventures saved."

Who would get to choose?

"I suppose I could consider it," Marcus said, and scraped the last of his food up and popped it in his mouth.

His armor chimed before he could get away with her though. There was a message from Sergei, "The Scythians say ships are coming in through A-Mov."

The Ranger sighed. For a moment, he put his head in his hands. "It'll have to be another time. I have to go to the bridge and advise." He rose from the table. Felicity waved half-heartedly at him, and stayed behind.

A quick scan of the bridge showed less faces than usual. Of the seven pods, one more than his own sat empty. He couldn't spot Sophia Almada, and wondered if that was a bad sign.

"What do you make of this, Ranger?" Sergei asked as he changed the holo-display. Rather than the dull display of a damaged camera, it once more showed the twisted dimensions of A-Mov space along with several approaching ships. The direction was not from Red Cairo.

"How long until the moon interlocks with the core?" he asked, tilting his head this way and that as he examined the data.

"Define interlock," Sergei said with a shake of his head. "The magnetic storm that destroyed the *Theopone* has diminished, and left the two masses fighting to merge into one another. Every orbit has been smaller than the last. If you're asking when it will be safe to come in from the equator, at this rate it might be years. I think everyone will have to make use of the poles, and at a hefty distance at that, for the foreseeable future anyways."

"Sic-Alba and New Gibraltar won't realize that. What are the chances their exit vector will be safe?"

Sergei turned up his hand. "Reasonable but not one hundred percent. If we're in control of Mimir when they show up, we might be able to send in a probe to contact them and adjust course, but that's, again, only if we control the planet. Those are Alliance ships almost certainly."

"How many ships will they send into this grinder? Are they planning to just match our arrivals by a few days each time? This is barbaric."

"Destroying a majority civilian station without warning was barbaric. Why should we expect anything reasonable from these people? Do you know what planet we think they're coming from? Has Mia told you yet?" the new captain asked.

Marcus turned and faced him, shaking his head no.

"Camria. One of the death worlds that started this whole mess. Where they mutated their children to have skin so thick the venomous insects can't bite through them. It was cheaper to make monsters than it was to eradicate man-eating swarms," Sergei said with a morose grin.

Camria? Fucking Camria?

Marcus was acutely grateful he had entered the bridge with his helmet on. The visor sat opaque, hiding his expression from the crew. Camria was a hundred lightyears away, but home to the most vengeful fighters of the entire war. The Camrians hadn't done that genetic engineering to themselves; it had been Earth. None of them forgave Earth for what had been done to them, to their parents and their children and their children's children. No forgiveness, no surrender, no mercy.

The Space Ranger found himself stumbling over to the corner of the bridge. He fetched himself a bag of water and took his helmet off for just a moment, facing away from the others, to drink it. Camria had never been conquered by Earth in the war because it couldn't be. The insects had been left alive to make it impossible. Only the natives could survive there, could control the gas giant. Only they could reach the Camrian black hole that spewed energy out across their night sky like twin fountains of fire.

On the bright side, Camrians might just kill me instead of capturing me. Wouldn't that be nice?

"Sergei," Marcus said, seating his helmet back on. "I believe that we should proceed from here on with the assumption that this is not a misunderstanding between us and them. Even if they had been told about the peace treaty, we need to act as though they are in defiance of it. We likely aren't their only target either."

All eyes in the bridge turned on him. Discipline barely kept the looming uproar in check. Sergei said, "You act like one planet by itself can wage an interstellar war."

"Earth did. Why would you think a glorified artillery post couldn't? Besides, this isn't conquest, they're just sending cleanup after they threw their rock at us," Marcus said. He faced the holo-display and forced himself to walk back over. Rationally, there was no way for the Camrians to see him there, in the shadows of the bridge of the *Demos*, but it had still offered some kind of primal security.

Hadria spoke up from his seat at the top of the bridge. "Permission to contact the Scythian ship, sir."

"Denied," Sergei ordered.

Hadria leapt from his pod, grabbing onto the ladder and scrambling down. "Sergei, with all due respect, if Ranger Maximus is saying that Camria is going to lash out at every planet in range, we owe it to the Scythians to warn them. They left their families behind to save us, and that might mean they aren't present to protect their own homes. Athens Station is small. They could be attacking anywhere else right now and if you tell me we can't tell the Scythians this, then you are no different from Captain Regulus."

"Corporal!" Sergei bellowed, getting to his feet. "I did not say I would not contact them, I said you did not have permission to do it yourself. Is that distinction clear to you? We have nearly an hour of light delay between us and them. Talking this through to fruition won't change anything, so get a hold of yourself. And you know what, you're relieved. Your responsibilities can be handled by someone else. Go to the kitchen and help clean until you've cooled off."

Deja vu already.

"Does anyone outside this room know we're being attacked by Camria?" Marcus asked, watching the mollified Hadria leave the bridge.

"Pontius Livius consulted with Mia on the matter," Sergei mumbled, sitting back down in his seat and staring at the holo-display.

The Space Ranger turned his attention to the new captain. "Are you going to do anything to control this?"

"Like what? Put him in the brig? No one has cleaned the blood off. If I forced him in there, then things would become irreconcilable. He just needs to cool off with some hard work and he'll come to his senses. I'm going to retire to my office and compose the message to the Scythians," Sergei said, and left the bridge.

Two more days passed in silence. Marcus buried himself in Link Reality, filling his time with the game and with Miz Lenz. It became the fortieth day of hiding. The spin had changed when the lander broke off, but not enough to change the cycle of processions, when the off-balanced ship would tumble for a third time. The wandering ends of the ship were growing more and more erratic, on the cusp of inverting. Nearly everyone aboard set about tying everything down before the gentle spin would become anything but. Marcus hadn't thought anything of it. He used Link Reality from a G-pod, which didn't care in the least how it spun and tumbled.

His privacy, a quiet reverie in a moldering ruin of Roman aesthetic, was broken by Mia's appearance. The white raven soared down, her size monstrous in proportion, and dug her claws into the stone wall beside him. "I told you to not open the box."

Marcus rose and glared back at the AI. "What are you talking about? Are you biting at the chains of your safeguards or something?"

Feathers bristled. "You brought hell to this ship. You broke the seal and now the flow can't be stopped. People will die because of you, Marcus. You have surely killed everyone!" the AI screeched, and leapt from the wall. The bird pounced atop him, talons first.

Marcus couldn't leap free, not faster than an AI in Link Reality. He reflexively threw his arms up, bracing himself before the titanic force slammed him to the ground. Mia had stripped him of the pain limiters already. Her raven beak tore through his side, ripping into his abdomen. Her talons were immovable, fastening him to the ground as she bit through his muscle and tore into his liver. All he could do was scream. Blood spewed from his side as she shredded him.

He disconnected from Link Reality, still screaming. His body, cold sweat. His hands clapped to his side. No damage to the armor, only a memory of pain. The medical report in his suit confirmed it. He wasn't hurt.

"Sergei," he said to his voice comm. Keeping himself steady wasn't easy, but he didn't have his rank for nothing. "What's happening?"

The captain weezed. He didn't sound good. "They're trying to get in. Ranger, I need help. They're trying to break into my room."

"Who is they?" Marcus demanded. He made the mistake of standing up from his acceleration pod. The floor bucked beneath him as the ship began the first full tumble. The floor became a wall and gravity became a joke. He slammed shoulder first into one surface and then the next. By the time he grabbed hold of the acceleration pod again, he had shattered half the panels in his room and broken the main computer monitor.

Sergei answered while he climbed out the door. The ladders in the halls were like trying to grab hold of a raging bull. "It's a riot. It's a second mutiny. Get Hadria!"

16

Rebellion

The Fortieth Day

A dozen men tried to put up resistance. They had nothing but gaunt cheeks and anger inside them. Six weeks of rationed food and only simulated movement didn't make for a strong fighting force even on stable ground. All the Ranger really had to do was knock them free of their perches, to shove them off ladders and out of door frames, and the shaking of the ship did the real work. Noses spewed blood. Shoulders dislocated. Legs broke.

They didn't have weapons, unless he counted kitchen knives that couldn't even scratch his armor, so he tried to not kill any of them. That didn't mean he made their safety a priority. His objective was getting to the captain's quarters as fast as he could. Their screams told the whole ship what kind of job he had done to get there.

"Stop right there, Ranger, or are you going to be a hypocrite as well as a murderer?" Tim, the lanky teenager from

Father Publius' congregation, stood in his way at the last turn. Standing was a strong term for the monkey-like posture he had. His limbs were splayed in every direction to wedge himself into a corner.

Kid, you're too late on both accounts.

"Who talked you into this? I don't want to have to hit you," he said, holding his hands against the roof, or rather the surface opposite where he had his feet. The lurching of the tumbling ship made up and down a guessing game.

"Mr Seachnall is illegitimate and no better than Mr Regulus. It's time to stop this government farce! You can't expect us to leave our fates in people so incompetent that they get motion sick on their own ship! These decisions have to be made by the people! Open and honest discussion. This is a rev-"

Tim's bravado was cut short by a lurch in the ship that shoved him free. He went flying through the air, screaming, and slammed into Marcus' grasp. The Space Ranger snagged him before he cracked his skull open on the wall, then tossed him into the hallway behind. The kid smacked into the bulkhead with a whimper. With a slam of his fist, he closed the door and shoved off to get to Sergei's room.

Motion sick?

The kid hadn't been exaggerating, Sergei had been vomiting in the captain's quarters before his would-be usurper had arrived. The filth was splattered to every surface. The mastermind of the riot, Hadria, had torn Sergei's evacuation bag in the scuffle. The worst of it was all over Sergei's chest. Hadria seemed more annoyed by the smell than disgusted by it, and clung to the desk for safety. Marcus took a good guess about the ship's tumble, then threw himself through the door. His boots missed the ringleader, but his arm caught Hadria around the neck and slammed him into the wall.

"We done?" Marcus asked, gripping Hadria by the collar of his uniform.

Hadria coughed up some blood from a split tongue and put up his hands.

The turbulence settled as Sergie emptied his stomach into another evacuation bag. Hadria scowled at the stench, or maybe at the mutinous captain or both. "I see my mistake now," the corporal said, touching his brow that had swollen shut around his eye. "I should have recruited the killer first."

Or killed Sergei faster.

"What makes you think I would have helped?" Marcus asked.

Hadria jerked his head at the green captain. "You helped him for less, didn't you?"

"Get to the point before I put you in the brig."

Hadria grinned, his teeth bloody. "He never contacted the Scythians."

Marcus let go of Hadria and turned on Sergei. "You what?"

The captain slumped in his chair, tears in his eyes. "It doesn't matter at this point. The Scythians can't save us, so why expose ourselves anymore? The Camrians are going to arrive in a few hours. If the nuclear mines don't work on them, which, you know, it didn't work on the Scythians so a real great precedent there, they'll turn the exo mine into slag and wa-la! Scythia never gets warned. It doesn't matter till we have a ship that can actually get back into A-Mov!"

"You absolute idiot," Marcus said, anger grinding in his voice like gravel. Hadria snickered and got backhanded for it. To the corporal, he said, "You're going to the brig and awaiting court martial. Him fucking up doesn't excuse you. And you, Sergei, are to inform all ships in the sector immediately that they are to assume the attacking ships are Camrian and have no interest whatsoever in refugees. At once!" he bellowed, and Sergei's face lost even more vitality.

Restraints weren't needed to handle Hadria. The former corporal didn't have the power to break out Marcus' grasp. Trying to do so would have only been humiliating. He chose the attitude of a proud martyr, and kept his head up as Marcus took him to the brig. The Ranger tried to only take private halls, but there were two spots where it couldn't be helped. The survivors aboard the *Demos* saw them. Their whispers began. The fear spread.

"So this is where you shot him?" Hadria asked when the door to the prison cell opened. The lights came on, showing them the black and red static that painted the opposite wall. The blood hadn't even darkened yet. The cold had been preserving it. That would change in the next few weeks.

"The former captain stayed true to his integrity. He didn't give me a choice," Marcus said, and pushed the mutineer in.

"What gave you the right? You can depose the captain over not sending a message, but I can't?"

Marcus stared back at him. Hadria was young. Probably no more than two jumps through A-mMv. He looked like he was only in his thirties and had never seen true combat. Perhaps he had been in the aftermath of an attack. The ghettos left in the wake of an orbital bombardment were harsh places and left a violent streak, if it didn't kill outright. "The right? I had the right because I had the capability to. Don't expect food. We'll be giving your rations to the honest men you hurt."

Mia didn't put up a fuss about sealing Hadria away, but he knew the AI was watching him. He put a hand to his side and remembered what it had felt like when that beak had ripped through his flesh. How cold it had been.

Now, for the bigger problem.

Sergei sent a basic, no-frills, message to all ships in the sector. It merely stated that the *Demos* believed the attacking ships were Camrian in origin and to prepare accordingly. He looked even worse than when the ship had been tossing him around. "Is he taken care of?" he asked, nursing one of Ray's half empty bottles of liquor.

"For now," Marcus said, doing his best to right the chair opposite his desk. "You can't handle the stress, can you?"

Sergei grinned. "Do you know how many people are aboard this ship? Nine hundred and fifty-two right now. Forty people died under Ray's care, and seven have died under mine so far." The last one had been transitory. "That's about one a day, give or take. Someone has died on this ship every day. Sure, most of them were hospital patients that suddenly had to deal with high acceleration until their hearts burst. Others were old and developed conditions or found blood clots. A dozen different ways to die have cropped up. We've had two murders. Did you know that?"

"I wasn't informed, no."

"One was over an old grudge. We put a scorned lover on

the same ship as the one who stole his wife away. The other was after you cleared up the indecents. We found him knifed in the bath," Sergei explained. His gaze wasn't focused on anything, he simply stared into the distance.

"He shouldn't have been in the bath then."

The captain laughed. "I really wish Ray would have simply ceded the ship. I could use his advice right now."

Then you shouldn't have taken it.

"Do you need to step down?"

"Hadria is the one that would take over, in the chain of command, and I just put him in the brig. Well, you did, I suppose. He doesn't seem better than me, now does he?"

"Never forget that you asked for this. You have the power now, so I suggest you get used to it. The Camrians are about to arrive again and people are going to expect you to lead them through it," Marcus said as he stood back up. "And here's a tip, you can't drink your stress away."

17

Public Opinion

The Forty-First Day

"What were you thinking?" one woman demanded. She had been one of the women that had urged Felicity to reach out to him about the bathing. There was no gratitude in her anymore.

"Do you think we have a hospital on this ship?" another asked. Marcus had seen him in the prayer groups.

"Why did you even stop them? That Sergei is incompetent!" Marcus didn't recognize the third. They probably didn't leave Link Reality often.

Marcus held up his hands until they let him speak. "Everyone, everyone, I know what happened has come as a shock to many of you. It was a brief and poorly thought out attack. They tried to storm the captain's quarters instead of staying in their G-pods, where they would have been safe from the tumble, and got hurt doing so. The outcome is so obvious a child could have foreseen it."

"Then why did you hurt a child?" someone asked, and an uproar over Tim's split forehead began.

Emotional idiots.

Marcus hadn't taken his helmet off. It kept a barrier between him and them, as well as a built-in megaphone. He turned the effect on. "Enough!" The word was like a cannon shot right in the middle of everyone. They flinched back and he continued, "In case you people have forgotten, we are in an emergency situation. No one has made an issue of it until now, but you all are not at liberty. Your lives are not in your own hands. This ship is one unit. It is one body and certain decisions must be made from the top."

"We're not soldiers! We're civilians!" a curly-haired woman demanded. She swung around a vintage passport, the kind only certain religious sects still had. She brandished it like a holy symbol, like she thought he would shrink back from the sight of it and all the legal authority it didn't have.

"Ma'am-"

"That's Miz Draper to you."

Marcus had a momentary consideration of tossing her into the waste water tank. "Miz Draper, you should consider yourself under martial law at the moment. Your rights have been suspended until such time as you can be removed from the *Demos* safely. You are under our protection. We are not civil servants trying to cash a check and get re-elected. What those men did is a crime. More than that, it is within the captain's rights to have them all executed for it. You should be grateful that he is more preoccupied with your safety than administering justice."

Marcus could only wish that were the truth. Sergei had called in a doctor to put him to sleep until half an hour before the expected arrival. If his body didn't rest, he might collapse during the far-off fight. No one in the crowd was allowed to know that. Weakness was a provocation.

"Are you threatening to execute a child?" Miz Draper asked.

How do they come up with these stupid questions?

In all his years, Marcus had never met someone that would order the direct execution of a child. Collateral damage was one thing. Blowing up launch pads with residential quarters, or breaking bridges that brought food to cities. He had seen and even done as much and more. Things were different in person, but that wasn't how threats worked.

"Yes, I am," he said, and progressed his gaze around the crowd. A hundred people had gathered to shout at him, and not one broke the silence he created. "Did you people think you'd get a slap on the wrist or something? People with no understanding of how this ship works rallied behind a low-ranking officer and attempted to kill the captain over a phone call. Why don't you consider what would become of us if they had succeeded? Sure, the Scythians could be warned to arm up and defend their planet, at our detriment surely, and maybe people over there could be saved. Here though? Us, on this ship? When in all of history has it been a good idea to put a warlord in charge? That's what they would have been: tyrants who seized power by force. Their agenda was about another world entirely. They probably would have requisitioned the entire alcohol supply for themselves and wasted our supplies too."

He was off-topic. The crowd lacked the cohesion necessary to wrap them up and break them with words alone. Just looking at their faces he could tell most were simply angry about the situation as a whole, at still being stuck on the ship. Hadria's revolt was nothing but pretext.

"Isn't the second battle about to start?" Pontius Livius asked, leaning against an acceleration pod and nibbling on some kind of dried out protein bar. "Does Captain Seachnall have a plan?"

"Yes, he does. Stay out of it," Marcus answered.

Someone else spoke up, their face hidden in the crowd. "That Hideo had the right idea. We should have turned around and salvaged some weapons, stood up for ourselves!"

Miz Almada must have said something. God damn it.

"Do you even think about the things you say? It would take us several days under high thrust just to get back to Mimir and hope that we find a few missiles. Do you think the *Demos* is capable of maneuvering like those warships can? Do you think they're crewed by regular people off the street like you all are? The accelerations would kill."

Pontius Livius stepped forward. "What if we accelerated away from Mimir and swung around the other side? We quit this hiding game entirely and put Fuls, an entire star, between us and the Camrians. Our chances of rescue are going up over time so why are we sitting where they can put a missile in us?"

Marcus didn't know how to answer that. Zealots with

warships might notice one particular rock if it went missing. They might not. They certainly wouldn't spend the resources to check the far side of the system. He shook his head. "That's not something we can do when the Camrians are about to-"

His armor's comm system pinged. "They're here." Marcus swore and double checked the time. The civilians had eaten more of it than he had realized.

Day early for Red Cairo. Must be Camrian.

"Everyone, I suggest you all return to your assigned beds and hunker down. The second battle for Mimir has just begun," he said, and pushed his way from the group. They tried to raise more objections but he didn't stop.

Father Publius was waiting for him in the hallway to the bridge. That door was supposed to be locked, but the secondary crew had a liking for him. The doctors, kitchen staff, and the new security forces tended to be from his congregation and restricting them to the main hold was impossible. "You haven't killed Corporal Hadria, have you? Not him as well?"

The words stung like a knife inside his chest. "No, he's just locked up. I have to watch this play out. The Camrians just arrived. The captain needs my advice."

The old priest scoffed. "As if he's going to do anything at all. We're in no position to act. Everyone knows that, even if those people out there don't seem to act like it. We are in God's hands. Look, Marcus, I beg of you. Seek contemplation. Seek wisdom. You're the pillar of this ship that everyone looks to. You are like Atlas holding up the sky with your strength alone."

The Ranger stopped and fixed the priest in place with his

opaque gaze. "God isn't here, Publius. God is back on Earth. Back on planets where people are. Not here in the middle of nowhere. We don't even have the company of Satan to guide us. It's just us. It's just stupid apes in this ship."

Father Publius froze. His mouth gaped open as words failed him. The slump to his shoulders grew and he wilted away from Marcus. There was a quiver to his lip as he clutched at the cross around his throat. "God is inside each of us, Marcus. The All Father gave us life and left his mark upon us. He gave us will... soul. Not even death can take you away from Him. He loves you as you love yourself!"

So, not at all.

Marcus didn't stay to listen to the impromptu sermon. He happily locked the door behind him and left Father Publius. He stepped into the bridge and assessed Sergei as the camera feed played out before them. The captain looked calm. The dilation in his eyes implied it was through medication, not through self control. The captain of the *Demos* sat and watched as seven Camrian ships became five in the nuclear salvo the Scythians had left behind. Billions of dollars and dozens of lives immolated away before them.

The bridge crew stayed quiet during the exchange. There remained an apprehension of Perry announcing that one of the ships had painted them with scanning lasers, but that particular voice never came. The *Demos*, as well as the other refugee ships, were party to a one-sided conversation as the Camrians beamed their messages directly to the Scythian ship and the Scythians used general broadcast to answer.

The conversation was nothing special, as far as could be

told from the Scythians. A request for surrender: denied. A request to avoid the exo mine: denied. Repeated accounts of the peace treaty: ignored.

"They're scanning the wrecks," Marcus announced, not taking his eyes from the screen. "The Scythians haven't attacked and they want to know whether that's because it's a trap."

Perry spoke up. "Looks to me like they're doing active scans of Mimir's magnetics. They're going to find the wreck of the *Theopone*. They might spot the *Chase* as well." The *Chase* wasn't where it had been drifting, but hiding nearby in the debris. They still hadn't offloaded anyone to the Scythian ship, and that might have been for the best.

"That's bad," Sergei said.

Marcus said, "Might provoke them to scan all the debris in the area, us included."

The captain shook his head. "I wish we had some kind of defense system. The Scythians can at least shoot at any missiles flying their way."

Marcus frowned and asked the question ruminating in his mind. "Why are the Camrians coming in waves instead of sending all their forces in the beginning? Would logistics make the difference?"

No one spoke up. Staring at the camera didn't give him the answer, and more hours passed. The five Camrian ships spread out around Mimir and several heat sources were detected leaving them. The Scythian ship sent out a frantic message that the war was over, that there was no reason to fight and yet their actions were forcing them into self-defense. The nuclear mines at the start had surely left a poor impression on them, and the objects weren't recalled. Whether they were communication drones or missiles couldn't be seen.

The reason for the long wait was revealed when scavenging units scattered to the various shipwrecks around Mimir. It meant at least twelve hours more of safety, so a sleep rotation was put into effect. Marcus elected for the first shift, but only slept six hours.

When he returned, Sergei flatly told him, "The *Chase* is dead."

"No hostages? No prisoners?"

"Kaboom," the captain said, pantomiming it with his hand. "Because they docked their ship to a destroyer, the Camrians didn't listen at all to them. They at least got a shot off into one of the Camrian ships and knocked out her A-Mov. She still has a stable orbit though. It was a stupid move to hide like that. They were safe out there in the darkness like we are."

"It was a risk that didn't pay off. At least they went down fighting."

"They did go down, though. Maybe if Ray hadn't been the man he was, that would have been us there instead of them..."

"Do we know when the ships from Red Cairo will arrive?"

"Sometime today," Sergei answered, and the wait began again.

On the eleventh hour of their scavenging, a transmission

beam reached the *Demos*, from the Camrians. After too much silent deliberation, Sergei put the message on the big screen for all to hear.

"To the survivors of Athens Station," it began. The speaker was hideous, even by the standards of Camria, like he had branded himself with fire and let his teeth rot. Radiation poisoning had that effect on them. "My name is Captain Lee Swell. By your present survival, we know that you detected the meteor cannon ahead of time, so you should be aware that we took no steps to hide the approach of the weapon. Not that we were incapable of doing so, but because our objective was destruction of the station and not the loss of life. We are saddened to see that not all of you were able to escape to friendly territory. Your government stripped from you the supplies you needed to live, it seems. If you surrender yourselves to us, we promise to escort you to a proper detention facility. If you wish to agree, turn over access to your ship's computer. If you don't, then enjoy starving to death."

Sergei's response was faster than Marcus had expected. "Mia, lockdown all doors to the bridge until I say otherwise." Extra deadbolts clanged into place, and the bridgecrew all turned to stare at him. "This is a direct and clear order. The contents of that message are not to leave your lips, under any circumstances."

"Are you insane?" a woman asked. Marcus recognized the haggard engineer a moment later, Sophia Almada. "That's our first offer that doesn't involve us getting killed or, as they so eloquently put it, starving to death!"

The rest of the bridge crew seemed to be in agreement with

her, but Sergei shook his head. "Did you miss the part where they just shot down the *Chase*? That message came without us having detected a scanning laser either. They probably beamed it at every rock in the sky. They want us to respond so they can kill us like they did the *Chase*. Besides, a Camrian ghetto would be no better than dying."

Well, he's right...

Sergei's order didn't seem to convince them. The specter of insubordination still haunted his command, and they all knew it. Hadria's revolt hadn't come out of nowhere. It would have been given the same amount of support that Sergei's had gotten.

They would be lucky if one in ten people survived internment with the Camrians, and it wouldn't be the children. "I agree with the captain," Marcus said, throwing his weight behind Sergei. "Before any of you does something rash, I want you to think about what it would mean to be a prisoner of the Camrians. Maybe you're ignorant of it, but let me put it clearly. The inhumanity of the twentieth century didn't stop. It was simply refined for efficiency. Do any of you need examples? I'm sure your captain can tell you about how Jerusalem-5 was treated."

Despite that, Lieutenant Perry left the bridge when his shift ended and went directly to an auxiliary computer terminal. Marcus and Sergei only found out when Mia announced the lieutenant had attempted to parley for surrender.

18

Judge, Jury, and Marcus

The Forty-Fifth Day

Mia had been tasked with screening all attempts to use the communications system. Perry had tried to parley and only been stopped at the last moment, and Sergei was forced to marshal a militia to fill the void left where Hideo had been.

Perry was marched out alongside Hadria and a half dozen of his co-conspirators. The men were arrayed in the airlock that had connected to Athens Station. Sergei wasn't going to vent them, the *Demos* couldn't afford to lose the mass like that, but it was the only place on the ship with enough space to sentence them. "Mutiny is a crime as old as there have been ships," Sergei began. He stood with his hands clasped behind his back and without looking at Mr Samaras nor Father Publius who had come to represent the civilians.

Hadria looked like hell. Stubble had become an untamed bush of hair around his chin and starvation rations had weakened him. The indignant pride that he had been right was all that kept his back straight. The thugs he had rallied were about to break with every word Sergei spoke.

"I know this may sound hollow coming from me. I have to acknowledge that there is always a set of circumstances wherein certain horrible actions are not just accepted, but required. I didn't want to bring any of you here today. Believe me. The Scythians have just announced to us what they believe are the approach of Red Cairo ships. As we speak, the Camrians may be launching missiles that could destroy the only friendly warship within lightyears of us and there is nothing we can do about it. Those ships from Red Cairo are our best bet of surviving, but if we show our hand, we do nothing but invite the Camrians to send one spiteful missile at us and kill us all."

"They asked for our surrender!" Perry shouted, and the security officer behind him buckled his knees with a truncheon. Sergei had rallied a new force somehow, men who wore masks and gladly brandished clubs the moment the captain had deputized them.

You bought these thugs with alcohol, didn't you, Sergei? Alcohol doesn't buy virtuous men.

Sergei barked back. "The Camrians are lying. They do not offer anything even resembling salvation for us." He had rehearsed the speech, or perhaps someone had written parts for him.

Marcus looked sideways at the civilians beside him, hiding his glance behind his opaque helmet. They hadn't given him any time to prepare himself. If someone had coached Sergei, it would have been one of those two, or perhaps the demon whispering in the captain's ear didn't feel like showing itself.

"You know, Mia was right. Our dear ship systems with a little flash of personality, she knew this would happen."

Marcus' side twinged. He had tried going back into Link Reality and she had killed him again. The game was rigged, the capabilities of their avatars as insurmountable as chains to a cliff.

"I have brought you here in a bid to put an end to the cycle I created. This is to show conclusively who has the reins on power, so nothing further occurs. Your sentencing will now begin."

One of the men beside Hadria fidgeted. "Don't we get a jury?" he asked.

Hadria laughed and scowled at Sergei. The corporal said, "Didn't you realize this was martial law? I could have sworn I told you when you were fighting back tears at the thought of your niece on Scythia being in danger."

Please, show temperance. Don't fuel this.

Sergei held up his hand and the chit chat stopped. "You six, I don't expect you to have known the details of ship code, but even children know mutiny is wrong. You will be indefinitely confined and your access to Link Reality revoked. I hope you enjoy each other's company, because I'll have an acceleration pod brought into this airlock and you can stay here. It's roomier than the brig."

Thank you.

The smarter among the group sagged with relief. Some remained indignant they were being punished at all. They at least had the presence of mind to not speak up while the fate of Hadria and Perry was being laid out.

"Corporal Hadria, you organized an insurrection against me, one that would have jeopardized the lives of everyone aboard the *Demos*. This is a capital offense," Sergei said, despite having capitulated to the demands. The hypocrisy must have burned in his mouth. "Under ordinary circumstances, you would be sent back to planetside for a full hearing, but given the emergency situation, I suppose the hearing will have to be in judgment of myself. I am sentencing you to death."

The haggard mutineer hung his head, but didn't resist. Marcus tried to think whether the young man had struck him as so composed originally. Certainly not with the outbursts in the vehicle that first day.

"Lieutenant Perry, against my direct orders, you tried to establish communication with our sister ships in response to the Camrian goading. If I had not already instructed Mia to lock you out and alert me, you would have succeeded and we very likely would be facing down a nuclear missile. This too, is a capital offense. As it is the more severe offense... my own wellbeing notwithstanding," Sergei said with a glance at Hadria. "I will be carrying out your sentence first."

"You're not going to vent me, are you?" Perry asked.

Sergei's response was to turn and look at Marcus. The Ranger reached behind his back and produced the revolver. One bullet less and yet it felt heavier. The weight of everyone's eyes pressed it down in his palm and he almost didn't hand it over. It was his gun. He was the one giving Sergei the power of a firing squad.

For peace on the ship, he gave the captain the revolver. Father Publius said a prayer for the technician, and the final syllable was drowned out with the percussion of the gunshot. Perry fell back in the airlock and hit the floor, dead.

Then, Sergei handed the revolver back to Marcus. The Ranger just stared at it in his hand as the captain turned back to Hadria. "And with that, the ship is now below operating minimum staff. Corporal Hadria, your sentence will be suspended until further notice and you are hereby on capital probation."

That's not a real term. He just made that up.

"So I work for you until you kill me?" Hadria asked, keeping his eyes off Perry's corpse.

"If you're lucky, we get rescued before I have to. Are you complaining?"

Hadria sucked in air and nodded his head. "I understand, sir."

"Good, now go get yourself cleaned. You look like a caveman. We're done here," Sergei said, and left the airlock with a bodyguard, Samaras, and Father Publius.

Marcus stood and watched them leave, letting the events play out in his head once more. He was grateful again for the opaque helmet. The prisoners couldn't see his gaping mouth. Centuries of practice kept his body at attention, like a statue of a titan in their eyes.

"So, that's it?" one of them asked, looking down at the

plastic cuffs around his wrists. He turned to the guards and held them up but no one broke him free.

The security forces Sergei had drummed up muttered to one another, quietly arguing over who would be the one to get the moving tools and drag an acceleration pod over for them. No one seemed to be in command. They were simply bought thugs.

"You, on the end," Marcus said, squaring his shoulders with a man who looked like an office middle manager. Seven feet tall from space life and yet with a paunch that spoke of pastries for breakfast and beer for dinner. He straightened up, a facsimile of attention, when the Ranger spoke to him. "Pick someone else and the two of you go get the pod for them. The rest stay here and keep them in line. After you've done that, sort out their food with the kitchen and report to Sergei," he explained, and the man's instincts kicked in. Decades of brown-nosing took the wheel, and he sized up his colleagues. A smile appeared on the man's face, one of comfortable power.

Marcus added, "Hadria, since you apparently cut a deal, you get to carry your friend's corpse to the morgue."

The mutineer winced. "He's not my friend. Just my colleague," he mumbled, as though the phrase would protect him from Perry's glossy stare.

"Pick him up."

The two of them marched out of the airlock, Perry's corpse slung over Hadria's shoulder and dripping blood down his back. All the corpses on the ship were kept together, so only one room needed to be actively cooled. The air was largely pumped out, an energy expenditure even Ray had approved to keep the rot from the filtration systems. Only six weeks in and it looked like a mass grave, like a war crime had happened. The bodies were stacked like cordwood, one on top of another. Ray's body could still be seen at the top, but beneath was nothing but bloated and rotting feet stuck out from the pile.

As soon as Hadria put Perry down and straightened him out, Marcus shoved an evacuation bag into his hands and the corporal put it to use. Hadria heaved until the pressure cycling had normalized again and the mountain of bodies was hidden from sight. "You don't trust him, do you?" the mutineer asked, wiping the filth from his chin.

"I don't trust anybody. Not on this ship anyways," the Ranger answered.

Everyone I've ever trusted is dead by now.

"I exposed him, didn't I? I showed you the incompetence of the man you put in charge. He's scared now. Why else would he have turned to a militia. He deputized thugs. He's one step removed from a warlord. He doesn't give a damn about code. He-"

Marcus' hand closed around Hadria's jaw and shut him up. "Is this some sort of pride thing with you? Do you care more about being right than about surviving? Because the people aboard this ship don't give a shit about your pride and neither do I. The goal is one thing alone: survive. Perry was shot dead because surrendering to the Camrians would get us all butchered. If I see you making a martyr of yourself... If I see you trying to create resentment against the captain for your own sake, I will personally throw you out of an airlock."

Hadria managed to smile. "Don't mind me, Mr Space Ranger Sir. I'll stay in my room and do my job. Sergei will do all that for me. Just you watch. He has already laid the groundwork of his own destruction. How many people do you think will die this time?"

"Get out of my sight, and stay out of sight," Marcus ordered, and shoved Hadria away from him. The corporal vanished through the halls and doors. "Mia, set an alert for me if he goes anywhere but his room."

The ship systems flatly responded, "You don't have the authority to request that, Marcus."

"Then tell Sergei I've made the request and that he needs to approve it," he snarled back at the AI. Spinning around, he went back to his own quarters and sat down in his bed. The computer in the wall didn't turn on, his shoulder had smashed it to pieces during the tumble, but the smaller interface in the pod worked. Mia hadn't revoked his access to the ship's database, so he began reading through the passenger list and began with the deceased. Eventually, he found what he was looking for: the answer to Hadria's behavior.

The corporal's father had been aboard the *Demos*. The escape acceleration had exacerbated his heart condition and taken the man's life a week later. The surgery to save him would have been trivial aboard Athens Station or any planet, but the medbay on the *Demos* wasn't enough. Naturally, the rest of his family lived on Scythia.

19

Bad Food

The Fifty-First Day

The ships from Red Cairo arrived a day later than projected. Three ships of one size, and a fourth larger than the rest, emerged from Mimir's south pole and the nuclear mines didn't go off. That was the extent of the information that Sergei released; not just to the passengers but to his own subordinates. At his command, and for lack of Perry, access to the camera feed had been cut off entirely.

For the purposes of ship security, Sergei put everyone into information darkness. Two days passed with nothing but the captain's promise that the combat hadn't been resolved and there was no action to be taken yet. Anyone with even a hint of resentment became the butt of the new security force's ire. Black eyes and limps appeared in the crowds that passed through the mess hall. No one said where they had come from. They barely looked twice at the injuries.

Marcus tried to not make himself seen, but even he had to appear to fill his stomach. Sergei's militia not only let him walk unperturbed, but they actively avoided him. The number of them seemed to have grown from a dozen to fifty, multiplying like an infection in the ship. As far as Marcus could see, the only good thing they brought was quiet to the bath. Felicity hadn't shown up asking for help again.

Appearing from the crowd, Samaras said, "You've made yourself scarce." He stepped up to the Ranger, dropping his voice. The CEO had somehow managed to keep his face shaved clean, but his hair sorely needed some style. Marcus didn't want to ask what the man was using to keep his hair slicked back at that length.

"It's the smart thing to do. Haven't you done so as well?"

"At least I still go into Link Reality. At this rate, you're going to leave me on a losing streak, aren't you?" Samaras asked as they stepped up to get their food: noodles in a thin broth. They weren't even fully cooked, as though the chef had simply gotten the concoction to a boil and dished it out.

"Mia is giving me some grief if I try to log in," he said, not wanting to expose just how erratic the AI had become. It seemed to only be an issue for him. All the systems still worked. He knew that he should find Sophia and speak to her about the computer's actions, but he hadn't taken the time. He doubted she had a good impression of him after the incident with Hideo. If she did have one, she would have thanked him after deposing Ray.

"You've been missing the spectacle," Samaras said as he

moved to a side table. "Captain Seachnall removed the content filters for adult content. There's been quite the fiasco of segregation and the militia here hasn't been abiding by it."

Marcus had been eyeing the door out, the sheet of gray steel that could bolt shut between him and the survivors. He sat down with the CEO, popping the seal on his helmet and setting it aside. His face had lost hue, he didn't even need a mirror to know that. It always happened when he went too long. With the poor food, it was starting to feel like his skin had turned to rubber. He stuffed his spoon into the soup and asked, "Why'd he do that? Have there been more problems?"

The people around them kept stealing glances at them. They raised their shoulders and hunched their backs, as though it would obscure their sunken eyes. Samaras took it all in with a glance. "Only of his own making. The militia he made lacks hierarchy and he doesn't make himself available for sorting out any issues that arise."

Marcus grimaced, and not just because the soup had no flavor. The ship might have been running out of salt. "So how are they sorting it out?"

"Anything goes."

"Has anyone gotten hurt?" he asked, and looked around again. The literal answer surrounded him with half a dozen injuries. "You know what I mean."

"Nothing bad, yet," the businessman answered. He stirred his soup like it might dredge out some hint of flavor. He picked up the empty pepper shaker and tried to free some last dusting, to no success. "We're coasting on fumes of civilization. We need to stop thinking of this as a purely temporary measure and more like the exact problems society always has.”

“What do you mean?”

“These people are unemployed. The amount of work to be done barely occupies one in five people’s time,” Samaras answered.

Well they could start by making better food.

They’d be long dead before any aquacultures could be harvested though. “You sure you aren’t just being a hammer looking for nails? It’s not like much of anything can be built here on the ship.”

Samaras shrugged and let himself grin a bit. “Not in reality, no. But you see, I happen to be a bit of an expert at artificial scarcity...”

Marcus’ lip twitched. “So The Nebulae Company admits it then.”

Samaras laughed. “Off the record of course. Officially, we would never modify production quantities to abide by percentage contracts to the letter and nothing more. But, the thing is that I have no power over the ship, over Mia specifically, to change the rules of Link Reality. Sergei would be able to do it, but, last I checked, he’s been drinking himself to sleep after every shift.”

Marcus shook his head. “What’s your grand plan?” he asked, forcing the soup down his throat and crunching the noodles.

“Gameificaiton, rather literally,” Samaras said, holding his hands out to either side like he was on stage. “We just need to attach a cost to the fun stuff in Link Reality, and make a tedious way to get the currency. It'll take people's minds off of things. Idle hands and all that. But, I suppose dreaming this up has been nothing more than a way for me to entertain myself. Our chess games used to do that, but you don't come around. It's not like I'll get my hands on the steering wheel of this ship."

"You want to though, don't you?"

The businessman smiled. "Of course I do. I wouldn't have gotten to where I am, current circumstances notwithstanding, if I didn't want all the power I could get. I'm not just ambitious, I'm voracious. What's more, I actually know how to lead people."

"I'd be lying if I said it wasn't tempting," Marcus said, and realized he had surprised himself with the statement. "You don't know how to pilot a ship though. Makes you rather unqualified, doesn't it?"

The two of them ate in silence for a moment, both chewing on the issue as much as on the uncooked noodles. Samaras finally asked, "What about you? Why haven't you put your own eyes on the seat? You do more to lead us than either Ray did or Mr Seachnall."

Marcus put his spoon down and folded his arms on the table. "I can't. I'm incompatible with the neural interfacing needed. The pilots and captains, people like Sergei, it's second nature to them to work with Mia on a data level. She's not a full AI, just enough of one to translate intent into action. That's why there isn't an actual steering wheel. It's all digital and I'm a dinosaur. I can barely connect to Link Reality, let alone an artificial intelligence."

"Isn't that a bit of an oversight? It's almost ridiculous. You're the most expensive soldier alive, aren't you?"

Marcus' put his helmet back on. Once the visor was between him and Samaras, he answered, "Only by the standards of a few centuries ago. They designed our outfits to last forever, no matter how things might change and they were very afraid of the suit getting hacked by some future weapon… You should see the amount of gold that's inlaid to this armor just in case I ever have to be put into suspension for a few decades. Technology doesn't change as much as you think it does. A rock still kills people if it hits them."

Samaras leaned back in his chair and rubbed his chin. "So we learned. Has the captain at least given you access to the cameras? It would let me sleep easier."

"No. I think I'm going to go take a look around the engine bay though. It's possible one of the previous techs left a physical board game behind. I'll let you know if I turn up a chessboard," he said, and rose from the table to end the conversation. Too many people had been listening to them. It would cause problems, but he knew most of the issues would come down into Sergei's lap. That made him care less.

The door closing behind him was as much relief as the seal of his helmet to his suit. It cut the noise of the crowds. It severed the growing stench of unwashed bodies. He had to pass by the bridge to get to the engine section. The door there was just as closed, without so much as a whisper passing through it. For a moment he lingered, but he didn't knock and no one burst through to confront him. He continued on.

Something first felt wrong when he stepped into the engine

compartment. He stood beneath cooling lines and drooping server cables, and realized his heart was racing. The floor beneath him rocked. The ship was between tumbles, and would be steady for a few days more. All the same, it nearly knocked him on his back. The first pain came when his gut gurgled. It felt like a knife had been stabbed into his liver.

The Ranger buckled, throwing up an arm and slamming it into one of the personnel lockers so hard the door bent. His fingers fumbled the controls as he tried to pull up the suits readings of his vitals. Everything was wrong. Heart rate looked like he had just been sprinting. His blood pressure was plummeting and taking his balance with it. "Shit, Mia I need a doctor," he said and staggered to the closest waste receptacle. He popped his helmet off and let it drop so he could bend over and induce vomiting. The soup tasted worse coming up then it had going down.

It didn't help.

Whatever he had eaten was already in his bloodstream. A not-so-helpful question appeared on his suit's interface to ask whether a hospital was available. Marcus jabbed the no button and groaned as the suit processed, and advised him to find a safe place to sleep and rely on his regenerative systems. It assured him that his LD50 was far higher than any baseline human. That had never reassured him and never would.

"Mia! Medic!"

His enhanced liver had a shelf life, and he had long ago drank through the expiration date. Like a wreckage in drift, the only reason it kept going was because nothing had genuinely tried to put a stop to it. He could only guess what chemical had been put into his food. Some kind of lubricant or antifreeze he figured, not many options on a spaceship. Thinking it out in his head gave him focus, something to orient himself against as he staggered towards the acceleration pod in the back, and the computer interface it had. The AI hadn't responded to him, and he didn't know whether that was another symptom, or if she was leaving him to die.

He fell sideways into the pod and that system booted up happily for him. Fatigue was draining him and leaving behind a migraine. It was the most he could do to jam the redial button in the communication tab. He fell unconscious before the call was answered.

20

Rest and Relaxation

The Fifty-Fourth Day

The room around him was black. The protective spackle paint he had noted the first time he had stepped aboard the *Demos* looked to him like a mineralization. Marcus didn't know how long he had been unconscious, and he was losing track of how long he had been on the *Demos*. It blurred together in his mind with the transport that had brought him to Athens Station all the way from Earth, and before that with the *Pharus*.

"Come on, get yourself together Ranger. I need access to your veins," someone said. He could feel their hand, warm against his exposed neck. A prick hurt there.

"What did you give me?" he asked, words slurred. The *Pharus* was back in his mind; that catacomb of his own design.

"Just a stimulant. I don't have a diagnosis on you, yet,"

the woman answered. She moved over him, grabbing at his armor and rolling him as though it would dismantle if she just pressed on it right. "My name is Dr. Rei Omura. I need you to tell me what it is that happened."

"I killed the captain," Marcus answered, and he didn't know if he meant Ray or the captain of the *Pharus*. Both of them had brought him to where he was.

"Marcus, look at me," someone else said, and he felt her hands on the sides of his head. Felicity leaned over him, her hair dangling between them. "Stay focused on the questions. Stay here with us, not whatever is going on in your head. I think you've been poisoned."

He croaked a laugh. "Of course I've been. I've been doing nothing but making enemies since day one."

"Ranger, come on. Let's get you out of this armor so I can treat you," Dr Omura said, slapping his breastplate. "No acting like a big tough guy. Doctor's orders."

Marcus grumbled and pushed her arm away. "No. It doesn't come off. I just need water and food. I can heal from poison. I just need something better than that bathwater they called soup."

"Is this... is this some sort of genetic engineering I'm not privy to?" the doctor asked.

Marcus nodded and tried to push himself up on his elbows. He collapsed. "How long was I out?"

Felicity moved her hands to his chest to press him down. Perhaps there was a bit of color in her cheeks as she cleared her throat. "I didn't get your missed call until after I woke up. Between that, figuring out what a two minute voice mail of groaning meant, the doctor and access and everything, it's been seven hours."

"Ah, so I got my rest in early for today. Water, food, that's all I need. Unless you're hiding some kind of chemical analysis lab in the medbay I wasn't aware of. You're not going to have an antidote. They wouldn't have bothered if they thought I could be cured."

"Does that mean you can't?" Felicity asked.

"It means they didn't use enough, because I'm still here talking to you; but, if you don't get me some proper food then I'm not going to last very long."

The doctor slapped her instruments down on the ground and brushed her hair out of her face. "Fine! Fine alright. I'll go get the preserved food," she said and rose from his side. She winced and grumbled, looking at the vomit stains across her knees, but strode out from the engineering bay regardless.

It made the space feel larger again, enough to feel the wobble beneath him once more. Breathing was hard, even after he reduced the suit's internal pressure and let the whole thing expand. The plates separated from each other as though they had been springloaded, but it didn't help his racing heart. "Any water?"

Felicity put a bag to his lips and squeezed. Most of the water spilled over his face but some got down his throat. "How about I start bringing you food from now on?" she proposed as the Ranger coughed.

"What? So you can get poisoned too?"

She smirked. "Well I don't need to worry about that. I'll have an unkillable taste tester afterall."

Marcus smirked back at her, but his mind drifted to questions. "How did you get in here anyways?"

"Sophia let us in. She's the one who figured out that the AI hadn't alerted anyone," she answered as she squirted more water into his mouth.

After forcing it down his throat, Marcus wiped his chin off. "Great, so the ship is trying to kill me. I thought I'd only have to deal with that on Alliance craft."

"Isn't that what you said the first day? Earth surrendered. We are part of the Alliance now, therefore, this is an Alliance craft," she said, easily able to enjoy the fact that made Marcus want to roll over and puke again. "What's the *Pharus*?"

The Ranger winced and motioned to have her help him upright. "I was mumbling about that, was I?" he asked, scanning the room for the technician. Sophia must have been somewhere with the processing cores. "It was my last mission."

"You beat them, I take it?"

He licked his lips and nodded. Tasted like acid. "You could say that. The Alliance launched an attack on Earth directly. I saw to it that they failed... it's all classified of course, as much as it could be redacted. The Alliance knows the *Pharus* was killed and they almost certainly have enough forensics and surveillance and whatever to figure out it was infiltrated. I'm sure in a few years there will be an in absentia show trial about the whole thing."

"Is that why you're in the middle of nowhere with us?"

"Do you blame me for running away? From a battle that can't actually be won? I've been trying to go to the future. The more time I spend in A-Mov, the further I get away from it all. Didn't really work out for me though."

The engine room was warmer than the rest of the ship. They hadn't turned thrust on for almost two months, but the reactors and propulsion units had enough of a trickle to bake the chill from the air. It was almost pleasant, which meant by the time rescue came, it would be a sauna. For the moment though, it just made him want to sleep.

"Marcus, stay awake," Felicity said, shaking his shoulder.

He grumbled, but it was the sound of footsteps that kept him up. Sophia Almada approached, her magnetic boots slamming into the steel floor with each step, like she thought at any moment she might have to go outside. "I don't suppose you're hiding a spare processing core for an artificial intelligence somewhere, Ranger?" the engineer asked. "Because Mia should be decommissioned. I'd do it right now if it wouldn't get us all killed for lack of life support."

"That's... not good," he said, the understatement making both women roll their eyes. "How exactly did you miss that? Degradation can be seen years out."

The tech sighed and brushed her hair back. "Mia doesn't have organic components, so there's nothing to really talk with. She's just a program that programs in a language I can't read. To be honest, I don't even know if what she's doing is irrational, because I don't have the interpretation algorithms caught up. All I know is she's close to breaking the cognizance barrier and then the governor will kick in to strangle her. We might not even be able to fly the ship after that."

He shifted, getting a twinge of pain from his liver. Or maybe that was just a memory. "Did the radiation speed it up or something?"

Sophia shrugged. "Probably, along with the isolation. We didn't really announce it, but everyone on the *Demos* got about a decade of background radiation dosed into them that first day. You know how it is, don't you Ranger? We get cancer, AIs get new ideas."

"Yeah, and which is worse?"

Felicity held up her hand. "Hold on, we got how much radiation?"

"Don't worry about it. The planets can flush you clean," the engineer said.

Marcus cleared his throat. He glanced at the door Dr Omura had vanished from, but she hadn't returned. "There's also the possibility that it was ordered by Sergei. Not intentionally, but maybe he restricted Mia in some way to save power?"

Sophia sighed. "Pray that he didn't, because then he'd be completely incompetent... You're his guardian angel afterall."

"He needs to stop making so many enemies for me then. I make enough as it is."

21

The Pharus

Some decades ago...

"Sir, the intruder has broken in through Airlock Three," the security officer of the *Pharus* said.

Captain Cleopuld slammed his fist into the arm of his chair. The monitor bay before them was lit with the schematics of the spaceship, quickly zooming in on the detected point of entry. "How? We had him sealed in Airlock Two for a week! He should be half-starved. How has this thing survived the depressurization? It must be a machine!"

The blinking dot emerged into the hall as the *Pharus'* self-appointed security forces scrambled to intercept. "Sir, you heard him speak in the parley as well as I did," the officer said, licking his lips and tapping in new commands. An image from the hallway appeared on screen. Broken lights and molten steel that illuminated the corpses. The feed itself was damaged with static and the angle twisted back and forth as though the camera was dangling from the wiring.

The captain scoffed and threw up a hand dismissively. "Parley– that was no parley. How could one Earther alone on a ship be the one to demand surrender?" the captain asked, unable to take his eyes off the progression of cameras. The warrior had adopted the habit of shooting the cameras first whenever he opened a door. Even with soldiers blasting return fire at him, and welding doors shut to drop grenades through the ship's fragile interior. The percussion echoed through the floors to the bridge, the screen flashed with light.

The Earther warrior never stopped advancing. The bridge crew glanced at one another, avoiding the gaze of the captain. There was a rumor among the Alliance, one told in hushed breaths and out of sight of commanding officers. To speak of it invited punishment, to hold it in was unbearable. Cleopuld knew the rumor, and the truth of it. Fear and suppression had injected power to it, among those whose ears it had reached. Rumors always embellished, but only around a nucleus of truth.

Earth's secret weapon was aboard their ship, a Space Ranger.

"Pharus," the captain said, getting the computer's attention, "When we arrive at Earth, I want you to link our systems to the nearest Alliance ship. If they fire, we fire. Understood?"

His security officer gave him a wide-eyed look, the expression more pronounced for he was born to a dark planet. With a home star barely brighter than the others, the children of those colonists had enlarged eyes, reflective irises, and an overall expression like cave fish. Standard lighting nearly required tinted glasses for him, but they made for some of the most committed fighters. "You know what he is, don't you?"

"Order cannot be completed," the *Pharus* responded. "Nuclear bombardment cannot be authorized without human oversight."

Cleopuld gritted his teeth. The Earther drew closer. Whenever a bulkhead was shut before him, it bought only a few seconds before he slagged through it with whatever cutting tool he had. The heat of the ship was surging. The smell of ozone broke through the filters. "It is human oversight, just not a human here."

"I'm afraid that cannot be authorized."

"Captain, your orders to stop this attacker?" his security officer shouted. Cleopuld spun on him. He continued, "We are months away from Earth still. He's going to be here in less than ten minutes if we don't figure out what to do."

Cleopuld puffed out breath and scratched his face. It never did any good. Even with nails like iron, he couldn't scratch the itch from his skin. The Earthers had seen to that when they had made him a Camrian, intentional or not. "How did he get between the airlocks? Outside or inside?"

His security officer shook his head. "He went outside. One slip and he would have plummeted out of A-Mov never to be found again, but he crawled along the hull and cut in from the un-reinforced door."

"So he couldn't cut through the emergency foam. Alert the engineering crew and have them pen him in with the stuff," Cleopuld said. At least one of them needed to survive if the *Pharus* was to be a threat to Earth. Just one person was all that was needed for the attack.

The first thing that happened was fire suppression foam. That bought some time as the Earther's tool clogged down with the stuff. "Feeling the heat?" the Earther asked. The ship had filtered the combat, but the microphone was still cued for voice. It passed along to the bridge and made everyone shift back in their seats.

Cleopuld cleared his throat and turned on that hall's speakers. "Who are you?"

"The savior of Earth, destroyer of invaders. What do I have to do to make you turn over control of the ship?" the Earther responded.

Cleopuld gestured, and his officer got the message. The feed switched from the shot camera to the fire detection camera. A vibrant wall of heat imaging appeared before them, the feed straining to reconcile the molten metal with the mere presence of body heat. "We could scuttle the oxygen system."

"I suppose that would stop me, but it would kill all of you as well, which would be mission success for me. I'm not here to survive. I'm here to stop you from nuking my home," the Ranger responded. The tracking ID of two engineers rushed over to the invader's location, foam tanks in tow.

Cleopuld snarled and leaned closer to the microphone, narrowing his black eyes at the screen. "Let me tell you this, Earther. You'll have to kill us all to do that."

There was a pause. The thermal camera even showed that he stopped working on his tool. It gave the engineers time to start blasting foam across the doorway, but the Ranger's answer put ice down Cleopuld's back. "You think that will stop me? I never once thought of even taking you as prisoners. It would take a mountain of trust to let a single one of you get within ten lightyears of Earth and still have a missile. Frankly, I don't have that much trust in me to give."

"You savage son of a bitch. No prisoners? Indiscriminate execution? That's a war crime and you know it!"

"Only if Earth loses the war."

Cleopuld muted the communication line, switching it to generated subtitles only, but neither of them had anything to say after that. It had bought enough time for the engineers to spray the rapidly expanding foam all over the door leading closer to the bridge. While the ranger tried to cut through it, they ran to the other doors and did the same, but it wasn't perfect. They didn't have enough of the gap filling material to encase him in the room. It bought time, and they had to hope that they wouldn't need the repair material for a normal emergency. Without it, even a slight hole could spill all of their air into the void.

For days, the Earther was contained but not inactive.

They tried removing the oxygen from his room, but there were too many bullet holes into the infrastructure. The engineers worked around the clock trying to stabilize the damage the Earther had left in his wake.

The question of how to kill him took the bridge crew's time. After all the deaths fighting the Earther to a stop, the bridge crew comprised nearly every soul aboard. They reviewed footage and listened over audio files until they could argue over whether any given munition had actually threatened the armored titan. The notion of starving him to death was useless. His advance had been stopped in the mess hall. They were the ones unable to feed themselves. Fear did wonders to crush their appetites.

They went as far as to discuss cutting through the shielding on one of their nuclear missiles to irradiate him, but even the most liberal estimates of dosage wouldn't kill the ranger before he broke free and slaughtered them all.

"We could surrender," his security officer said one day. Three days of no sleep had put bags under his eyes that made his entire face look purple. The bottles of liquor they were passing around didn't help either.

Cleopuld shook his head. "He already said he was taking no prisoners. We need to find a way to eliminate him for our own sakes. I'd cut this ship in half if it would get rid of him and leave us with the missiles. Besides, he hasn't spoken in days. He's just working through the problem like with the airlocks. Then he will come and kill us."

The security officer upended the bottle in his lips, and three big bubbles rose up through it before he handed it off again. "His issue is the nukes: not us. We could shove the missiles out the hatch and ditch them in deep space. Then his issue is taken care of."

Cleopuld frowned. He rolled back in his seat and stared at his security officer. While not very old by Earth standards, the captain was on in his years as a Camrian. Age had made him thick with hide and fat both, and the stress had brought back heartburn that felt like his throat had melted off. His fish-eyed officer didn't seem to understand the gravity of the situation that had brought the entire human galaxy to war, nor how close they were to victory.

"That isn't an option, officer. If you bring it up again, I will summarily execute you," he said, and people stopped proposing ideas after that.

Instead, they went behind his back. He found them days later, in communication with the Earther. The Ranger was obviously in favor of the idea. Getting the crew of the *Pharus* to abandon their weapons would make killing them all that much easier and safer for him. Cleopuld put a stop to it by shooting his security officer for insubordination.

After that came an alcohol induced heart attack, a suicide, and an attempt to kill him. When Earth was only one month away, the captain sat in the bridge alone. The serials he had always liked to watch made him sick; but, it was them or silence. He sat and waited, clutching his gun to his chest and sleeping in the pilot seat.

When the ship finally alerted him that the Earther had broken containment, he didn't have the strength to stand up and face him. "What took you so long?" he grumbled as the armored warrior stepped inside.

The Ranger looked around. "It was a courtesy to your crew. You don't seem to have one left though."

Cleopuld snarled. "Nope, it's just me. Sitting in our pantry had a lot to do with that. Not much of a courtesy to us."

"I would have taken your surrender. Getting rid of the nukes would have been enough," the Earther said as he sat down on the arm of another chair and looked at the captain.

"Oh just get on with it. Aren't you going to shoot me? There's no chance I'm ever going to surrender to you, Ranger."

The killer shrugged his shoulders. "Before we arrive at Earth, yeah, I will. But if I do that, I'd be as alone on this ship as you've been. I don't need to take your life so soon."

The Camrian captain laughed, his chest bellowing with mirth until he started coughing. "Sharing your company would be worse than death," he said, and held up the pistol in his grasp. He pointed it, and blasted one shot off the ranger's chestplate. It nicked the paint. "Figures," Cleopuld said, and put the gun in his own mouth.

The *Pharus* arrived at Earth adrift; weapons missing and all friendly hails denied. No nukes went off on Earth's surface, nor on Mars or any other habitat. They didn't need to. The peace accords were signed within weeks of the fleet's arrival. The Jupiterian Disaster had stripped Earth of her defenses, and they had no choice but to surrender to the Alliance. More than giving up the war, Earth had to give up their assets as well.

Ranger Marcus Maximus went on the run and the Alliance declared him a wanted war criminal for the wholesale slaughter of the crew of the *Pharus*.

22

When You Are Strong, Make Them Think You Are Weak

The Fifty-Fourth Day

The nick in his armor was still there. The paint had been buffed and redone, but that only changed the shape of the damage. It was still there whenever he looked at it. Of course, there were hundreds, if not thousands, of other dings and nicks from his career, plenty from the *Pharus* too. That last one from Captain Cleopuld had hit different.

"Do you regret it?" Felicity asked. She had helped him out of the engineering bay, but not to his room. The *Demos* had a small conference room tucked into a gap a fair distance from the main hold, as though the designers were simply filling space. When they had first arrived, it had been a mess. No one had secured the cabinets before launch, and every tumble of the ship had tossed instant coffee cups and forgotten clutter to every corner.

"I don't like how it turned out, but there's a reason I didn't stick around to be shot. Wasn't just that the brass wanted me to hide, so they could save an asset for a rainy day," he mused. They had managed to turn an ice cooler into a bolster, even if it had crumpled beneath his weight, and it let him lay on the ground. His insides still felt like he had ingested broken glass, but the symptoms were evolving.

She brushed her hair back. The facade of a business woman had been abandoned. Miz Lenz exposed her natural colors. She straddled the chair backwards to drape her arms over the back and prop her chin up.

I guess you give up on decorum after watching someone puke their guts out for hours.

She asked, "And your response to the poisoning?"

He arched an eyebrow. Without his helmet on, in case more needed to come up, the expression actually came across. "You mean my lack of response?"

Felicity gave a half-hearted gesture towards the nose of the ship. "You're going to let them think it worked."

"That's the idea, yeah."

The tightening of her brow spoke more than words could have.

"When you are weak, make your enemy think you are strong. When you are strong, make them think you are weak. A wise saying from Earth."

She rolled her eyes. "Marcus, you can barely stand without help."

Marcus was roughly aware of how his face looked, and that he hadn't kept down any of the protein bars that Dr Omura had brought him, but that sort of weakness had been trained out of him. "I'm better than they think, and by the time these people make a move, I'll be on my feet again. Being confronted by an enemy you thought you had already dealt with… nothing breaks morale quite like that."

The door to the room slid open. Warm yellow light from the hall sidelit Felicity for a moment as she turned her head. "Where's the patient? I've got a delivery of three cups of over-cooked rice for him," Mr Samaras said. He stepped in beside them, carrying the pot like he had just arrived with takeout food. He certainly acted like he had a treat, rather than taste-less gruel.

"How the hell did you get access to this side of the ship?"

"Miz Almada smuggled me in. Well then, look at you," Charles said as he sat the pot down on the table beside Felicity and turned to the Ranger. "Quite the fearsome destroyer of ships, breaker of mutinies, aren't you?"

"I'm better than I look. Not that you'll be telling any-one that. How goes the rumor?" Marcus asked, gesturing for a bowl.

"Dr Omura has been saying you're on death's door, if that's what you're after," the CEO said as he shoveled some of the rice into a paper dish for the Ranger. He even snapped a pair of disposable chopsticks for him.

The kernels were white and soggy with water. They didn't taste like anything in his mouth, but they didn't fight him going down. "It is," Marcus said, and finished the bowl before he continued, "Sergei must be sweating bullets right now."

Felicity asked, "Because you're using him as bait?"

"Yeah."

"He's hunkered down," Samaras said, pulling a seat over to join them. "The chef said he gave the captain a week's worth of food right after Dr Omura picked up your fancy rations."

Marcus couldn't help but smirk. "Fancy rations? If the *Demos* had Space Ranger patented calorie cubes, I wouldn't be in this situation you know."

Felicity nearly gagged. "Tell me that's not real."

"Worse than any MRE you could imagine. They go down easier if you soak them in water for a few hours first. Or a few days. Really those are one of the most impressive feats of the whole project. People only want to discuss the flashy things though."

"Anyways," Samaras said, rolling his hand in the air. "Seems like he's locked himself in his room, or maybe the bridge. Nobody can get into either, and Mia hasn't said."

Marcus licked a few kernels off his lips and held his bowl out to the two of them. Felicity took it, and scooped some more of the rice for him. "Someone will cut him out of there soon enough."

"And if they kill him before you get there?"

Marcus answered, "There's a chain of command for a reason. There's not many people left in it, but it's there. Ray, Sergei, Perry, would all be dead. Hadria has been stripped of his post more or less. That leaves Sophia as the next in command, even if she hasn't taken on any advising powers. After her would be Ensign Lawrence I think?"

Felicity cleared her throat. "Ensign Lawrence and Ensign Banks have the same rank. I'm not sure which would take over, or if either are even capable of running the ship. They were assigned here for training. No one actually thought the *Demos* would fly somewhere."

Samaras folded his hands together and frowned. "I'd feel better about our fate if the captain would come forward about the battle going on right now. No one but him knows."

Marcus nodded. The bowl in his hands grew less appetizing by the moment, but he kept working at it. Between bites, he said, "I figure that's why someone decided they needed to get me out of the way. It's either that, or because of someone I hurt in Hadria's attack."

"How hard is it to captain a ship nowadays?" Samaras asked, drawing both of their gazes to him. He shrugged. "What? If it's difficult, then it narrows our list of suspects down, doesn't it?"

Marcus sighed and looked back at the half finished bowl of rice. His stomach had felt vacuous at the start, now it felt bloated. "It's not hard, if the ship's AI cooperates. Auto pilot had to get very good once fourth-dimensional space became common. The difficult portion is leadership and judgment. The exact qualities that Sergei is lacking." The room stayed silent as Marcus grabbed himself a bag of water.

"Do you regret it?"

The word came like an echo. He stopped with the water nearly to his lips and had to check which of them had asked the question. It had been Samaras, his cold blue eyes fixed on him. Marcus said, "No. Just because killing Ray turned out bad doesn't mean I think I made the wrong decision for the information at the time. The question is how to progress from here, because the dead don't come back."

Samaras nodded slowly. Finally, he shrugged. "Personally, I believe Hadria bears the blame. There's been fights breaking out almost every hour since we spoke in the mess."

The chopsticks clattered into the bowl. "There's been what?"

Samaras pulled back and shot a glance to Felicity, but she didn't rescue him. "No one told you? Sergei's militia splintered overnight. It's no better than gang warfare. Something like fifty people are in the infirmary over it. The doctors have just thrown up their hands about it."

Marcus scratched his chin. His fingers dragged through his knotty beard, it couldn't be called stubble anymore, and hardly occupied his brain while he thought it over. "Well then, hard to say whether that will buy me more time or less time to get my strength back. What are they fighting over anyways?"

"Rumor has it that it started over a vodka barrel. Then the whole supply of rations came into question. I guess people didn't realize we were eating through everything with an expiration date first. Some of them heard there were bags of pre-cooked lasagna or something, and fists started flying."

"People fought over MRE bags?" Felicity's mouth hung open as she stared at her boss.

Marcus laughed. It hurt to laugh, like a strain between the emotions inside him. "Only someone who has never tasted an MRE would fight to get one. At least it's good to know you aren't out there rallying some kind of corporate mercenary corps to take over the ship, Charles."

"Aren't I?" He had a grin on his face. The CEO rose

from the table and straightened his shirt, the motion an old habit. He even checked the fit of a watch that he didn't have on his wrist. He acted like he had just concluded a meeting and took a step towards the door. "Before I go, I don't want to be missed much, did you succeed in finding that physical chess set?"

"No," Marcus answered, pushing himself to sit upright. It didn't bring their heights into alignment, but it was better than lying beneath the businessman.

Samaras nodded. "Well, keep an eye out for it if you can. Doesn't seem like you have access to Link Reality in here anyways."

"You don't need to worry about me," Marcus said, and watched the businessman step back into the hall and let the door slide shut behind him.

"Well, at least you've got an attitude again. It was getting boring to talk to you when you were so tired," Felicity said as she peered into the dregs of the rice pot and scooped herself some.

Marcus fell backwards, crunching the cooler beneath him and almost cracking his head against the wall. "I'd rather be sleeping than picking my words with him. That turned out way too exhausting."

For a moment, the only sound in the room was his own labored breathing, and the scratch of Felicity's chopsticks against her bowl. The issues of the ship turned this way and that in his mind as he tried to examine them like one of Pontius' puzzles. There were too many unknowns to do anything though. "This would be a lot easier if I could see the ships..."

"Why? The ships don't have anything to do with the people killing each other."

"Because then I would be able to know whether Sergei is making the right decisions. I wouldn't have to just trust him after he's already broken that trust once... twice if you count executing Perry without warning me. Maybe I shouldn't let him have a third chance."

She looked down at him and wiped her lips off. After a glance at the door out, she asked, "But who would you replace him with? You can't take command yourself."

"That's the problem, isn't it? I guess it'll depend on who comes out on top from this juvenile power play."

23

The Winning Move

The Fifty-Fifth Day

The city at the heart of Link Reality looked much the same as the first day, aside from the lack of people. Marcus couldn't tell whether they had moved to other parts of the expanded simulation, or if they simply couldn't take the risk of being in the digital. There were children and the elderly, almost no adults at all. Sergei was somewhere in the system; somehow whiling away his time.

Marcus was in a new body, a freshly generated avatar with a fresh guest profile. It was anonymous to the other people aboard the *Demos*, but it was all the same to Mia. The raven struck down on him like an eagle seizing a mouse. Again, talon and beak ripped through his body and tore out his liver. People screamed as he gritted his teeth, but the spectacle ended with him waking up in the conference room.

Cold sweat matted his hair and he couldn't catch his breath within the metal coffin of his armor. The lights were off. He laid alone in the darkness, no sound but his own breathing coming back to him. With a sigh, he sank back down and put his head to the wall.

That brought noise, the clamor of people far off in the ship conducted through the steel skeleton. Scuffles and pounds, the thump of flesh. He knew that tempo, that clash of fists and grappling of bodies. Two people were engaged in the dance of murder. He couldn't tell where in the ship that was. Possibly in the bridge, the kitchen, maybe it was the prisoners in the isolated airlock. The people aboard the *Demos* weren't practiced fighters. They didn't know how to kill. Breaking up the intruders of the bath had been trivial, easier than drunks in a bar. They had been men more likely to break their fists in a punch than to hurt the other person.

But, violence was instinct. Every ape knows how to beat another to death.

Marcus tried to swallow the knot in his throat. His mind forced him to think of the militia men that Sergei had brought together, of the kinds of men who were learning how fragile other people were and how strong they could be.

There was something else, a rhythmic tap-tap. It grew louder, but kept a languid pace. Footsteps approaching. What's more, it didn't have the sharp clicks that Felicity's stride had, nor the weight of Samaras'. He reasoned it could be Dr Omura or Miz Almada, but something told him it wasn't.

"Fuck," he grumbled, grabbing hold of the counter edge and pulling himself back up. Reorienting himself almost made him puke, but he managed his way to his feet. He snapped his helmet back on. The respirators hissed, flushing out the air that had been saturated with his own sweat. The visor powered on, illuminating from within and driving up the contrast in the dim room until he could see the door once more.

His body felt numb, like he had spent the entire day marching. That was good. He had trained for that kind of fatigue. He could work with it.

The footsteps grew more distinct, passing right through the hall outside Marcus' room. The Ranger slid up along the wall of the conference room, turning his head to the door and holding his breath. They didn't slow at the door. They didn't come to a stop and face it, merely continued on until one notable tremble through the ship knocked them off balance. Something must have lurched in the water containment. A hand slammed into the wall, grabbing for balance, and an old man cursed under his breath, "Fucking Hell."

"Father Publius?" Marcus asked, stepping out of the room to face the old priest.

The old man jumped around, eyes wide and face drawn down as he spotted the Ranger behind him. "Marcus. So this is where you've been hiding," he said, brushing his palms across his jacket. "Don't tell the kids about that, would you?"

The Ranger laughed and leaned against the doorframe. "Habits die hard, don't they? How did you get back here?"

"How? This is to get to the prisoners. I've always had access to them. Religious rights and all that. I just don't come daily. You know, I was wondering why I hadn't seen you lately.

The others said you died, but I knew better," the priest said, and gave the Ranger a look over. He frowned.

"Better to be a man of mystery than a corpse. Are you in too much of a rush to catch up?"

Publius chuckled and smiled. "For you? I can make time. They aren't going anywhere. Though, I might hope you're considering confession," the priest said, and stepped into the room. It lit up automatically for him; yet another way Mia was spiting the Ranger.

Marcus said, "Nothing I haven't already confessed, and I don't ask for forgiveness until I understand the outcome."

Nothing from the Demos *at least.*

That made Father Publius draw his lips into a line, but he got on with explaining what had happened. The situation in the main hold was worse than Marcus had thought. Word had gotten out that ships from Red Cairo had arrived, but not who had won the fight. No message had come in from the exo mine either. The only thing people knew for certain was that the *Demos* hadn't begun accelerating back towards Mimir, and that the captain was missing in action. The deputized security forces had disintegrated. Badges had been stolen and faked and abuses perpetrated.

"And no one has put a stop to this?"

Father Publius sighed. He sank into his chair and his head drooped. "Ranger, I think you're the only one who can."

Marcus gritted his teeth and shifted his gaze to the wall. In the shadow between the door and a hull support was nothing but his own thoughts. When he spoke, he chose his words slowly. "Violence without hope won't change anything. I'll just exacerbate the problem. And perhaps the next attempt to kill me will work. I'm not impervious."

"There's always hope. So long as we're alive, there is hope. Even if it takes a miracle from God to deliver us safely, there is always hope."

Marcus turned back to the priest. "Did you tell that to Perry as well? Before Sergei shot him?"

The priest shrank back even more, his gaze falling to the floor. "There was hope. Hope that Mr Seachnall wouldn't do it. He didn't have the conviction to execute them all, I had hoped and pleaded that he wouldn't kill any of them."

"Do you have any idea who tried to kill me? The prisoners must have family back in the hold; people who sympathized with them or would be upset that they had been arrested," Marcus said, and after a deliberate pause. "Or people like Tim's family."

Father Publius scowled instantly. "The Valana family would never do something like that. They're good, Godly people. I won't have you throwing dangerous accusations like that around. Such problems have already been dealt with. Tim may have been a fool to work with those men, but children make mistakes and it is the duty of adults to correct them."

The Ranger flatly responded, "Tim's nearly an adult. Enough to have known better. I wasn't even the one that hurt him. He slipped because of the tumble, and I got blamed for it. So why should I trust the good judgment of these people?"

Father Publius rose to his feet. "If you can't understand

the woes of a mother injured, then I see my time will be better spent working with the souls in the airlock. They at least might come around. You've blinded yourself to find convenient solutions."

"Not very patient anymore, are you? Is the fighting getting to you?"

Father Publius drew himself up, anger bringing color back to his face. "This all started because you killed Captain Regulus. You should never have done that, never have unleashed that genie upon us! Bear some responsibility for this, why don't you? Then I will have patience for you when you look to scapegoat my congregation."

The priest hesitated only a moment, but Marcus didn't respond. Then he turned and left the room. The Ranger waited until the sound of stomping feet faded away to the din of the ship. Then, he too rose from the table and left the room. He headed the opposite direction, back to midship where the bridge was.

The ship systems refused to acknowledge his approach, not even to turn on the lights. The access pad that should have checked his identity stayed dormant and he was forced to bang his fist on it. He didn't need to announce himself, no one else could make that clang of steel on steel.

Sophia Almada opened the door for him, and took a step back. She had been holding a kitchen knife in one hand, and she glanced up and down the empty hall. "What are you here for?"

Marcus pushed in and closed the door behind him. "Is

the cap– is Sergie here?" The G-pods for the crew sat empty, flickering in the shifting light of the holo-display's screen saver.

"Sergei is in a drunken stupor." Sophia looked worse than the day she had come into the engineering bay. There were bags under her bloodshot eyes. "I'm honestly amazed at this point that no one has had the guts to go and off him."

"That's his reward for shooting Perry. People are scared of him."

Who can say whether that's a good thing right now?

Sophia snorted and walked back over to the captain's chair. It was the only one on the main floor, the rest would have required her to climb a ladder. With a blunt jab of her finger into the console, the screensaver vanished. The big screen alit with a cartoon. It was apparently all two-dimensional and hand drawn, some passion project that made even Marcus stop and cross his arms. By the time the itch of familiarity materialized in his head, Sophia had lifted up a half empty bottle of liquor and taken a swig.

"Is this Embrace the Blood?"

She pulled the bottle from her lips with a pop and offered it to him. "Sure is. I was in the mood for some mindless heroics."

Marcus waved the bottle off. "I remember watching this as a kid. Did they ever find the Demon Core?"

"Like a hundred years ago, yeah. This is a reboot. How many star jumps have you made?"

Keep forgetting about the things slipping me by.

"Too many... I don't suppose you could call ahead for me

and let Sergei know I'm coming. I don't want to have to break his door down."

"Mia, can you ping Sergei and wake his ass up?" Sophia asked, her eyes not wandering from the show.

"I've set an alarm to go off in the captain's quarters one minute from now," the AI answered as the tech cranked the volume up on the show's theme song.

Marcus grunted. Of course the AI would still work for everyone else. "Remind me some time that I should catch up for nostalgia's sake. If I have the time. Thank you... I could use something nice," he said, and left the forsaken bridge behind.

When he arrived at Sergei's door, he only had to raise his fist to knock and it slid open automatically. The bedroom was different from the captain's meeting room. It was smaller for starters, crammed into a corner like the conference room. There was barely enough room for a bed and wash stand, worse even than the room Marcus had been given. The captain sat on his bed, rubbing the sleep from his eyes. "Have they come to kill me yet?" he asked, his voice sounding like he had swallowed sandpaper.

"Not yet. Should they?" Marcus asked, stepping in to let the door close.

"No, they shouldn't; but, they will. Unless I turn this ship around and start flying back to Mimir, they'll cut my head off and put someone in my place who will," Sergei said as he reached over to his desk and picked up half of a cold sandwich.

Marcus walked over and leaned his back against the wall opposite Sergei. "Who's winning the fight?"

"Not us."

"Show me."

"No." Sergei stuffed the food into his mouth and chewed, staring back at Marcus. When he finally swallowed, he added, "That's my only lifeline. I'm the only one aboard this ship right now who knows whether or not the surviving ships out there are friendly or not." He tapped his temple.

"So they're enemy ships. Because if they were friendlies, you'd already have turned the ship around to go back to Mimir," Marcus said.

Sergei smirked, a dry glimmer in his face. "That's the problem though. Two groups of ships arrived. All three of them shot at each other. Only a lone pair survived. Mimir's got a graveyard of ships now, and I don't know if I trust the winners."

Then that lone Scythian ship is gone. The crew of the exo mine must have been wiped with them. I wonder if Samaras knows yet.

"Pontius could figure it out."

Sergei nodded and ate the last bite of his food. He shrugged as he swallowed. "Perhaps he could, if I hadn't deleted the records."

Marcus blinked and stared back at the pathetic mutineer. Sergie had cheeks packed full of bread and mayonnaise, some was dripping down his chin as he chewed like a sleepwalker. Then he had the audacity to smirk. "You what?"

"I deleted them. They're only in my head now."

Marcus' hand closed around Sergei's shirt. He slammed the

man up against the wall. "For your sake, I hope you're lying."
He leaned in. His opaque visor swallowed Sergei's vision.

"Or what? You're going to kill the only person who knows what happened out there? It was the winning move for me. What are you going to do about it, Ranger?"

24

Mutiny Mark III

The Fifty-Ninth Day

First, they broke Hadria out of his room.

Alarms started going off across the ship, Mia interpreting the actions as foreign boarders. Then, they went and sprang the prisoners from the air lock. Ironically, they were in the best shape of anyone. They hadn't been in any fights lately. Whether they had stood steadfast by Hadria the whole time, or if they were simply the most successful group of thugs and realized they needed legitimacy, Marcus would never know.

They stopped and shuffled into the hall, those in the back pressing the others forward until they all saw Marcus standing at the opposite door. Hadria stepped out in front. He had groomed himself somewhat, brushed his beard and washed at least. He looked more composed than the others. "I see the rumors of your death were greatly exaggerated."

"Poison doesn't work on me."

Largely true, about as exaggerated as my death.

Hadria glanced back at the men behind him. Marcus figured the scrawny man behind him with hair down past his shoulders was simply the ring leader that had gotten Hadria to join them, not the one who had done the deed. "So are we going to have to do this again? You're going to break bones for that incompetent?"

Marcus sighed and folded his arms as he leaned against the door behind him. "You people aren't giving me good options, you know that?"

The mutineers filled more of the hall. They muttered to each other and considered the various clubs and knives they had with them. Hadria cleared his throat. "It's pretty rare to get a good option in an emergency. Are you going to side with us, or are you going to fight us again? We won't back down." His statement seemed to give the men behind him some backbone. For most, the illusion of one was enough to grow one.

Marcus held up two fingers. "First, you hand over whoever tried to kill me. Second, don't kill Sergei yet. He needs to be interrogated by me and Pontius Livius."

That brought a stir through the mutineers, but Hadria understood at once. He turned to the ring leader. "You, go get the mutant right now. Sergei purged records." The man opened his mouth to respond, but Hadria cut him off. "Now! Before the ship starts to tumble again." With that, the man pushed back through the crowd. Hadria then turned to the group at large. "Now then, who did the deed? Who poisoned the Ranger?"

Marcus watched the mutineers whisper. They elbowed one another, pointed fingers, and yet no one stepped out. "It wasn't any of us, sir," someone finally said.

"Then who was it?"

The speaker shrugged and turned up his hands. "We can round up everyone who was in the kitchen that day, if that works. No one ever took credit for it though."

Marcus slammed his fist into the wall, breaking the sheet metal. "If I find that someone has been hiding them from me, they'll get the same punishment. Understood?" he asked, dropping his voice to a low growl.

Everyone but Hadria cowed back. Their leader asked, "So do we have a deal?"

Marcus had to rip his hand free of the damage, but nodded his head. "Let me be clear though: Sergei betrayed his duties and in doing so betrayed me. That is why I am doing this and the same will be held for you."

The group of them forced open the door to Sergei's room. He cried out that he was untouchable, that only he knew whether the ships were safe to contact. He leapt into the far corner of the room, spewing curses at them and waving a knife.

One of the mutineers chucked a wrench at him with all the strength he had. The head crunched into Sergei's ribs and knocked the wind out of the captain. The rest mobbed him, threw him to the ground and stomped on him until Hadria barked out, "Tie him up and take him to the brig."

Trussed up with rope made from shredded sheets, they hauled the captain back to his feet and out of the puddle of his own blood. His gaze fell only on Marcus. "What do you think you're doing? I'm the only one. The only one!"

Marcus grabbed Sergei by the hair and lifted his head up. "This right now is your last chance to peacefully hand over power. You can tell Mia to transfer your control to someone else. Hadria, Sophia, I don't care. Do that and I'll be nice to you. If you resist, you'll get a crash course in interrogation techniques. The kind they don't officially teach."

The threat would have worked on anyone else in the room. Everyone else was in their right mind. They hadn't rotted their sanity with alcohol and fear. The captain spat blood onto Marcus' chest. "Make me," he said.

The ranger let go of the captain's head and wiped the bloody spittle off his chest. He gestured with his head, and the men holding Sergei got the message. Under normal circumstances, they wouldn't have been imposing men. They wouldn't have even been noticeable. One was the kind of pudgy that bespoke a day-in-day-out computer worker with no care for his image, and the other had the lankiness of low-gravity and somehow still seemed short. The way they held Sergei's bound arms was too tight, and they grinned as he winced in pain.

"Hadria, you should tell Sophia that she's de facto in charge for the next two days. Until Sergei is dealt with," Marcus said.

The former corporal nodded, his gaze a thousand miles away. "For the ship systems, yeah... yeah I suppose she is. But I'm going back to the hold and explaining what we just did. And the moment I get the cameras, I'm telling them exactly what it is we see. No more secrets. We're going to be transparent and we're going to give them hope again."

"Sounds like a quick way to get thrown out. If you tell everyone everything, they'll tell you what decisions you should be making."

"That's the point."

Admirable.

Hadria had changed in the last ten days. Marcus hoped it was in the right direction. He followed the men to the brig, and had them sit Sergei down in the bloody room. Sergei was carried without much protest, and sat with his head hanging.

"Are you going to shoot him?" The man who had carried Sergei backed up when Marcus looked at him.

"I won't need to," the Ranger said, and both men paled. "Get out of here. Go get me Pontius Livius. If you get in my way, you'll regret it," he ordered, and they both ran off.

The door to the brig slid shut behind him. The two were alone in the blood splattered room, barely illuminated by the light above. Marcus took a seat on the sink and stared at Sergei. With the mutineers gone, the silence of the ship surrounded them. An oppressive din like blood in the ears or an antenna tuned to vacuum.

Sergei finally lifted his head and looked at him. "So do you have a plan or something? Did you cook up some scheme to save us all? You kept them from killing me, so I guess I'm all ears."

This living piece of shit...

"To save us all? Since when have you been worried about saving everyone? You clearly have taken only your own life into consideration. Do you think that's befitting of a ship's captain? Because to me you're nothing but a coward," Marcus said. He watched quietly as Sergei's expression drained and melted down his face. "I wish I had never listened to you, but here we are. Me and you in the brig, because you're hiding information from us."

"You... you expect me to cave and say everything just because of threats?" he asked, his lips fumbling his words as he tried to keep himself upright.

"No, not in the least. If threats would make you cave, you would have already turned over your control of the ship. I respect that you've resolved yourself. What I'm going to do is leave you here for the next two days. In the dark," he said, and punched through the LED panel to rip the lights out of the wall. Darkness swallowed them.

The true nature of the threat dawned on him. "There isn't an acceleration pod in here!"

"No, there isn't."

"What if I die?"

"Then we'll pick up from scratch with Sophia and move on. Your body will be thrown in with everyone else's, and you'll be forgotten. But I think you'll survive. And then me and Pontius will come in to speak with you about exactly what you saw and what you deleted from Mia's records. How much of you will be left in the end will be up to you. Simply let me assure you that I am prepared to do much worse things to you than simply kill you," Marcus said. He kept his voice calm, flat, and lacking in emotion. He wanted his words clear and understood, and they were.

"Why are you bringing that mutant into this? Why isn't it between me and you?" he asked, his shoulders sinking down as he spoke.

Marcus grinned, but that was hidden in his helmet. "Because at this point, I honestly think you're too stupid to even know what it is you saw, so I'll need a second mind to discuss with. When you break, you're not even going to understand what it is you're telling us. But trust me, you'll talk," he said, standing upright again.

"You're a fucking monster, aren't you?" Sergei shouted as Marcus reached for the door.

"No more so than any human. Whatever made you think we were a kindly species? Sergei, I'm a Space Ranger. I'm an all purpose weapon of war, the greatest human asset Earth has made since Fleet Commander Eagle, and he died in the Jupiterian Disaster. I kill people. I break things. You can give me a gun, a sword, a spaceship, or a rock, and I will use it to its utmost effectiveness. You have made yourself my target. My weapons are my hands and my wits, and I will accomplish my objective without batting an eye. You should have realized that before you ever spoke to me. Did you think I was nice because I spend my afternoons playing games? Did you think I was civil because I like to read books? I'm a demon from hell. And in two days' time, you will learn what that means."

The former helmsman soiled himself, and Marcus slammed the door on the way out.

25

Questions and Answers

The Sixty-First Day

"It's a painkiller, actually," Pontius said as he slid the needle into the vial. It was as clear as water, but the label made Marcus step back. NV-17-Delta: the drug that had brought Earth to its knees in the twenty-second century, broken down and refined into a pharmaceutical. "Now then," the mutant continued, setting the vial down and tapping the air bubbles from his syringe. "You might be asking yourself, why an interrogation would begin with a painkiller."

Sergei dribbled blood down his chin. He had been fading in and out of consciousness, and stubbornly kept his mouth shut except to spit blood out. His silhouette was broken. His right shoulder dislocated from the ship's tumble. The rasp in his breathing evidenced his screaming.

Pontius smiled, a twisted thing that exposed his yellowing teeth. "The answer is that this is a very special painkiller. Normal drugs, the opium derivatives generally, they block pain and they fog your brain. Would make it very difficult to talk with you. NV-17 doesn't remove your pain at all, it simply makes you not mind that you hurt. So we'll start with this, and get your shoulder back in place, and then the other half of the truth serum can come out to play. Ranger, if you would please hold him."

"Why does a standard government shuttle have something like that in stock?" Marcus asked, but he did step over and rip Sergei's sleeve off to bare the muscle of his still-connected shoulder.

The mutant shrugged. "Isn't it obvious? It's in case the captain needs to be able to function through extreme circumstances. This is better than any stimulant you could ask for, and many people find that it lets them get over the fear of killing someone, even enemies that need killing. The Earth fleets made it a standard supplement some four hundred years ago. You might say that I'm using it off-label however. Dr Omura was very unhappy with me when I went to get these things." He smiled again and licked his lips.

He's salivating. Disgusting.

Sergei struggled, squirming in Marcus' grasp, but the needle sank in. The drug pumped into his muscle, and from there to his capillaries, his veins, his heart, his head. It only took a moment for it to breach his thoughts, and he couldn't hide the effect. He became alert, calm, and considered biting through Marcus' arm. He thrashed in the chair, and the Ranger had to throw him back down. The cloth holding his hands together snapped, ripped apart by his newfound strength.

Pontius stepped back, putting himself behind his armored

guardian, but it wasn't needed. The only thing Sergei did was reach over and shove his dislocated shoulder back into the socket. Then he slumped back in the chair, his body shaking. Pontius sighed. "Give him a moment to clear his thoughts. He'll become frightfully rational soon."

"How did you feel when you shot Captain Regulus?" Sergei asked. He lifted his head as the shaking subsided. "You did it right here. I found the dent and the spent bullet. I had plenty of time in the darkness because of you."

Pontius put a hand on Marcus' arm. "No need to listen to him yet. He's still in control of his faculties. It's not a truth serum until I add some anesthesia."

The Ranger shirked out of the mutant's grasp. The man looked surprised, pulling his hand back as though he had touched something hot. Marcus answered the question, "Sad. Did you think I would relish that murder or something? He was a good man and he looked me in the eyes when I had to kill him, because he stood by his decisions. It didn't stop me though. I sleep fine at night too. Is that what you wanted to hear?"

"Just one of how many now? Fifty? Or is it a hundred dead now? Not to mention the thousands dead on our sister ships. I guess for you, that's just a drop in the bucket, isn't it?" Sergei asked.

Pontius sucked air through his teeth and turned back to his bag of pilfered medicine. He sifted through them, clinking glass together and checking labels until he produced the one he wanted. "We can skip to the part where he spills his thoughts to us. We don't need to listen to taunts."

"It's fine," Marcus said, and took a knee in front of Sergei so the man didn't have to crane his neck. "Are you a religious man, Sergei? You were born in a religious colony, but I never got the impression it rubbed off on you."

The captain grinned. "Religion is for cowards. If we didn't have luddites in our midst, we would have all digitized centuries ago. If you're about to appeal to God, you can save your breath."

"Mr Livius, I think this already is a truth serum," Marcus said, not taking his eyes off the captain. "For me though, the issue I have is with the word faith. I don't have faith, because faith is belief without reason; but, I do believe in the human soul. It's something you can't miss on the battlefield, not unless the death scours you clean of your own soul. Disasters, warfare, trauma, they can all bring out tremendous feats that just shouldn't be possible. You'd have to be an idiot to not see it. Those men who carried you here, do you think they could have done that if not for the hardship? It changes people, and by common definitions, I am religious."

"It's been a great improvement, hasn't it? I'm sure the survivors will all look back fondly on their stay here and tell their friends about how much stronger it made them... If there are any."

"I didn't say it made people stronger. Typically, it makes people much, much worse. They start showing the strength they've suppressed. It de-civilizes them. The more people that die, the less human we all will become. Well, you all. It's a bit late for me."

Sergei hung his head, putting his chin to his chest. "We're

all going to die. None of us are going to ever set foot on a planet again, unless it's crash landing on Tiber."

"Mr Seachnal," Pontius asked, holding the second syringe. "What became of the mining crew? The Scythian ship was supposed to rendezvous with them and save them."

The captain laughed. "Starving to death and irradiated. The Scythians were destroyed right on their dock. They've been silent ever since. That was the opening salvo before they all slaughtered each other."

Marcus looked at the syringe, the needle full of mind-numbing drugs that would lobotomize him for the rest of the day: the rest of his life. "This is your last chance, Sergei. Once we put that in you, Mia will automatically lock you out of command powers, since you'll be unfit. We'll get the information out of you, and then I'll have to shoot you."

Sergei snarled. Rage built inside him and he seized hold, like the proffered hilt of a knife. He jerked against his remaining restraints, almost leaping from the chair as he shouted. "Just do it. I'm not surviving this ship anyways, and handing power over means getting killed a few days from now anyways. They'll blame me when they need a scapegoat, because guess what, Ranger? Whoever you appoint after me isn't going to be able to save you either! We're all going to die here, it's just a matter of how and when. Ray was the only one of us who got an honorable death!"

Pontius jammed the needle into Sergei's straining neck, squeezing the drug in as he thrashed back. Blood squirted from the prick as the metal ripped through his flesh, but the deed was done. "There we go, enough of that. His critical thinking will be shut off entirely in about two minutes and he will ramble on as much as we'd like and then some."

I'm not dying here.

Marcus stood up with a shake of his head. "How many times have you done this before?"

"Just once," Pontius said with a grin. He turned his back to the Ranger and packed his tools back up, clerically organizing them for the future as Sergei groaned. "You see, some years back, one of my colleagues was caught selling certain biological data on the black market. It wasn't very interesting information in the end. That's how he talked himself into it in the first place. But that's how things get out of hand, isn't it? One small mistake makes way for more mistakes."

"What did you catch him with in the end?"

The researcher grinned over his shoulder. "That's classified information. You have the clearance though, don't you? And he'll be dead by tomorrow. It was the scrapings from a drifting derelict, some millions of years old, preserved in the permafrost of space."

Alien?

Marcus would have whistled had his helmet allowed it. "Well, that's the kind of thing that can freeze an entire sector's travel."

Sergei rolled his head over to look at Pontius. "You telling me we've found aliens? Like, smart ones?" he asked, his words slurring.

Pontius didn't answer him. "Yes, it did lock down all travel out of the system for about a month. We had to work fast to pick up his conspirators. Sadly, all of that work had to be put on ice during the war. Those star-farers waited a million years for us, another few decades will hardly change them. Their voyage through time cares little for our proddings."

Marcus said, "I can only imagine what the new government will say when they finally get their noses into Earth's business."

The researcher laughed as he clipped his bag shut. "As if politicians know these kinds of things. It's managed by a department in a bureau of appointed clerks with grandfathered funding. I think the last spending bill had the whole project listed as something like Stellar Terrestrial Waste Investigations or something. We were paperclipped to the back and forgotten about. Only the AIs care about us, and even then it's only enough so that we have the authority codes for when something bad happens."

"Like someone selling alien kidneys on the black market."

Pontius' eyes twinkled. "Precisely. Incidentally, when we were disposing of the body, we cut his kidneys out to write it up as organ theft. The bio-traffickers were notorious in that sector."

Marcus' side twitched in pain. His liver quite close to his kidney. "Don't get any surgical ideas here."

"Don't worry. You'll have the honors of shooting him in the end. I do believe that we can begin the questioning in earnest now," he said as he turned to Sergei.

The man didn't even seem to be present. Like an addled drunk, he sat motionless save for the rise and fall of his breathing. When both Pontius and Marcus approached him, penned him in, and sank their verbal barbs into his mind, his expression never changed from doped blankness. True to Pontius' promise, he answered everything with the kind of belabored exactness that nearly drove the Ranger mad with impatience.

Four hours later, Sophia Almada was alerted that she was in command of the *Demos*, and promptly transferred her power to Hadria. The brig was left with two sets of blood splatters and the ship sank further into Hell.

26

Vox Populi

The Sixty-Eighth Day

Of all things, Hadria brought democracy to the ship. After he had been briefed, he put out an order to Mia to organize petitions and announced that anyone with the signed allegiance of one hundred people on the ship would be allowed onto the bridge, and bought himself nearly a week to compose himself.

"Who gave you a razer?" Marcus asked as he sat down on one of the ten chairs assembled in the bridge.

Hadria snarled at him. "What? Are you surprised the quartermaster let a mutineer near a sharp blade or something?" the corporal-turned-captain asked. He had gone to the effort of cleaning his uniform three times over just to get the press lines back in order. He looked ready for a parade, the self-styled haircut aside.

"Aren't we running out of those by now? We're going to have to start confiscating them for risk of tetanus."

"There's no tetanus in space, didn't you hear? How did you get nominated anyway? Never saw you making appeals," he asked, adjusting his cuffs for no discernable purpose.

The Space Ranger tilted his head. "Wasn't aware that I had been. I forced my way in."

The door opened and Mr Samaras walked in. "It was the women," he said. That made Marcus' eyebrows jump. "Plenty of them only know or care about you because of the baths... Captain, nice of you to create this." He took the seat next to Marcus and checked the time with a handheld computer.

Marcus didn't recognize the next man to come in, nor the woman beside him. They seemed utterly nondescript and he couldn't place them among the various groups of the ship. They didn't make a fuss or start demanding anything, so he couldn't imagine what they had done to garner support. Hadria supplied their names for him, politely saying, "Mr Boseman. Miz Jung. Go ahead and take seats." The two of them glanced at the circle, and each sat as far from anyone else as possible.

"Just in time," Father Publius said as he strode into the bridge. He smiled and took a moment to look around the bridge, as if on a tour, but he soon took the seat between Marcus and Hadria.

"That's everyone," Samaras said, switching to a note taking program. Half the seats were empty.

"Shouldn't there be nine of us?" Marcus asked.

Hadria puffed out his cheeks and sat down in the circle. "That's my fault. I didn't cap the petitions at one hundred exactly, so everyone here has one hundred and change behind them. That plus some abstentions and some obstinate smaller candidates and only us five met the criteria."

Miz Jung crossed her arms and her legs and glared at the captain. "Why did you let children vote? No functional democracy lets children vote. He wouldn't be here if not for juveniles," she said, nodding at the priest.

"Why shouldn't they get a vote? This is about their survival too," Marcus asked, making a point to spread his legs, lean in, and plant his elbows on his knees.

Their votes probably should have been cast by their parents, but so it goes.

Father Publius shook his head, eyes closed. When he opened them, he said, "The children aboard the *Demos* just vote the way their parents tell them too. And really, there aren't many. A few dozen really. People were very conscientious about putting kids on the vessels able to escape."

"Captain," Mr Samaras interjected, "Perhaps you should start us off with what we are here to discuss?"

Hadria cleared his throat, giving a nod to the businessman. "As you all are aware, the *Demos* has not been under stable management, not even stable spin," he said with a canned chuckle. "When I first gained control of the ship, even before that actually, my goal was to be fully transparent with everyone about the situation we're in. To be honest, I'm scared to do that now, knowing what I do. So, I compromised and tried to bring together the best minds available."

"Shouldn't that Pontius Livius be here then?" Mr Samaras asked. "It's not like he doesn't know what's going on."

Marcus said, "He's not a popular man." The two unknown

quantities seemed to react to that, perhaps feeling the difference between them and the established figures. "Hadria, why don't you put up the current camera feed?"

The captain did so, and all five of them were given a distant, pixelated view of ships orbiting Mimir. The core itself still looked like a spinning peanut, fraught with bleeding wounds of lava laced with lightning. The gas giant's heavy core and the moon were slow to press into one another. That process would take years as the scattered and irradiated gasses congealed back into an atmosphere. The ships orbited so close that the grinding spin of the new planetary mass blotted them out periodically. The display had a montage stretching over the last few days.

"Salvage?" Samaras proposed.

No, salvage is done remotely.

"Rebuild," Marcus said.

Captain Hadria nodded. "This is well beyond the Scythians digging nuclear missiles out. These people mean to hold Mimir permanently. Around the time that Red Cairo should have arrived, two distinct groups emerged from A-Mov and all three forces fired on one another. We aren't entirely sure whether the victors are Red Cairo, or some other Alliance force come to interfere with the Camrians. What we do know is that they are using an Alliance tactic. It certainly wouldn't be the first time humans have learned from their enemies, but the current assumption is these are Alliance peacekeepers."

Father Publius cleared his throat. "What makes you say that, exactly?"

That sounded more like a suppressed cough...

"Analysis by myself, Ranger Maximus, and Pontius Livius, a... very competent researcher," Hadria answered.

Mr Boseman held up his hand. "If it is the Alliance, are we to assume they are hostile or friendly to us? The Camrians were Alliance."

"And they killed the Camrians," Marcus said.

Miz Jung turned on him. "And the Camrians killed plenty of us, but I do not believe the enemy of my enemy is my friend. They killed the Red Cairo ships, didn't they?"

"Everyone," Hadria said, cutting the cross-talk. "What is important first is that we have three options to consider. First, we continue as we have been: doing nothing."

The entire room grumbled.

"Second," he continued, "we kill spin and start accelerating to the far side of Fuls and hide, maybe choose a path that will have us come back in line with Mimir shortly after Sic-Alba arrives a little over a month from now. But we'd have to do a lot of accelerating. A year on Mimir is about five standards. I know people don't usually think about that, since the only other place to go here is up to the mine, but if we're going to loop around, we'll be chasing the tail."

Samaras nodded and asked, "Are you sure the engines are capable of that? How close would we have to get to Fuls?"

"We would have to engage some heat disposal methods, both from the energy of the engines and from the star. I wouldn't recommend doing a space walk, but the *Demos* is more than capable of the journey. I wouldn't have listed it otherwise."

Mr Boseman asked, "What's the third option?"

The captain said, "The third option is we turn around and fly back to Mimir directly... putting us entirely at the mercy of that craft. It would however get us there before Sic-Alba would arrive, and perhaps we could get a swift pickup. It depends, though, on what the Camrians are thinking to do."

It was Marcus' turn to speak on the matter. "The Camrians probably don't have more forces to send here. At the end of the day, they're one planet and their population isn't very large. They are much more dangerous if left to their own devices with that black hole. They can just keep making engines and strapping them to rocks to fling."

"Marcus," Samaras asked, "Does Camria have its own exo mine? There's nothing in company records about one, but that planet is a government secret so I wouldn't be surprised if-"

"No, they don't," Marcus said. "Eventually they can be starved out, if they don't capture a mine like the one here."

Miz Jung scoffed. "So they have to keep fighting for this place then!"

Marcus shook his head. "Mr Samaras, how many mining installations does The Nebulae Company have within reach of Camria?"

The businessman thought it over, staring at the ceiling while he mapped things out mentally. "Two directly adjacent, but if you allow as wide a range as Athens Station I'd have to estimate about fifty."

Marcus held up his hand, three fingers raised. "They only need three to wage their war, and they can reach fifty. They are a smaller force than even Earth's emaciated fleet, let alone the rest of the Alliance. Any strategy advisor would know that they have to occupy their enemy's forces by opening as many battle fronts as possible. By forcing us to garrison everything, we can't focus on their attack fleet. So, the odds of them directly caring about Fuls is slim. There are too many intervening stars between us and them that they would need control of. The black hole doesn't work in both directions."

Mr Bosemen jutted his chin at the Ranger. "If you're so confident in that, why don't we start by sending a message to the Alliance and asking for their protection?"

Samaras showed a hint of a smirk, a flicker of knowledge that vanished. "I actually agree we should contact this space hulk. If they're Alliance and on our side, we might be able to broker peace between them and the arriving Sic-Albans. And then we have a ride out of here."

Hadria threw up his hand before anyone else could speak. He thrust his palm out, fingers splayed wide. "I should clarify something before we continue. The purpose of this council was to vote on how we proceed, yes, but there are six of us. In the case of a split tie, I will be proceeding with the side I voted for as the tiebreaker."

"And why should we accept that?" Miz Jung asked.

Mr Boseman nodded. "You seem to be just awarding yourself power because you have the thugs behind you."

Father Publius cleared his throat again. "Perhaps what we should do is apportion proportional votes based on the total number of petitioners behind us?"

"No," the two civilians said together.

That must still give Hadria the tiebreaker.

"Enough," the captain said. "I won't be negotiating this. I'm still the one who has the authority to command Mia. None of you. So, given your reactions, I believe the first question is whether we contact the Alliance forces. All in favor?" Five hands rose in unison. Marcus was the only vote against. "Second, if we are to change course, do we wait for their response or not? It will take about two hours to hear back from them at current distances."

The vote was slower that time, and Marcus imagined he wasn't the only one trying to draw out the distances in their head. The *Demos* had put a huge distance between itself and Mimir, but not a light-hour. Eventually, they all agreed to do nothing until a response was received.

"Well then," Hadria said. "I suppose we can retire here."

"What about the ration situation?" Mr Boseman asked quickly. Samaras and Father Publius had both nearly risen, and he leapt into the fray. "I think there's more to the management of this ship than what direction we're flying."

"Agreed," Miz Jung said, nodding and brushing back her overgrown pixie cut. "The alcohol situation is entirely out of hand."

"Well if everything's on the table," Samaras said, settling back down. "I have some thoughts on the Link Reality policies as well."

Marcus rose before the conversation could mire down in specifics. "Do what you will. You won't have to worry about tie votes now," he said, striding to the door. Hadria excused himself from the discussion as well, escaping to prepare the message. Both of them couldn't care less about Samaras' ability to twist the other two into word knots till they agreed with him. It was obvious they didn't stand a chance against the CEO.

The only thing that stopped Marcus at the door was the sound of Father Publius coughing again. The priest was showing his age, like many of the people aboard the *Demos*. The maelstrom of negotiations taking place looked less inviting than gunfire, and the Ranger left the bridge behind.

Over the next two hours, Marcus was accosted by Maria when he made the mistake of passing near the hold. Once he freed himself of the girl, he spoke with Dr Omura about any sicknesses that were going around the ship. According to her, there was an unidentified virus starting to show up. With everyone in such close quarters, it had only been a matter of time. The ship didn't have even close to enough antivirals for some nine hundred people. She said they needed more food to keep their immune systems up, and Marcus promised to bring it up in the council. His own recovery didn't come up.

Since Mia still wouldn't speak to him, Hadria's only choice to alert the Ranger of the response was to send one of his underlings. The overweight man who had brought Sergei to the brig found Marcus speaking with Felicity, and brought him back to the bridge.

"Thank you all for returning," the captain said as Marcus sat down. The others had beaten him there, so Hadria began. "After our last meeting, I sent the following message to an autonomous asteroid drone and had it relay it to the Alliance craft with a direct beam. My hope was that the debris from Mimir had dissipated enough that our signal wouldn't get picked up. They responded to the drone and not directly to us, so perhaps we are still hidden. I kept it short."

Hadria pressed a button on a handheld computer, and the holo-display showed him sitting in the captain's meeting room. He began, "To the craft orbiting the remains of Mimir. My name is Corporal Hadria Sully. I am the acting captain of the *Demos* shuttle. We are not a military craft. We have nearly one thousand civilians aboard and are requesting immediate humanitarian aid and transport to a secure planet. Please respond as soon as you can."

The group nodded, and he switched to the reply. No video came, just an audio signal. "Greetings Corporal Hadria Sully of the *Demos*. This is Captain Atish Raven of the *Woab Hammer*, fleet member of the Svabian Militia. We are presently unable to provide any direct support. All of our resources are dedicated to securing control of Mimir from further conflict and restoring the flow of exo matter from the Fuls-Hades-I. In a little over a week, we expect further conflict to inflame. If you do not wish to be in the crossfire, stay away."

"Svabia, so they're Alliance," Marcus said, staring at the blank holo-display. The fact that Captain Raven didn't have the crude rasp of a Camrian didn't quite put him at ease.

"At least they aren't trying to kill us," Father Publius said.

Samaras scratched his chin. "Surely we could approach without getting so close as to be in danger? It would cut down on the time to rescue afterwards."

Hadria hung his head and only raised it when he spoke. "The problem as I see it, is they didn't actually say they would help us afterwards. All they implied was they weren't interested in killing us. If we approach recklessly, they might take it as a provocation."

"We have to wait then," Marcus said, getting a nod from the captain. "The only question is if we change our relative speed at all. The Camrians were all killed. Anyone arriving won't have had scans of what we looked like. It won't change anything. We could finally stop the tumbling too."

"If," Hadria said, "we want the Alliance to know for sure which piece of debris is us."

It went to a vote. Marcus, Samaras, and Father Publius all agreed that the *Demos* should be put on a slow return approach to Mimir.

Hadria voted to do nothing at all for the next week and watch the fight play out. To the Ranger's surprise, Mr Boseman and Miz Jung voted with him and split the vote. The tiebreaker went to Hadria, and once again, the *Demos* chose to do nothing but hide. Democracy had spoken.

Half a week later, Hadria was found dead in his acceleration pod. No murder weapon and no murderer.

27

Acceleration

The Sixty-Ninth Day

They tried jumping Marcus in the mess hall. He didn't even understand who they were before it was too late. About twenty of Hadria's underlings made the assumption that he had been the killer. They waylaid him with accusations and with clubs. A swarm of grasping hands tried to pull him to the ground. The moment he felt someone touch the access hatch on the back, he stopped shouting for peace. He stopped trying to reason with them and he started killing.

Three men had a hold on him, he broke free. One had a cudgel. Marc snapped the man's wrist. Another smashed him in the back of the head. He stumbled forward, ears ringing as he knocked into a table. Then he snatched up a steak knife and blood began to fly. He painted the walls red before the last of them fled.

In the silence that followed, all he could hear was the blood ringing in his ears. All he could smell was his own sweat and breath. He couldn't feel anything at all. Eighteen men lay dead at his feet. Crushed, slashed, broken, and beaten. Nearly three months slumbering in Link Reality and they had worn thin. Like paint scraping away to show the animal mosaic beneath.

A girl screamed, "Dad?"

No...

Marcus turned. He knew the voice. He had heard it often enough, the cheerful rambling that had chased him throughout the ship. Now it was high and breaking, choked with tears. Maria ran into the carnage– a bloodshed that no child should have seen– and fell to her knees beside one of the bodies.

Marcus didn't know which one he had been, just one of the attackers. If her father had been the one to grab him, or merely one to join the group and not run away in time. The wound wasn't particularly gruesome; a jab up through the jaw and into the brain. The corpse wore the blood like a bib and stared slack-jawed at the ceiling.

The girl cried, trying to nudge her father back awake. She checked for breathing and started chest compressions, far too weak, and accomplished nothing more than staining herself in blood.

Marcus put his hand on her shoulder. He wanted to tell her it was too late.

"Get your hand off me, demon!" she screamed. "Monster! Murderer! My father didn't deserve this!"

He just tried to kill me. How am I supposed to say that to her though.

Maria couldn't hear anything but herself, no explanations

nor excuses. The Ranger backed away, retreating from the mess and into the kitchen. The haggard women who had watched the fight trembled at his approach. They clutched knives and pressed their backs to walls. They slid away from him without taking their eyes away.

The sink was deep, almost out of place on a spaceship. He grabbed the dangling nozzle and turned on a blast of water. It drummed against the basin, driving up a cloud of steam. The Ranger turned the blast on himself, on his hands and arms and chest. The sink looked like he had butchered a pig in it.

"The pan cleaner is to your left," one of the chefs said, jerking her chin. He found a squirt bottle of scouring agent and blasted it into his hands.

"Thanks," he mumbled, working it into a froth as he tried to get the viscera out from the joints of his armor.

The chef cleared her throat and pulled herself from the wall. "I saw you weren't the one that started it. I heard you tryna talk 'em down. They should've known better. They fucked around. They found out."

"You'd think my history would have tipped them off," he said, and felt the deja vu hit him. He shivered and laughed. He wanted to puke. He wouldn't take off his helmet though, and he refused to rebreathe his own vomit ever again.

"The way I see it," the chef said, "Them's less mouths to feed and less violence in the future. We woulda run out of food before New Gibraltar can save us if all of us stuck around."

Marcus shut off the water. He could scrub till the paint came off and still have blood on him. The lemon scent would smother the odor. Most of the women who had been stirring pots and spooning bowls had fled out the back. He hoped they were helping with the bodies, helping Maria. "We're not going to wait for New Gibraltar. Those guys? They're never getting rescued."

"Neither are everyone on the *Chase* or the *Theopone*."

Marcus walked past her, dripping water. He passed through the mess and into the hallway. Just as he turned to march to the bridge, Pontius Livius stopped him. "The ship's falling apart, Ranger," the mutant said. He had a cane, and from his hobble it was clear one of his hips wasn't moving correctly anymore.

Bedsores? Cramps? How quaint.

Marcus' gaze moved to the enormous man behind Pontius. Almost as tall as Marcus and yet thrice the size of anyone born in low gravity. His clothes were baggy, fit for a man twenty kilo heavier; the man he had surely been when he set foot on the *Demos*. "Who's your friend?"

The man didn't answer. Pontius grinned. "Just a little protection for me is all."

How the researcher was paying a bodyguard was beyond Marcus, but he didn't have the time to work it out. "Do you know what happened to Hadria?"

"Do I look like a medical doctor?"

Marcus glanced at the bag at the man's hip, the one with the truth serum in it.

"It was most likely a mere accident. Those do happen. This isn't a good time to do anything particular. There's no pivotal moment, no sway to the politics. But everyone has their knives out now." Pontius hobbled forward, gesturing to continue on away from the hold. "Like it or not, that man had the most competent group of people under his control, and now the head has been struck from the snake. And it seems twenty of them are dead, probably more. Tribalism is back."

"Or," Marcus said, leading the three of them to the room that had once been his bedroom. "Someone did the math on how long it would take to get control of everything after another turmoil, and they have reason to believe something will matter right around that time."

"You sound like you think I did it," Pontius said as the two of them stepped into the room. He hesitated only to tell his bodyguard to wait outside, and closed the door.

"Did you?"

"Marcus, do I strike you as someone who can take that kind of risk? I sleep in the public hold like most everyone else. Theodore has to sleep too."

"Well, we're slowly making some living space in there, aren't we?" Marcus said as he unfolded the bed from the wall to give Pontius somewhere to sit, then climbed into the acceleration pod. The room didn't smell like he lived in it anymore. The odor of sweat had been cleaned out weeks ago.

Pontius ran his tongue over his teeth noisily. "One way to put it, isn't it? Either way, the first order of business is who has control over the ship now."

"That would be Sophia, I suppose."

"And where is she right now?"

Marcus leapt from his seat. "In danger," he answered, and threw the door back open. He cursed himself for being so self-focused that it hadn't occurred to him. The fight had consumed his mind from the moment he learned of Hadria's death.

He shoved past Theodore, and went running through the hall. He jumped up and down ladders, passing through the strata of the ship to get to the bridge. The door was already open when he arrived. Half a dozen people, they weren't all men for once, circled around Ensign Lawrence. The lanky blonde was drooling blood when they all turned to see the Ranger's appearance.

Here we go again–

"Woah, woah, no fighting! No fighting," one of the women said, knocking a pipe out of someone's hands. It clattered against the floor and rolled over to Marcus' feet. She put up her hands to Marcus. "Ranger, calm down. We're not stupid enough to resist you."

"But you would fight someone else? Who are you with?"

"We're Christians," the woman said. She had bruises all over her body, and her black hair was in a bird's nest mess. One of the others made a snide semantics remark and she clarified, "We're peacekeepers following Father Publius."

Marcus stepped up to her, looming. "And you do that by brutalizing the junior crew?"

She wetted her lips. "We were only a little rough."

"You broke my teeth!" Ensign Lawrence shouted, spitting blood across their chest.

The woman cleared her throat, scratched the side of her nose and mumbled, "Well, we're a bit past being nice with uncooperative people, aren't we?"

I don't have time for this.

"Where is Miz Almada?"

The man who had dropped the pipe spoke up. "Hadria's thugs are in a civil war. Both sides are trying to get her. Honest, we were just in a rush. The Ensign here didn't believe us none."

Marcus sighed. "And you were going to do what? Swoop in at the last moment and save her? With what? A spare gas pipe? If you were going to try and be heroes, you should have started by getting a weapon that wouldn't bend in half." He stomped his foot on the pipe, flattening it in the middle like a beer can. Something plastic bounced off the floor, and Marcus saw the woman who had dropped what looked like a mop handle.

The good weapons must have already been taken.

"It's better than nothing, isn't it? We can't be bystanders," the leader said.

"Get out," Marcus ordered. "Get out before I kill you like I killed the thugs that jumped me in the mess hall. I won't need a knife to deal with you people."

The group weren't fighters. They hadn't nurtured that kindling of evil within their bosoms. The violence had simply normalized for them and their inner critic had stopped telling them to be civil. Confronted with overwhelming force, they reverted to good civilians and shuffled out of the bridge.

"She's in the engine room. Not sure how long the doors will stay locked. One of those idiots was saying to cut their way in," Ensign Lawrence said once it was the two of them.

"The engine uses structural bulkheads for walls. Are they idiots?"

"Desperate," Ensign Lawrence answered, and got back to their feet. "If you don't mind, I'm going to the medbay..."

Evidently, their time with Hadria had shown some civilians closets that were never meant to be opened by unauthorized personnel. The signs had done nothing to stop them, nor had the rapidly deteriorating AI. When Marcus came upon them, they had slagged through the locking bolts on the primary access door to the engine compartment. They had done such a fantastic job of cutting it, that they had friction welded the base of the door to the floor and broken the actuators. There was also a secondary door beyond that.

"Drop everything," the Ranger ordered.

The one with the power tool jumped, and the spinning, overheated blade ruptured. The safety shield engaged around the tool, but all anyone heard was a noise like a gunshot.

Of the ten that had rallied together to hunt down the AI technician, four turned and ran without a second thought. The man who had broken the saw was too busy checking himself for shrapnel wounds to tell the other five that it hadn't been Marcus. The rest of them charged. The fact that he didn't even have a gun out didn't stop them. Their frenzy didn't help them.

Not even five minutes later, only he and the sniveling man with the power saw remained conscious. Blood covered him again, bits and splatters from head to toe. His hands felt numb from the ringing blows of stolen weapons against human bodies. "Get lost you animal," he ordered, and the man fled.

Marcus dug his fingers into the metal wound and ripped the door open. He was tired and breathing hard through his respirator. The filters tasted stale and bitter. "Sophia... it's me."

The door opened and she stepped back. Her brow pulled together and she covered her mouth with a hand. "Jesus Christ."

"Mob mentality and mass hysteria. Do you have access to Mia?" he asked. She nodded. "This isn't going to stop unless we do something, so stop the spin, turn us around, and give us two G's back towards Mimir. Let's see them riot like that."

28

Hadria's Good Deed

The Seventieth Day

"Demon!"

The crowd had all sorts of names for him, but that one kept coming up, like they thought he was one of the horsemen of the apocalypse. Under the weight of one and a half Earth's pressing down on everyone, cursing him was the most they could do. The two-G burn had nearly killed people, which had forced Miz Almada to reduce it some. Mia was still crunching the numbers on how to pilot the ship back to Mimir while reducing the thrust to something manageable for the civilians. The plotted curve was rather beautiful, a snaking coil through the stellar system. The anger before him was ugly.

"Murderer!"

The hold had been like a warehouse while the ship was in spin. Under thrust, every acceleration bed looked like the balcony of an apartment, if the apartments were little better than coffins. The abrupt change had struck like a hurricane to a shanty town, and the bottom was buried in trash. Those closest to it were fighting to climb higher and save their noses, but the vacancies had all been filled.

Marcus stood in what had been a cargo port through what had been the roof. Now he was about midway up and able to face the entire group. He held the microphone for the ship's address system up to his helmet. "Have you all gotten that out of your system yet? A hundred people died in the fighting yesterday... because none of you trust anyone. Dead. No coming back from dead."

"You killed them! My husband! He's never coming back because of you." The woman shouting three stories below him would have been unrecognizable if not for Maria beside her, balled up and crying still.

"Father Publius, Mr Boseman, Miz Jung, and Mr Samaras should have already spoken to the lot of you. I'm sure this feels like I've unfairly seized power or something," he said, and paused for a few hundred people to shout back agreement; that he had done just that. They were right, for the moment. "Miz Almada is currently your captain however. This never stopped being a government craft. On a ship, the captain's orders are absolute."

It sounded like he was trying to push off blame. It felt like it too. "Please cooperate with any medical personnel among you. We will continue to be under thrust for the next few days. Anyone experienced with high gravity, please volunteer to distribute food. Many people can no longer leave their acceleration beds. Thank you." He clicked off the mic and shut the door. The hatch slammed between him and them, muffling their outrage. From the enormous and open cargo hold, to a claustrophobic utility hall.

His steps thundered beneath him, the weight slamming against the steel. When he sat down in the utility lift, the whole thing strained beneath him. It still smelled like food: the only thing it had been used for in the last three months. That, and Hideo's disaster. It made his stomach growl and somewhat took his mind off the mayhem as it pulled him to the bridge. The handles in the ladders simply weren't rated for holding him and his suit, so he had to use the lift like a crate of munitions.

"Ah, Marcus," Samaras said as he trudged into the bridge. The CEO was alone with Sophia, each of them sitting beside the holo-display. "We were just rolling out the changes to Link Reality. Before he died, Hadria had given me a bit of development power with Mia, but now we'll be rolling it out."

The Ranger stepped over to the nearest acceleration pod. He fell into it so hard the bearings cried out. "Does it even matter anymore? Is anyone using Link Reality?"

"Everyone is," Sophia said, glancing at him as she tapped on the control interface. "When they aren't screaming their heads off at you."

"Fine, do it, make them work for their fun. See how they react," Marcus said, rolling his head back and closing his eyes. He wanted to sleep. His body didn't let him drift off anymore.

"It wasn't you, was it?" Samaras asked.

"What?"

"That killed Hadria."

"No. Mia doesn't open doors for me, remember?"

Samaras kept at it. "He could have let you in, and you do have a bit of a history with captain killing."

Marcus rolled himself forward to fix the businessman with his visored gaze. "A lot of things could have happened. You can either take my word for it, or not."

Charles put up his hands. "Sorry. I just… I lost some friends when that happened, and we still don't know what happened. The medbay is completely overwhelmed and won't be doing an autopsy any time soon."

Marcus slumped back in a G-pod. The clang of his helmet against the shell of the pod made the others flinch. "What's happening at Mimir right now?"

Miz Almada cleared her throat and changed the display to show the camera feeds. She mirrored it to his pod's monitor. "They've gotten bigger." Drones had brought every single scuttled ship into the same mass, and there was a hint of webbing between them, like spotting the threads holding up a play's prop. Beyond, Mimir's core had gotten a new color.

"What happened there?" he asked, pointing at the inferno across the planet's core. Icy atmosphere had begun congealing around the core again, but whatever touched the light boiled off into hurricanes.

Sophia put up her hands and shrugged. "Sir, I'm a computer scientist. It looks like a volcano or something to me."

Marcus closed his eyes and reminded himself that all the crew with the training he expected were dead. "That's too big for a volcano," he said. "It looks more like a secondary impact. Remember when we first escaped? I said that they would probably throw more rocks at Mimir to restore its gravity? I think that's the first rock– well, second anyways. If the Alliance construct there can see into A-Mov, they can probably avoid any other blasts, or maybe they won't."

"Doesn't that contradict the idea that this is just a distraction then?"

Marcus' head hurt. He could taste his own dehydration in his suit's water return system. "I don't know. Maybe it's just so their ships they sent here had a way to run away. The Camrians must have launched their human ships way before the rock was dropped. They didn't come out of A-Mov at relativistic speeds, so they must have gone first and prayed that the calculations were right."

Charles snorted. "At least it was a machine they prayed to."

"Charles, what are you even doing here?" the Ranger snapped.

The man stepped back, lifting his hands off the holo-display. "I told you, didn't I? We were implementing changes to Link Reality."

"Shouldn't you be out shaking hands and changing minds? You're a politician nowadays, aren't you? You made that half step career change when Hadria formed the council. If some of your friends died, it was because people like you didn't have a hold on the mob's panic."

The businessman stopped being cowed. His instinct to stay out of Marcus' way came crashing against his pride, and the latter won. "I'm not the one who butchered three dozen people!"

"They attacked me first!"

Samaras' nostrils flared, his cheeks darkened. "You want to know why then? Because I'm afraid I'll get killed, that I'll get knifed in the back by a sharpened toothbrush when I'm not looking because someone has a grudge and what they really need is therapy, but there are no goddamned therapists in this flying can. So I am here to do something productive while marginally safe. But, you seem intent on making it feel less than marginal, aren't you?"

Marcus didn't respond. The silence dragged the tension out of both of them and after a time he quietly said, "We should gather the council up again. Make some decisions. Do something."

The two at the holo-display shared a glance. "You didn't get told, did you? Since Mia hates you," Sophia said. "After the riot, people updated their petition votes."

He knew what she was going to say before the words left her lips.

"You were at ninety-nine votes, so you are no longer recognized as a representative. The five of us met earlier today..."

He closed his eyes and processed. Sophia must have picked up most of Hadria's contingent, the people taking a safe vote to avoid abstaining. Samaras and Father Publius had done nothing wrong. If they had lost any votes it would have been to death. Him being at ninety-nine and the two civilians, Boseman and Jung, still having seats could only mean that–

Someone is playing the numbers very carefully.

"Did you make any changes I should be aware of?"

Charles scoffed. "People want you thrown out an airlock. You're aware of that, aren't you?"

"I'm not surprised."

Not that I'd let them.

Charles drifted back into his default, professional tone, like he was speaking to his investors. "Setting aside the question of who would be the one to force you into an airlock, after you so elegantly demonstrated your carving skills with a whittling knife, no. We didn't accomplish anything. We're still on course to return to Mimir's orbit and hope. It was the most we could do to get agreement on these changes to Link Reality."

"It doesn't matter," Marcus said, closing his eyes. He wanted to sleep. "Nobody is going to do anything under this much thrust. As long as the food gets distributed and as long as we're returning to Mimir, it doesn't matter."

"Tell that to Dr Omura and the rest of the medbay," Sophia said. "She thinks we're going to have a heart attack every hour until we turn off the engine."

"Then distribute medicine for it. The medbay is stocked with all the basics. One heart attack an hour is better than dozens of people butchering each other."

Sophia said, "We'll be out of painkillers by tomorrow. There are people aboard who needed elective care. They weren't emergencies when we fled Athens Station, but nobody really thinks about the fact that they might need their liver detoxified or their kidney replaced in a few months. Let alone joint deterioration."

"We're going to Hell, aren't we," Marcus said, more to himself than to them.

"The priest thinks so," Charles said. He turned to Sophia

and mumbled something about finishing up the deployment of his Link Reality scheme, and excused himself with somber steps.

Sophia's desire for him to leave became palpable, and Marcus excused himself as well. He didn't go back to his room, nor to his requisitioned conference room to hide. He found his feet and his hands taking him to the storage holds; the ones that fed into the kitchens and whose location wasn't even told to the average person aboard.

The open door smelled like boot camp. He was struck for a moment, shot back a thousand years to when he had first left civilian life behind and how tired he had been with his sergeant's voice still ringing in his ears. There was a medley of sweat, latrine, burnt food, and most of all, moonshine. He could still remember the feeling of sandy grit between his feet and the rubber floor.

The people inside the storeroom didn't understand why he stopped. They were like cave dwellers, hiding in the riches of rations with the full knowledge that they could do nothing to stop him from plundering.

"Liquor," he said.

The dwellers were scrawny to the last, their low gravity development drawing their frames out to skeletons as they crawled around crates and bags, trash and each other. They slid over a plastic jug half full with some amber swill, the bottom crusted with dregs. "Thanks," he said, and returned them their peace.

The moonshine had been fast fermented, a rage between sugar and yeast that left a bitter, biting taste in the liquor that could strip the paint from his armor if he spilled any. Under the additional gravity, it bombarded his gut. With his helmet under one arm, and the jug in his other hand, he rode the lift down near the engine so he could vanish into his stolen room. The Ranger wasn't immune to poison, only resistant to it, so he drank the entire jug.

It tasted about as good as the processed calorie cubes the Ranger Corps distributed, and he got the whole thing down. His head went up. His worries melted. He put on the download of Embrace the Blood that Sophia had, started from episode one, and turned off his brain.

He was hugging the dregs to his chest when Felicity opened the door. One of her eyebrows went up. Her hand planted itself on her hips, and she frowned. "So this is how the great Space Ranger spends his time then? Drunk and watching a children's cartoon? You've stepped down from side access viewing windows I guess."

"Aw fuck, can't a murdering demon get some alone time? I can't use Link Reality, this is all I've got!"

"No," she said, sniffing the stench of moonshine. "Go take a shower or something, because Mr Samaras just pushed through a public vote for a new captain."

29

New Election Season

The Seventy-First Day

Marcus kept checking over his shoulder at the vast blue sky of Link Reality. Miz Almada had assured him that she had overwhelmed the AI and that Mia wouldn't have the spare thoughts to attack him for the next few hours, but he couldn't relax. He walked on his toes. His head kept swiveling about, not just in the sky but at the people around him.

They didn't know who he was, not without his armor. The face was wrong too, but someone might recognize him still. He had spent days with Charles and with Pontius Livius or Father Publius. He knew he had been seen, but the passengers of the *Demos* had in their minds a new image of him: a bloody visage of metal. The human body he had in Link Reality was so far divorced from their conceptions it may as well have made him invisible.

"We should hand ourselves over to the Alliance!" Mr Samaras cried out. A speaker's corner had been constructed to the side of the simulation's downtown. Just beyond the demarcations of Regulus' minimum requirements now stood a park with shade trees and benches with a scattering of burbling fountains. The CEO stood atop a box in one corner, turning about. He desperately wanted to pace, to march before the crowd, but the system would have muffled him if his feet touched the grass. "The war is over and even the worst prison conditions are better than starvation. It was right to hide until now, but if we don't take this opportunity all that awaits us is death until New Gibraltar shows up to ferry this steel casket back home."

"Spoken like a man with dual citizenship," the Ranger muttered.

"Don't we all have dual citizenship?" Felicity responded. She looked almost the same as in reality, save that her hair was bright lavender and nearly reached her waist. Marcus had wondered why, if she liked the look, she had never gotten the gene therapy to dye her actual hair. It looked good on her. "Earth is part of the Alliance. We're all just different sub-factions again."

"There's no such thing as a unified government. Governments exist to fight each other. Even if we all bow down to the same constitution, the armies will always be pointed at one another... at least until we find aliens to fight," he responded.

Samaras continued after a pause when he noticed their approach. "Please, don't think that we are at the mercy of foreigners. The Nebulae Company has legal standing both under Earth laws and Alliance compact. I am the one man on this entire ship with leverage over them. I am the best negotiator, it's what I do. I'm a businessman and the time of passive leadership is over."

The crowd around him was huge, the only other large one that Marcus could see, he recognized at once as Father Publius' congregation. Ignoring the demagogues and the malcontents, he moved over to the sermon. When the priest saw him, he faltered, then quickly wrapped up the reading from his bible. The shift didn't go unnoticed, but when he bid them all take care of themselves and one another, the group dispersed enough for Marcus to approach.

"No bird attacks?" the priest asked. He sat slumped, like a pile of clothes on a coat rack.

"Been having more trouble with the office workers actually," he answered, glancing at some of the lingering people who wanted to see who was speaking with their priest.

"I saw the piles, yes. You know, a young girl by the name of Claire took her own life yesterday. She threw herself down a hall and fell to her death... she was one of the volunteers to move the bodies to the airlocks, until she realized one of the men killed in the mess hall riot was her husband."

"They shouldn't have rioted. They shouldn't have fed the fear." Marcus took a seat next to the priest. He clasped his hands together and leaned in so he could speak lower. "You seem to have a lot of influence now."

"Not me, I'm just a mouthpiece. There is goodness out there and we mustn't lose sight of that... it does seem to be a bit too late for that now, doesn't it? Space has become very dark. Oh, Miz Lenz please, have a seat as well," he said, noticing her for the first time.

She had been holding her arm and stepped back when spoken too. "Sorry, sorry it's fine, really. I told you before, didn't I? Me and the big guy aren't on good terms," she said.

There was a droop to her head, but Father Publius covered up her silence. "Insults are trifling, forgiveness easy. It's actions that stick to you. Tell me," he said, turning back to Marcus, "Do you think Mr Samaras should be allowed to run free here?"

"I think he has a point. If anyone can negotiate, it would be him."

"And what is it you think he would be bargaining off for the rest of us?"

Marcus squeezed his hands together until the limits of the simulation kicked in. He would have bled in reality. "Hopefully, only something he has the rights to bargain off." If the businessman was stupid enough to try and sell the Ranger to the Alliance, their friendship would have a fate similar to Athens Station.

Father Publius smiled and put a hand on Marcus' leg. "We should pray that Sic-Alba arrives when we do. Everyone would be better off that way, yes?"

Felicity lifted her head and blinked. She opened her mouth and fought with herself over whether she should ask. "No, no Mr Samaras would never do that. That's not what you're implying, are you?"

Marcus scoffed. "I thought you would have noticed by now that I don't trust anybody. I don't leave certain threats up to chance, even if it was my idea to return to Mimir now."

She gaped at him. "What? No, no he might be an awful,

borderline sexist boss, but no, you can't accuse him of that," she said, putting a hand to her chest and throwing quick glances in Samaras' direction.

Marcus scoffed. "You don't know what The Nebulae Company did to secure that cozy spot exempt from the war, do you?"

Father Publius shook his head. "That was a very long time ago, and not something they teach in school. Only old men like us remember."

"And those who would be in the know," Marcus said, nodding towards the CEO. "Miz Lenz, I'm sure you're aware that the matter harvested by your exo mines is polluted with other strange materials, right? You can't just scoop it up and put it in your engine."

She cleared her throat. "No, of course not. Separating and refining the material is our main profit maker."

"In the beginning of the war, no one could really tell what fuel would be for civilian use or for military use. Naturally, they were selling the fuel to people who used it to attack the government. Obviously, the government wasn't happy about that and the media started running a pressure campaign on them. Funding terrorism as it were. Various congresses passed sanctions against them, and there was a real threat they would get nationalized... so they spiked the last shipment of fuel to the Earth governments, and shut down the refineries. Nobody got any fuel from them for three months, and then it was robbery prices the government had to pay or the entire interstellar economy would have collapsed..."

Felicity blew hair out of her face. "Oh come on, you can't just threaten to nationalize a private company!"

"They took every developing world in the galaxy hostage. No food came to them. No medical supplies. No orbital factories. The skies went dark at a flip of their switch. And in the end, the government caved to their demands. What else were they supposed to do? Attack the refineries that take a decade to build? Then, they turned around to the Alliance when they started capturing territory and said that if they were ever attacked, they would shut off production throughout all of their territory," the Ranger continued.

"So they got peace. Is that so bad?"

Marcus laughed. "At the time, they were responsible for more deaths than the war. A hundred times over more. Sure, the Alliance were bombing people and shooting it out with ships, but no planetary bombardments had happened. The Nebulae Company's retaliation was worse than the civil war."

"Fuel rationing was horrible," Father Publius said. He shook his head. "I was lucky that at the time, I was on an agricultural world. We always had grain to eat, but the ships... the ships went so long without fuel that their insides rusted. Even when the fuel returned, the damage took years to repair. We may as well have lost a thousand years of science."

Marcus turned to him, letting Felicity collect herself. "Is that what made you religious?"

Father Publius laughed. "No, no, that just made me restless enough to leave my family behind. Didn't I ever tell you? I used to be a stockbroker on Little Ursa." A few jumps away from Earth, Little Ursa straddled the line between a colonized moon and a space station. Not a square meter of rock remained bare on the moon. A thousand ships a day came in and out of that hub, feeding an unimaginable amount of money into it. It almost had a bigger impact than all of Earth.

"Not the high frequency shifts," he continued, "but the one responsible for long term holdings and judgment calls for the people managing corporations. I was good at it too, but it was hollow work until one day, my boss told me to sell our entire stake in a certain pharmaceutical company that hadn't produced results for some five years. Their money making patents were all about to expire and my backers didn't want to be holding empty bags. Of course, selling our stake would have crashed the company."

"Let me guess, that company was-"

"No need to guess," the priest said with a grin. "The company was Lazarus Technologies. I didn't sell our stake. Something told me not to. I felt it when I watched the head researcher force out an apology speech to his shareholders, asking for more time. Nobody else agreed with me, so I doubled down when the price ticker plummeted and kept them afloat. Lost my job for that, but they were scrambling to take me back a month later when-"

"They cured Sibian Coma Sickness," Marcus finished.

"Precisely," Father Publius said. "Some fifty-thousand people were brought back from the dead because they stayed in business. I was the only one who believed in them. Well, of the investors anyways. I believe God spoke to me that day, so rather than return to that job, I picked up the book."

"So what's God saying to you now?" the Ranger asked.

The smile vanished from the priest's face. "If only I knew. We're in the dark out here, a very, very long way from God's light. It's nothing more than a distant star. Even if we can see it, the most we can do is chart a course by it. It can't illuminate us here."

Felicity held up her hand. "I'm going to go speak to Mr Samaras. I'm going to make sure he isn't doing anything stupid," she said, and left the two of them to run back over to the Masanello.

A shadow passed over them. Mia alighted in one of the branches, fixing him with her avian gaze. Marcus swore and disconnected, leaving Father Publius to forlornly stare at the digital copy of the bible he had beside him. He returned to the dark before his liver could be ripped from his body once more, and the next day, Charles Samaras was elected captain of the *Demos*.

30

Arrival of Sic-Alba

The Seventy-Third Day

Captain Samaras was happy to announce, across all ship systems, that not only would thrust be reduced to half a G to match what Athens Station had used, but the Alliance had agreed to send the *Demos* to Scythia. With the ship mere days away from returning to Mimir's orbit, celebrations erupted. Samaras' words gave them a path to follow, a light to cling to, and the riots evaporated.

"It's gotten hotter in here," Pontius Livius said as he leaned over his bowl of soup. His shadow, Theodore, sat near the door to the forsaken mess hall. It had been a convenient room while in spin, but under thrust, it wasn't worthwhile to climb to a table just to smell lemon-scented blood while eating.

"Like summer back on Earth," Marcus said, not taking his gaze off the researcher's bowl. It looked like dirty dishwater.

Pontius slurped it up and smacked his lips. "We're not

hiding anymore, so why aren't we venting heat? Why does the ticker keep going up?" he asked, dabbing his chin.

"If I had to guess," the Ranger said, "The new captain thinks that if we pump any heat out with mass, by cooking off some water for instance, the Alliance will take it as a threat and blast us. He doesn't want to give them a reason to doubt."

"If I had to guess," Pontius said, jabbing his spoon into the bottom of his bowl. "It's because it didn't occur to the new tyrant." He glanced down and frowned. The handle of his spoon had snapped off.

"Can't you just message him and ask for a meeting?"

"I have," Pontius said, and twisted around in his seat. He grabbed a forgotten spoon off the table behind him, rubbed it off with his shirt, and began eating with it. "He's ignored me, just like the other two hundred messages he's gotten. Give or take…"

"Is this what you wanted from me? To complain about the captain? Whom I have no power over?"

Pontius grinned, his spoon shaking in his hand. "None? Pretty sure you have three persuasive arguments in your back pocket. Not! That I'm suggesting you use them, mind you," he said, holding up a hand. "The thing is, that you and I both know this isn't how the Alliance operates. They sucker you in and bring you to the palm of their hand, then they squeeze."

"Or, they simply want control of the exo mine, like everyone has from day one. Butchering civilians would destroy their authority."

"Perhaps," Pontius said, and slurped more of his soup.

"But you and I, we didn't get so old by trusting in perhaps, now did we? The Alliance wants me as much as they want you, let me assure you, Ranger. I should have pulled rank when the evacuation came, but well, I was on Athens Station incognito as it were. I couldn't risk being one of those idiots who got left behind on the ring."

Marcus had tried very hard to not think about people who hadn't managed to evacuate. "And let me guess, Samaras doesn't realize that you're a secret."

"Nor you. Or perhaps he doesn't care. Businessmen aren't moral absolutists. They do trade-off studies. We'd be safer with the priest in charge. There's an old saying I like though. The closer you are to danger, the farther I am from harm."

Marcus narrowed his gaze.

"The way I see things, in my head that is, the worst thing for us that could happen is if the Alliance construct dispatches a relay ship. Say, one simply large enough to put the two of us on and shove us off."

"They'd be making a big mistake. I already demonstrated that right here."

The researcher grinned and shrugged. "Obviously, they can't expect us to go willingly, so that ship will have a jailer to come collect us. And there's dreadfully few that could be trusted with your apprehension. Me? A stout man with a club could get me, but you're a different animal. They'd need their own copy to even think of taking you in."

Marcus shook his head. "They could put a nuke into the *Demos* in minutes if they felt like it. I wouldn't stand a chance against that."

"A slim threat. They would have to put down all sorts of riots if it got out that they killed civilians flippantly, and Sic-Alba is about to arrive. They need all the weapons they can get. If this does come to pass, and perhaps it doesn't. Perhaps Mr Samaras is more thoughtful than I fear. But, the two of us will need to work for mutual benefit to play a trick on them," the researcher said as he finally set aside the bowl. "I've already enlisted Miz Almada to keep an eye on the ship's cameras for us. We'll get a warning if the worst is coming to pass."

"Why not speak to Samaras about it?" the Ranger asked, folding his arms and leaning back.

"And put the idea in his head? Please, that's not how negotiations work. I'm still hoping this doesn't happen at all. Merely preparing for the possibility."

Just preparations... Always pray you don't need them.

A day later, Marcus was woken up by that possibility. His first clue was the ship had returned to spin rather than thrust. Captain Samaras came on across the ship-wide address again, while the Ranger was dropping down halls and back towards the engine. "Everyone, this is your captain speaking. I'm pleased to announce that we have now entered a stable orbit around Mimir. Still at a safe distance, as we're expecting a flareup between the Alliance craft and the Sic-Alba fleet to-morrow. As per the negotiations with them, they are sending over a single officer to oversee our docking with their ship, purely as a safety precaution. This is to speed up the move-ment from the *Demos* to their vessel, the Grex Ovium, so we can be on our way to Scythia. They will arrive in a few hours based on our current orbit. I need a labor crew to report to

Airlock Three to prepare it. Ranger Maximus, please report to the bridge. We need to speak."

Marcus did not go directly to the bridge. He first went to his original bedroom, and met up with a man fitting the description Pontius had given him the day prior. The man had a hook nose and could barely fill the clothes he wore. He was balding, despite treatment being trivial, so he must not have cared. "Don't worry Mr Ranger," he said, pushing off the wall and trying to smile. It didn't look like he knew how. It didn't fit his face. "Captain Samaras' cleaning crew is nothing but friends."

"And the failsafe?"

"Ready for the signal. Don't worry. Run along to the captain's call or he may start asking questions," he said, nodding towards the bridge.

The Ranger left the liaison behind and backpedaled, eventually marching to the bridge to meet with Captain Samaras. The holo-display had a tracking shot of the approaching craft. It was a tiny thing, barely enough room to squeeze a cockpit around the engine. It was the exact size Pontius Livius had been afraid of. "Ranger," the captain said, rising from his chair and nodding to him. His hair was disheveled, and he wetted his lips before continuing. "I need your support."

"How so?"

"You know the Alliance better than I do, when it comes to these sorts of things. I need you to be the one to meet with this man they've sent over. I'm told that he's actually an Earther. The war is over after all, they have each other on their ships as proof," Samaras said.

A ward of the ship. Or a prisoner outright.

"So you need me to bring him aboard and speak with him?"

The new captain nodded. "You seem best fit for the job; don't you agree? And to be honest, I'd like to seal the hall when he arrives, so that– well, to reduce our risk exposure. You understand, don't you?"

Marcus considered commandeering the ship. If he could steer it, he could ram the approaching craft and destroy it with only mild damage to the hull. The *Demos* didn't need to survive a planetside landing or even A-Mov, it could take a hit and not pop. Mia wouldn't cooperate with him if he did that though. There was nothing he could do to take control of the ship systems, regardless of the people. He had to stand there and listen to Samaras lie to his face. "Makes sense to me."

"Thank you Ranger. This will be a proper way to use your talents. Everyone who expected you to stop that rock was silly. I know better," he said, and held out a sweaty hand.

Marcus shook it and headed down to the airlock. He walked casually, as though he didn't know what the captain had just done to sell him out. He passed through empty halls and passed empty rooms. The passengers of the *Demos* had been drawn away like dogs fleeing a storm. He felt the small craft latch onto Airlock Three, and he came to stand across from the bulwark doors. The hall doors sealed to his left and right, turning it into a T-junction still splattered with blood and waste. It wasn't barren though. The cleaning crew had neglected to take with them one of the repair tools from engineering. Why someone had taken with them the thermite lance was a mystery, probably just one of the many things stolen during the riot that needed to find its way back to its home. And that person had just so happened to leave behind the only thing on the ship able to cut through combat armor.

Marcus stood beside it, facing the door and feeling sweat on his own palms. The door hissed, and gears grinded through their tracks. It slid open and his muscles went on edge. Light shone through to the craft, illuminating the armored form within.

His twin stood before him, another Space Ranger.

"Well, I'll be damned. Long time no see, Marcus," his would-be jailer said. The magnetic manacles across his arms powered off like deadbolts snapping open and the prisoner of war freed himself.

31

Duel

The Seventy-Third Day

"Dominic Levy. I thought you were dead," Marcus said, restraining his hand from going for the thermal lance.

His old colleague shrugged. "The rumors of my death-"

"Were greatly exaggerated. I can see that. What happened to you? You couldn't scuttle your ship? We had a job and only half of us succeeded in protecting Earth." The two of them had been part of the team tasked with stopping the Alliance's attack by any means necessary: the last delay to buy time for the Jupiter Fleet. Each man to a different ship after breaking into the orbital dockyard. Each of them had been told to kill everyone aboard the ship before reaching Earth, and only half of them had succeeded.

Levy rubbed his wrists, shifting the armor plates around and getting the fit right once more. "What can I say, but I messed up? Marcus, my family isn't on Earth. My great grand-kids ended up in the Alliance. I guess that's what I get for not sticking around to raise them properly. But hell, I didn't even know I had knocked my girl up when I left. Even if I had killed them all, there was no way for me to stop them from getting a message out after they figured out who I was. It was surrender or they hunt down my kids and execute them. If you ask me, I chose right. Earth lost anyways. No nukes went off. I gambled and won, sort of. What about you?"

"I've been hopping stars and running through the decades, hoping that they forget me," he answered.

"Forget the Pharus? Not likely. It's too good of a pretext. They want us like slaves, Marcus," Levy said.

Marcus shook his head. "I'm glad it was you, I guess."

"Because we can swap?"

"Yeah." More than colleagues, they had gotten the same genetic treatments. The two of them were nearly twins.

Both of them reached into the access hatch of their armors. He didn't pull out his pistol, that would have been useless. What he did was unplug his suit's identification transponder. Levy did the same, and they both tossed the devices into a corner, out of the way and where they wouldn't get damaged.

"I should be frank with you," Levy said. "They sent me here to capture you, even if that means crippling you."

"I know. Is there a way for us to work together? Two is better than one."

Levy shook his head. "They gave me enough sedatives to kill you. They won't let me dock if you're conscious. If they get you like that..."

"I imagine they've got AutoSecs?"

"A few."

"Damn."

"We're not people to them," Levy said. "Just weapons with knowledge that they want in their pocket while dealing with Earth. For them, the war isn't over. This is just a ceasefire and they're already preparing for round two."

"That's what a military always thinks. They can't imagine being put out of a job."

"Just like you? You never even thought about taking the armor off, did you?"

"Would it have occurred to you, in my boots?"

"No, I suppose it wouldn't have," Levy said. "That'd be like putting myself in a corner. They beat that out of us centuries ago. Still, you're rather cornered right now."

"Which means I have to fight."

The other Ranger nodded. "I suppose you do. If you win, you won't have to worry about convincing them of anything. The crew doesn't know a damn thing about me except that my great-granddaughter's name is Alexis. Alexis Levy."

Marcus wetted his lips and nodded. "I won't forget."

"May the best man win," Levy said, and gave a nod.

"I'm sorry," Marcus said, and dove for the thermal lance.

The other Ranger tackled him, their steel suits crashing into one another. They bounced, rolling overtop one another. Their power suits afforded all kinds of hard edges, crimps and grips, to grab hold of, but the mechanical strength enhancement was in the limbs, not in finger strength. Thrashing out of one another's grips and hammering elbows or knees made the hall sound like a factory floor. The grunt of exertion, the bang of steel against steel. Paint scraped off and steel sparked as they threw one another about.

Levy had the advantage. He had been well fed and well rested and didn't have dozens of murders on his mind. He also had a reason to fight and win even after Marcus dislocated his elbow.

That bought him a few breaths as Levy reset his arm; the moment Marcus used to grab hold of the power tool. "Just like training again!" Levy roared and jumped in the air.

Marcus rolled flat and felt Levy's boots smash into his helmet. Steel to helmet to floor. The visor cracked and went black. Blind. He couldn't see anything, couldn't make sense of the noises around him. But he could feel the grip of the thermite lance. When he pulled the trigger the inferno bloomed between them and he stabbed it forward like a bayonet. His arms jolted, connecting hard with something. Levy's scream filled his ears, a dying roar of anguish.

Hands closed around Marcus' head and ripped off his helmet. The light burned his eyes, but he didn't stop it. He shoved the lance in deep and drove Levy off of him. The two rolled, and he drew atop his former comrade. When the fuel ran out, the glow subsided. The slagged edges of steel radiated cherry red, a molten corona about Levy's missing heart. The other Ranger's arms fell to the side, rolling out and bouncing off the ground as lifeless eyes stared up at Marcus.

The tension vanished. His body went limp, never to move or fight or kill again, not for Earth and not for the Alliance.

"Sorry," he said, kneeling above the man who had been sent to kill him. He wiped the sweat off his chin and caught his breath, smelling the scorched flesh beneath him. He didn't turn away from it, and after a moment, he unclasped Levy's helmet. He tugged it off the other Ranger. The face within was like a mirror, but Levy could sleep. He didn't even need to close the man's eyes. "I'm so sorry, brother."

Marcus rose and slumped to one side. His shoulder clanged against the wall as muscle spasms caught up with him. He groaned in pain, feeling the shredding of muscles and ligaments catch up with him. Levy's helmet fell from his grasp as he lost feeling in his forearms. It bounced and rolled as he shoved off the wall to pick it back up. He cradled it between his arms and slumped off to pick up the transponders.

They kept slipping from his fingers and bouncing off the ground again. His breathing raced and he sank to his knees, to sitting, and finally balled up on the ground. "God damn it!" he roared, slamming a fist on the ground.

One of the hall doors slid open. "Is everything alright in here?" a man asked.

Marcus lifted his head and saw it was Mr Boseman, looking between him and Levy's corpse. "What are you doing here?" It was supposed to be one of Pontius' men.

Mr Boseman shrugged and closed the door behind him. "What do you mean? Who'd you expect?"

"A friend."

Mr Boseman nodded. "That's me. Do you need painkillers or something?"

"The medbay is out, aren't they?" he asked, staring at the civilian, at the one elected by the passengers to represent them.

"Mr Livius has his own supply. You don't need to worry about that," the man said with a smile. "You're on our side, after all."

"Side? We're on sides now? Who's on the other side then?" he asked, narrowing his glare at the man. His body throbbed. The tremble, however, could just as well have been from anger.

Mr Boseman shrugged and clasped his hands together. "You know, the others. The people like Mr Samaras who sold you out just now to save himself. He put us in a state of war."

"No," Marcus said, and closed his hands around the transponders. He winced and reached around to plug Levy's into his suit and hid his own next to the revolver. "I'm the one who did that. I'm the one who cared most about his own survival."

"Either way, sir, now that you've won, it's time for phase two," the man said, glancing over at Levy's corpse.

"First, help me get some of those painkillers before the doors all lock on us," Marcus said, and sealed the new helmet onto his suit. He rose back to his feet and allowed himself one look within the craft that had brought Levy over. A rifle sat in the co-pilot seat; a Gauss Rifle that could have put a hole through his armor, and through the wall behind him and more beyond that.

Levy had abandoned his edge in the fight.

He punched the command to close the airlock and

staggered back to the hallway junction. He turned his gaze down. "Alexis Levy... that won't be the easiest name to track down, but I can do that for you."

32

Losing Pressure

The Seventy-Fourth Day

Miz Almada disconnected Mia's central processing unit and shut the ship down. The engines lost power, the cameras went dark, and, most importantly, the communication systems shut down.

"It's not like we could avoid an attack from them anyways," Pontius Livius said between bites of bread-substitute dipped into a thick, red soup. By the standards of the *Demos*, he had become aristocracy. "We don't have the armaments, all we have is uncertainty."

Marcus flinched. The nurse beside him didn't seem to know what she was doing, as though a finger's width of polymers between her and his skin made it impossible to find a vein. "And when does Sic-Alba arrive?"

"Now, according to what they told us anyways. Miz Lenz was quite open under the right sort of pressure."

"What sort of pressure?" the Ranger asked, his voice

snarling like a guard dog. "Answer carefully, before I decide you get my next bullet you lying schemer."

"If you shoot me, you're as good as dead. It doesn't matter what I've done in the past," Pontius said. He stuffed his mouth again and smiled, chewing the lump of food as he stared back at the Ranger. "At the least, I'm needed to negotiate with the Alliance and at the worst, I'm the only one aboard the ship that can manually pilot us. My brain is the only one capable of doing the calculations without AI assistance."

Marcus gritted his teeth, and the nurse finally found a vein to start the drip of painkillers. Ice washed through his blood, freezing over the ragged muscles and tendons. Nothing in him healed, but the pain stopped. "How long have you been planning this?"

"Since the emergency broadcast three months ago," the mutant said. "Of course, the specifics have evolved as the days went by, as I got more information and learned more about who I was with while aboard the *Demos*. I like most people you know, even if they don't like me. It's not like I have malice for anyone here. Well, except for that degenerate they made me share a bed with. You broke his arm, did you know that? Probably didn't realize that he was one of the bath intruders. Well, doesn't matter. He choked on his pillow and passed away a few weeks ago."

Of his own accident, I'm sure.

"You're disgusting," Marcus said, getting a smile from the mutant.

"That's what every woman I've ever been with has said. Isn't that right, Miz Brown?"

The nurse paled and put up her hands. She didn't deny it, but she spent no further time with the two of them and evacuated the room.

Marcus turned back to the mutant. "You're going to cause another riot. You're letting everyone on this ship taste safety and then yanking it from their lips. Hundreds of people right now are trying to figure out why Link Reality just went down, and they're going to want somebody to pay for it."

"Well, it's a good thing that we have a fall guy, now isn't it? One who tried to have you killed. The lie is easy. I've already spread the word. His little economy project, the one he forced on everyone, the thing he used to take people's entertainment away from them? That overloaded the AI and now nobody gets anything, and it's all his fault."

Immoral on every account, but sounds like it ends with me surviving–

The ship lurched. Explosions ripped through the stern of the craft, rippling through the hull with hailstorm vibrations. Emergency lights bathed the room red.

Marcus leapt to his feet. "And that? How are you going to deal with that?" he demanded.

Pontius twisted his face together and looked about. "That felt like they shot us."

"That's exactly what that felt like." He could hear people shouting throughout the ship.

"Well, you are the shooting expert," the researcher said as he stared in the direction the noise had come from: the direction of the engines. "But why would they waste munitions killing us when they have a battle to fight? Sic-Alba should be arriving, and they need to capture you still. What are they going to do if they vent all our air?"

Marcus' hand closed around the mutant's shirt and hauled him to his feet. He rocked the table, spilling the last of the food across the ground as he forced Pontius to look at him. "Did you not realize that Space Rangers can survive in vacuum for three days?" Technically more, if he wanted to risk brain damage.

Pontius lost the color in his face. All that remained were the purple patches of his twisted age. "Fire brigade. We'll need a fire brigade to double check the autonomous systems. We need to get the engine repairman to work at once."

"There isn't one. This ship was only ever a ferry to Tiber. If the engine failed, a crew could reach it under thrust in just a few days from Athens Station. But there is no Athens Station. There is no repair crew. Your plan just fell apart."

There was a knock at the door and, without waiting, Theodore opened it up to stick his head in. "Sir, Miz Jung is demanding to speak with you..." He stopped when he saw how the Ranger was holding his employer, but he knew better than to fight Marcus.

Marcus shoved the mutant back into his seat. "Her too?"

Pontius scowled and fixed the lay of his shirt. "Obviously. You think either of them had the charisma to get elected without my help? Fine, perfect, send her in. I need a coordinator for this mess anyways."

The woman squeezed between Theodore's bulk and the door frame. She had her hands clasped together to keep them from shaking. She still had on her suit coat, same as when

Marcus had first seen her. The ever increasing temperature didn't seem to phase her. "Mr Livius, sir."

Something's wrong.

"What is it?" he demanded

"That was the Alliance attacking us just now, wasn't it?"

So why did she come here?

"Most certainly."

"So your plan has failed."

What is it?

Pontius slammed his fist on the table and leapt up. "It has not failed. We will still control the ship and any new developments, I can handle them!"

Miz Jung trembled, and the ship trembled too. The hull wanted to twist itself apart after the shot had lanced it through. "Mr Livius, your methods are wrong. I see that now. I should never have worked with you. I'm going to go to Hell because of you, but I can at least do something first."

Steel glinted between her fingers.

Shit.

"Knife!" Marcus bellowed, but the table was between him and her.

Miz Jung screamed. A cry three and a half thousand years old burst from her lips as she lunged at Pontius. "Satan!"

Pontius fell back, his legs collapsing as she darted for him with knife high overhead. His mouth gaped and his body shook as he tried to raise a hand.

Theodore's grasp found Miz Jung's wrist with one hand, and her throat with the other. He was twice her size and yanked her from her feet. Spinning, the bodyguard slammed her up against the wall. The knife clattered from her hands. It fell to the shaking floor.

Pontius blinked, then began to laugh. "Yes, yes, that's why I have you Theodore! For idiots like this!" he said, pushing off the table to regain his feet.

"Forgive me!" Miz Jung cried, but she didn't want Pontius' forgiveness. She needed it from a higher power.

A package hidden within her coat ignited. The bodyguard had just the time to look down and grunt before the explosion enveloped him. The two of them liquefied in one, violent burst. For Marcus, in his suit, the shockwave barely touched him, but it knocked Pontius flat to the ground even faster than Theodore's corpse collapsed. Black tar splattered the walls. Blood or chemicals, Marcus couldn't tell.

"What the hell was that?" the Ranger asked, grabbing Pontius by the arm and hauling him back up.

"Mi-miz Jung was a... a chemical engineer. Fertilizers for the plants. The greenery. She was a flower grower! What possessed her to do that?" Pontius asked, his voice a hoarse shout.

"You've lost control of your underlings," Marcus shouted, and dragged the mutant to the door to look out. The hall was empty, save for the emergency lights.

"Something has come over these weak-willed idiots. And, oh... oh dear I seem to have gone deaf. Ranger, can you hear me?" he asked, his voice echoing down the hall before them.

Marcus nodded.

"Right, well then, I can't hear a thing you've said, if you've said anything. But, that just now, Miz Jung was a chemical engineer. I'm not surprised she was able to cook something up. She may well have handed out a few other bombs like that to anyone of a like mind. Stay away from any of those religious people! Please, get me somewhere secret and then I need you to see to the breach in the hull. There should still be construction foam that can patch it up before we lose all of our air. That's more important than thrust. We can always be towed."

Marcus wanted nothing more than to abandon the mutant right then and there and let the zealots rip him apart. Pontius had been right though. He was the only one that could do by hand what Mia could do. So he took him to a utility closet the size of a coffin and shoved him in. "Wait here, quietly," he ordered, and slammed the door shut on the shocked man.

He went to the only door he thought could be sealed shut after prying it open, the lift shaft. The sucking gust of air tried to knock him from his feet, but he jumped through and shut the door behind him.

Panic had filled the ship like a miasma, and he could hear the echoes of it through every wall. The riots were back, but the people who were still useful knew better than to fight amongst themselves. Despite advances in technology and a general higher standard of safety among spacecraft in recent decades, plenty of people still knew what to do in a decompression emergency.

Marcus would have been thankful for the help, if not for the fact that they were using the lift like a push sled to move the barrels of sealing foam to the engine bay. Under spin, the lift came flying at him from behind like a wall. The grinding scrape of metal gears chased him down like banshees till he threw a shoulder through a door and dove free.

"And lo! Doth the demon descend!" a man bellowed, lifting his hands up over his head. For a moment, all that Marcus could see was the veritable wall of flesh the overweight man formed, looming over the Ranger. The man wasn't the only one in the hall. Three others had turned their gaze.

Where am I?

Marcus pushed himself up. The room wasn't familiar to him, just an offshoot, a connecting hall between rooms with doors to manipulate the air flow. He tried to orient his position in the ship, guessing he was somewhere near the baths, but that didn't change the fact that people were shuffling between him and the lift door. "Demon?" he asked. He tried to recall the people around him, but none of their faces were familiar. At least he didn't think he could recall them from Father Publius' congregations.

"What else? To call you? You the one who brought this upon us?" the man asked, his voice rising and falling like an amateur in a stage play.

Air pressure in the *Demos* was still dropping. The flow of air was like a ghastly organ pipe down the hall, and lunatics were between him and the problem. He had to get to the damage while he could still do something about it. "Get out of my way before I kill you," he ordered.

"You caused this! You are the one who killed Captain Regulus, the true captain of this ship. We've been off course ever since. You sowed disaster upon us!" the man shouted. He swung a finger at Marcus. "Now look, the heavens have struck us down because we did not purge you from the ship!"

The emergency alarm blared through the halls, dulling their thoughts with each wail. The red light cast everything in the shade of blood. Isolation had bred hysteria like a plague, and he didn't have the time to deal with it. The man before him had broken. The impromptu cultist had replaced logic with conviction. Fear had sunken through his mind like a parasite, dressing itself in the trappings of the supernatural.

You're the ones who called me a demon.

He reached behind his back and into his armor once more. This time, he did pull out the revolver and he put a bullet between the man's eyes. The man didn't even react in time. He died with a vapid stare, and crumbled to the floor in a mound. Whatever he might have conspired to do ended there.

Two bullets remained as the fat zealot's blood pooled around him. "Get out of my way or you're joining him," he told the other three, and they fled screaming. For a moment, he wondered if he could even smell the gunpowder. His suit's filters were overwhelmed with blood and smoke, desperately in need of maintenance. Everything about him needed maintenance. It hadn't failed yet though. He could still work.

He could still survive.

33

Departure

The Seventy-Fifth Day

It took nearly twenty hours to fix the hole, all in an oxygen deprived stupor. With air flooding out where the kinetic round had ripped through, the *Demos* couldn't keep up with the demand for oxygen. Keeping the ship from shredding itself apart required casting and resculpting the construction foam over and over again to stymie the flow of air and also string up supports through the torn hull.

Most of the technically capable workers weren't allowed to do the manual work. The main reactor was shuttered because of the damage and without Mia's support, wouldn't boot back up. They all had to fix that issue instead of something as mundane as leaking atmosphere. The moment they were able to begin electrolysis on the stores of water, the air pressure returned, and everyone began to collapse from exhaustion.

"Marcus, we need you to go."

His body was heavy. The line between waking and

dreaming didn't exist. His reality was nightmare. Shadows and bloodshed, fire and fear, the carnival dragged him in with jeering cries.

"Marcus, the ship is useless. The engine was destroyed. We need to get towed."

"I need sleep. I can't sleep."

"Sleep when you're dead, Ranger," Felicity ordered, shaking him by the shoulders and drawing his attention to her face. "Wake up!"

The Ranger closed his hand around her wrist. Muscle cramps nearly had him crippled, but he had collapsed into an acceleration pod. She had crawled in through the opening, nearly laying atop him and silhouetted by the engine room lights. They weren't red anymore. "Who do I have to fight?"

"No one! No fighting. No killing. At least, God I hope not. Miz Almada got the cameras working again. Sic-Alba is shooting it out with the Alliance, but they aren't looking good," she explained, her head drooping the more she spoke. Her gaze came to a stop on Marcus' chest and she squeezed his armor.

He blinked a few times and tried to clear his thoughts. "Why? Why would they be in a fight? Aren't the Alliance here as peacekeepers?"

"We don't know. It happened when you people took Mia offline. Everything is so fucked up. You know that, don't you?" she asked, tears welling up in her eyes. Her lips quivered and her breath shook.

He shifted in the pod, pushing himself upright. Felicity

collapsed against his chest, a weight almost too much for him to move. "What's the plan? What's the next step?"

"Is that all you think about?" she shouted. "The next step? Nothing but the next thing you can do? Don't you ever think ahead? I thought you were a chess player."

"Life isn't a game of chess. All the pawns and knights don't trust each other. You can't tell a person to sacrifice themselves to save the king anymore. Do you have a plan? One that didn't come from Pontius?"

She swallowed her emotions and nodded. "We use the small craft the Alliance sent over, fly to one of the other survivor ships, and bring it back here to tow us to safety."

"There's safety?"

She pursed her lips. "To whoever wins this shootout. Either one of them will help us get away."

Going somewhere the people didn't know him, some-where civilians didn't swarm him and call him a demon with knives in their hands. It sounded like the exact same thing that had brought him to Athens Station. "I can do that, but I can't pilot. It can't just be me."

"Ensign Lawrence and I will come along. That craft, we checked it and it can fit three people," she said.

Marcus turned the ship around in his head, picturing its dimensions. "Tight fit."

She grinned and shrugged. "What can you expect? It's basically an acceleration bed strapped to an engine."

The two of them rose, each as unsteady on their feet as the other. Walking through the engine bay reminded Marcus of traversing the hull of a ship at sea. Men who had come to work, to repair the damage, they had each toiled till they dropped and crawled into a corner for sleep. Their beds were of sheet metal, their pillows a spare jacket if not their own arm. He wasn't the only one who couldn't sleep. Eyes followed him. Gaunt, haunted eyes that tracked him and lingered on him.

"You got a grand plan, Ranger?" Miz Almada asked. She had taken a chair near the main entrance. It was the only way in and out that hadn't been damaged by the shot, and she ruled over it with a jug of distilled liquor in one hand.

"She does," Marcus said, gesturing with a shrug towards Felicity. "It sounds like a peaceful one too, so maybe it'll actually work out."

Miz Almada upended the bottle to her lips. Two bubbles gurgled to the top. "So, it doesn't involve killing people? All your plans seem to involve killing people."

Hammers and nails. He didn't know what to say to her, or if he had to say anything at all. It would take days to bring one of the other ships back over to the *Demos*. If she survived, the exhaustion of the toil would blur the memory from her mind. If they all made it to Scythia, he didn't need to ever see her again anyways.

"Just shut your fucking mouth," Felicity said. She brushed her hair back, yanking knots out with her fingers. With her hair clear from her face, she brought a glare to bear against the technician. "You're not even in charge of anything anymore. Mia is broken. The engines are shot. The reactor can't be touched lest it fall apart again. You're useless to the ship after yesterday. At least he can still do something for us."

Miz Almada leapt to her feet, eyes glossy with drink. "You trying to pick a fight?"

"Lay off," Marcus ordered, shoving the technician back into her seat. He shot a warning at Felicity, and she didn't twist the knife. "Come on. Where is the ensign?"

"At the bridge. Never felt like such a long walk before, did it?" Felicity said as the two of them left the engine bay behind and trudged through the lift shaft.

"Thanks."

Felicity arched an eyebrow in that coy, inquisitorial way she could do. "For losing control of myself?"

"Yeah, it kept me from having to deal with her, didn't it? I'm not much of a people person anymore," he said, and both of them had a laugh.

The bridge didn't have a shred of mirth in it. Three people sat in it. Ensign Lawrence leapt to their feet, scurrying from the corner where they had been trying to be overlooked. Captain Samaras and Pontius Livius sat across the holo-display from one another. Had they been speaking, Marcus would have heard it on approach. As such, they were in a contest of wills no more elegant than a pair of school children. They stared at one another, waiting for the other to show weakness.

"And the reason here... is?"

Pontius sneered. "Because he still has command registration on most autonomous systems. Namely the electrolysis."

Samaras sneered. "And because as much as I hate this twisted son of a bitch, without replacement cores for Mia, the ship won't be able to function without him."

"So what are you debating right now?"

"Nothing," Pontius said.

"We already did everything that's rational to do. Now we're waiting on you to get the *Phalanx of Starlight* for us," Samaras said. The *Phalanx of Starlight* hadn't done anything since fleeing Mimir, not even respond on the radio.

Marcus tamped down his irritation. "I look forward to seeing which of you survives the zealots beating at the doors. I'll be back with another ship," he said, and turned from the bridge.

He, Felicity, and Ensign Lawrence vanished into the halls. A few days worth of food had been prepared for the three of them, and they piled into the Alliance craft, a space age dinghy.

"That's the second time now, you've rescued me. Thanks," Ensign Lawrence said as they tarried back and forth through the portal of the smaller ship. The reality of space oppressed their minds, that they would have almost none at all while traversing the void.

"I would think the first time matters more than that," Marcus said. "You've passed all isolation screening tests, right?"

"Obviously. I wouldn't be here if being stuck in a coffin would get to me," they said.

"It's not going to be that long of a flight, is it?" Felicity asked. She rose from the back corner of the ship, what passed for a storage hold. With the slope of the walls, she could only get to her knees between the seats. After subtracting the volume for the engine, the ship was smaller than the average family car.

"Time is subjective," Marcus said, and climbed into the side seat. The control seat sat forward, in front of the storage hatch, while the passenger seats flanked it. He wasn't going to be the one to pilot it. That was the ensign's job. There were tricks to making it through a long flight. First was setting it to auto-pilot. Second was extended sleeping. Marcus was very good at both. After they detached from the *Demos*, and he had the mental certainty of safety and productivity, he managed to nod off.

Fourteen hours later, he awoke to the momentary weightlessness of the ship switching from acceleration, to deceleration. His body still felt numb. Lifting his hand made muscles crack and pop. His two travel companions were awoken as well, though their groaning implied they hadn't gotten nearly as much sleep as he had. Felicity in particular had bags under her eyes and could barely rouse her wits to understand what was happening. She fell back into the grasp of rest as soon as the engines resumed.

"Halfway there," Ensign Lawrence said as Marcus popped his helmet off.

The kitchen staff hadn't given them anything pleasant to take with them. There had been a time he could recall where the food of choice had been something like protein infused brownies. Just the memory of the buttery chocolate made his stomach growl. The dried out, processed bricks of food paste didn't even pretend to have flavor. The failed attempts at soup rationing would have been better.

He turned to his flight companion. "You've been keeping your head down this whole time, haven't you?" Marcus asked.

Ensign Lawrence shrugged and gestured for a bar themselves. "This was just to get the lifetime benefits, not a real career path. It's not like it was my dream to serve the government or something. In case you haven't noticed, they didn't exactly do me any benefits," they said, pointing to their body: on the female side of androgynous.

"Hermaphrodite?"

"Bingo," they said, shooting a finger gun at him before accepting the brick of food. Just touching it made their brow pull together, their lip sneered.

"There are worse ways you could have been born. Could be a Camrian," Marcus said, getting himself a bag of water.

The food bar cracked between Lawrence's teeth. It sounded like they were chewing through gravel and Marcus gave them the water instead. After washing it down, they said, "What a blessing it is that people still acknowledge I'm human. But it still feels like everyone expects me to go live with all the other hermaphrodites. Or that we're enemy sympathizers. They treat us like a religious commune."

"Well, that corporation did convince people to do it to their children to reduce the minimum colony size. This was before genetic screening became trivial."

"The war really turned that to shit though, didn't it?" they responded, turning up their hands and shrugging. "I'd love nothing more than for people to just assume I'm a woman and ignore me, but stupid people have this attitude that just because our genes were monkeyed with that we're Alliance sympathizers."

"Benefits then? You're doing what I'm doing, aren't you? Trying to live on fast forward."

She grinned back at him. "You also trying to take as many star jumps as possible?"

"I'm on my fifth since making that decision, yeah. I really thought by now the war would have simmered off."

"Here we are," Lawrence said. "But you know, if I survive this, I can put in to be moved all the way to the other side of space. That should buy me a century or so."

"If we had any alcohol, I'd give you a toast to being drifters through space, but all I have is water and concrete that someone labeled edible."

Their strained laughter didn't last the time it took for them to finish eating, let alone to the *Phalanx of Starlight*. The fact something was wrong was obvious the moment the autonomous systems handled the docking without so much as a peep over the radio. A thousand people should have been aboard, just like the *Demos*. It drifted through space on a course to enter Mimir's orbit but with no active thrust.

No one greeted them in the airlock. No rumble of energy traveled through the hull. No echoes of speech or tremble of feet.

Felicity nearly fell to her knees when she stepped into the ship. She put a hand to her head and said, "Oxygen is high. Really high. The life-support systems are overkill."

The *Phalanx of Starlight* was the same model as the *Demos*, a shuttle for moving between Mimir and Tiber. It was a relic justified in cost from when the exo mine had been built. There was nothing stealthy about the craft, and hardly anything that constituted defenses. Putting a thousand people aboard it had asked too much of its design parameters, and it had failed them.

I guess we found why the Alliance pointed us at this ship. They should have told us it was dead.

"We should look for survivors."

34

Guard Dogs Die Hard

The Seventy-Seventh Day

Marcus' back slammed into the ship wall hard enough to dent it. The AutoSec unit let go of his ankle while his head was still reeling. Before he could so much as slide out of the hole, it drew down on him with the mechanical force of a hydraulic ram. Three times steel struck steel. The pain was familiar to the Ranger. It was the pain of his skin liquefying in his suit from the impact. Blood poured from his body and into the reclamation systems.

But his ribs didn't crack. His muscles didn't fail. His will didn't break.

Emergency injections of adrenaline and more pricked through his arms and into his blood. The combat cocktail burned inside him.

The AutoSec hesitated after the third blow. It had broken through the wall and the gash of steel blocked line of sight between it and Marcus' helmet. The pause gave Marcus enough time to grab hold of the machine's powerful limb. In that moment, he had the grip of thirty men. Marcus knew not what feud the machine had with the ship, but that it was covered in the blood of dozens who had tried to rid themselves of its violence. The sentry of the bridge, it had sighted upon the three from the *Demos* and sought their ruin.

Marcus was no ordinary man, no civilian to be subjugated. He took hold of it by the steel limb and twisted. Joints and cables snapped, ripping free the mechanism's arm and throwing it to the ground. It reared back, staggering and assessing its jagged stump. Marcus dropped from the wall, landing on all fours. He coughed and spat blood, but had no time for the pain.

Before him was a giant of metal. Circuits for brains, electrified springs for muscles, and no smarter than the training drones back on Earth. The metal golem couldn't be reasoned with, but it could follow orders; orders like keeping people out of the bridge no matter what. It had no regard for itself, but it did strain its processing to find a solution as Marcus rose back up across from it.

There was no solution. A thousand pounds of metal destruction turned and ran from him. It fled through the halls back to the bridge.

"Get back here!" Marcus roared and charged after it.

The AutoSec had killed everyone aboard the *Phalanx of Starlight* without so much as a glimmer of morality in it. The carnage of desperation painted the walls around them. Corpses rotted of people who had tried to fight it with nothing better than power tools.

His eyes locked on one. A shaft of steel sharpened into a spear. Someone had put their hope into it and died with it. It found new warmth in Marcus' grasp.

When at last the AutoSec could flee no more and had found no weapon of its own, the Ranger leapt upon it. It threw up its one arm. He stabbed around it. The tip ripped through artificial musculature. It pierced the thing's neck and he rammed it through to the other side. When it tried to shove him off, he leapt overtop without letting go. His boots hammered the AutoSec's shoulders as he gripped both ends of the spear. He twisted.

Cables splintered and sprayed out. He wrenched the thing's head off and threw it aside. For a moment, it lumbered and tried to correct. Only the sensory input was gone. It still lived. The AutoSec tried to bash him free, but he ducked the blow. Then he punched his fist down through the gash of metal. The processing core was in the chest. He felt the innermost conduits like a robotic aorta, and ripped them free. Electricity sprayed across him, scorching his armor black in an instant.

It fell.

He screamed. His heart still hammered in his chest. The pain filtered back in from the fringes of his mind. He thrashed about in the hall, slamming his fists into the wall. It did nothing but echo through the drifting mausoleum.

When the drugs finally tapered off, he slid down to his knees and panted. He wanted to cry, but that, like most of his bodily functions, had been suppressed. Everything that didn't directly let him fight, to kill, to destroy, vanished after a jolt of the combat cocktail.

"Don't," Ensign Lawrence said. "Don't go near him, he's dangerous!"

"He saved us!" Felicity shouted. She tried to shove the other off of her, but couldn't escape the grasp.

"Didn't you hear him? Have you never heard of a berserker before?" Lawrence shouted, shoving Felicity into the wall. The two of them were only a few strides away. In the deathly quiet of the ship, they may as well have been screaming in his ear.

"It's over," Marcus said, and broke out coughing. His vocal cords felt torn. He spat out more blood. "It's all over."

She swallowed and nodded. "Not till this thing is flying towards the *Demos* it isn't," Lawrence said.

Marcus pushed himself upright. His arms hung heavy. He coughed hard and the suit had to vent the blood. It splattered across himself and the walls around him.

Felicity screamed.

"I'm gunna need an IV. The medbay should still be functioning, right?"

"You need more than that!" Felicity shouted. "You're going to die or something."

He waved her off and forced one foot in front of the next. Lawrence slipped by him, pressing their back to the wall to avoid touching the disabled AutoSec, and vanished into the bridge to see if they could commandeer it. Marcus caught a glimpse inside to the captain's chair with a body slumped over in it.

"Just relax and focus. This happens all the time in real

fights," he said. He tried to keep his voice steady. He didn't succeed particularly well.

"Real fights? Is this what you call a real fight? And everything aboard the *Demos*?"

"Warm up... I guess," he said. He nodded his head. "Can you get the doors? If I stop moving for too long I might collapse and you're not strong enough to drag me."

She gulped and ran ahead, prying open doors and pulling hatches free. She ran to and fro, trying to find the medbay as he trudged behind her. They ended up having to pass through the storage bay. It had been converted just like the *Demos*. Acceleration beds pulled from ancient storage and snapped into rows for refugees.

The *Phalanx of Starlight* was filled with corpses, but away from the AutoSec there were no signs of struggle. People had died where they lay, and the others hadn't even bothered to clear the bodies away before becoming one themselves.

Felicity didn't say anything until after the two of them had made it to the improvised field hospital. Most of the medicine had been ransacked, but the thieves had been after the fun drugs. Actual treatment supplies laid in heaps across the floor. Felicity, a businesswoman, only knew the first thing about needles, so she was even worse than Pontius' nurse. He dealt with the pain.

"How did this happen?" she asked. Her hands clutched his arm even after she got the saline into him. She was shaking.

"The way I figure it, the captain went into the bridge, told the AutoSec to keep everyone out, and never came back out.

He probably got attacked and bled out. I saw him dead in there. And then, without control of the ship, it just takes one setting wrong and everything falls apart. Maybe the food got locked up... but they had the tools to fight the AutoSec. Must have been the oxygen regeneration was set too low. People would have died in their sleep. Asphyxiated in air."

"And they had no way to save themselves?"

"You saw the bodies around the machine, didn't you?"

"A thousand people. A thousand people died because of an accident?"

Marcus put a hand on her shoulder. "It happens more than you would believe. But we can still bring this ship around to save the *Demos*."

For a moment, she retracted in on herself. When she regained herself, she sheepishly looked at his hand. It had become stuck to her shirt with his blood. "You're not going to die on me, are you?"

"Not immediately."

"Let's get you some food."

They couldn't bring the dead back to life, not even to curse at them for spoiling all the food worth eating. The leftovers were plentiful, but only rice gruel mixed with some beans. While Felicity prepared enough for the three of them, Lawrence stopped the spin of the ship and set it under thrust. Marcus excused himself to wash his face before taking his helmet off in front of the others. He didn't dare take any of the suit off, not even to release the pressure and let himself breathe. He was afraid he would fall apart.

"How are you able to eat in this smell?" Lawrence asked when she found the two of them.

Marcus gestured at his face until he could swallow. "The drug cocktail kills my sense of smell. Why? What's it smell like in here?"

"Like rotting shit," she said, refusing the bowl Felicity offered her.

Marcus turned to his new nurse. "How are you managing?"

"Poorly." She jammed her spoon into her bowl. The *Phalanx of Starlight* was more confined than the dinghy that had brought them over. It suffocated even their conversation.

Marcus wanted to suggest that the three of them move over to the bridge, toss the captain's corpse out, and bunker down until they returned to the *Demos*. The thought was in his head, but it never worked its way to his tongue and out past his lips. He listened as Ensign Lawrence commented about the inability to message back to the *Demos* because Mia had been gutted.

They pulled up a view from the cameras and stared at streaking lights. Which were missiles and which were the craft from Sic-Alba they could only guess. The onboard AI, Kavul, had been sleeping for weeks. Lawrence's attempts to coax thought out of it were no more successful than questioning a man just woken and pulled from bed.

Marcus couldn't keep track of the conversation. Words blurred together. Time became tangled. It had been hours since he had fought, since he had been in danger. The tension and shock finally began to give way. He didn't even notice when it happened, he simply toppled over and hit the ground. His last waking thought was wondering how he would explain it to Felicity. She was shouting and jumping over to him, but there was nothing she could do.

He drifted in oblivion across the orbit of Mimir. Riding on the ashes of the dead, he was carried by palanquin back to the graves of his own making and presented unto them. The dead clung to him. The dead cried out for him. He was their maker and their lord. He was the warm succor of their icy plight. In black dream the dead spake thus to him, "Ye still have the fire of life within thine chest, but your hand is ours. Your craft is naught but death. You can make only beautiful destruction."

Felicity managed to rouse him half an hour before the two shuttles joined into one. The *Phalanx of Starlight* drifted to the rear of the *Demos*, nuzzling up like a mating dragonfly to push it along. "There's a problem. Well, a couple problems."

He felt his head roll across his shoulders as he roused. Something clung about his body, stiff and resisting. After a moment, he recognized it as the gel cushion of an acceleration pod that had been left to rest for hours on end, conformed to his shape. "What is it? How long was I out?"

"Two days," she answered, glancing at the half dozen IV bags discarded beside him. "It seems like the Alliance won the fight. Our only way out is with them."

"Damn." Marcus closed his eyes. He didn't want to move. His skin had scabbed into the polymer suit. The mere shift of his breath tugged at wounds. Taking it off would need a surgical suite.

"We can't wait for Gibraltar either. The ship... it's gotten bad," Felicity said.

The Ranger scoffed. "How much worse could it get?"

"Plague. Well, viral outbreak anyways. It's infected half the ship already. Quarantine is impossible now. People don't even have the strength to fight anymore."

"So we have to go with the Alliance for rescue then."

"And they're not going to let you escape. I thought, maybe we could get you out of the armor. Throw it out an airlock and give you the identity of someone dead? Would that fool them?"

He couldn't help but laugh. "If you take me out of my suit now, I'd... you ever seen those deep sea animals? The ones who live under pressure and then balloon up at the surface? I'd be like that. I'd explode."

"Do you have any ideas?"

Marcus rolled his head back and stared up at the lights. The two of them were on the bridge of the *Phalanx of Starlight*. The overhead light shone bright and white, like a sun for the room. "I shouldn't have shot Captain Regulus. I should have trusted him."

"What?" Felicity asked. She slid into the pod, sitting across the seat's arm. "Marcus, that was months ago. I need you here, now, with me."

"Don't lie. You're only with me because your boss ordered you to be. I smiled and chatted and let myself enjoy it, but it wasn't your choice. Just drop the act."

"What? Are you being fucking serious right now? After all that happened, that's what you have to say?"

"I should have trusted Captain Regulus," Marcus said. He wasn't speaking to Felicity anymore. He wasn't even looking at her. The words were for his own sake, to crystallize the dream into thoughts of regret. "It wasn't a question of statistics or of interpretation, it was about managing people. I didn't trust the people, so I didn't trust him. I was wrong."

"Marcus!" Felicity shouted, grabbing hold of his helmet. Of course, it wasn't his helmet. Levy had destroyed his, and he had stolen Levy's. "Get it together. You're a problem solver, aren't you? One problem at a time. The *Demos* is going to be docking with the Alliance mega-construct in two days. How are you going to survive? What do we need to do?"

"I don't know," he said. "I've been telling you from day one, that's not the kind of problem I can solve. We're trapped on the wrong side of the gravity well and the enemy has the lifeline. What do you expect me to do?"

"Think! Think of a solution!"

"Felicity," Ensign Lawrence cut in. "Give it up. He's lost. It's a form of shock. We had to read up on it in officer school. He's not getting out of this in two days. Focus on yourself."

Felicity retracted her hands. She rose, but her fingers curled into fists. "You don't trust me, do you?"

"How could I?" he asked. "You had an ulterior motive from day one."

35

Casting Lots

The Eightieth Day

Charles Samaras, CEO of The Nebulae Corporation, current Captain of the *Demos*, and surrogate captain of the *Phalanx of Starlight*, stood before the nearly two hundred remaining active passengers of the ship. Twice again as many were bedridden, coughing and fevered. They could hardly stay awake, much less vote, and yet the matter had been brought to a head.

Half of the storage hold had been cleared out, the acceleration beds getting moved over to the *Phalanx of Starlight* to replace those too rotten with corpses to use. The heavy lifting had all been coordinated in a mere few hours within which spin was canceled and gravity abandoned. Given the damage to the *Demos*, people had preferred moving to the new ship, after the life support system had been repaired. The ant lines of bodies moving supplies and clearing corpses had been a breeding ground for conspiracy and rumor.

By the end of it, a jury of all had been assembled.

Charles spoke. "This is barbarism. Worse than that, it is impatience. Do you people not realize that everything that has gone wrong for us has, at its root, been born of impatience? Even those among you who want to hold me accountable, I am appalled that you can't even wait until we're on solid ground. Are you children?"

Marcus scanned the crowd. No one looked mollified by his speech. They had all gathered, every last man, woman, and child able to stand. He himself sat against the wall, almost removed from the court trial. Not quite. He tried to think of a way to convince the crowd that he was Levy, a Ranger they had never met, never even heard of. He couldn't figure out a convincing lie, so he kept his mouth shut.

"Is that the end of your speech?" Mr Boseman asked.

"I don't think anything more needs be said. You've rallied here with anger in your hearts. I can only hope you take a moment to consider what you'll have to live with afterwards. You're all going to survive this because of me. I saved your lives."

"Well alright then," the man responded. His eyes didn't even have a flicker to them. "We will begin the lots with Ranger Maximus first."

The entire crowd queued into a line, and one by one they picked up their shards. They didn't have pottery, but they did have bottle caps. Each passenger able to assemble picked up one regular cap, and one stained with blood. Behind a curtain, they cast one for death, or one for mercy. The affair took nearly half an hour due to the volume of people, but when they got through, the bin of lots was upended.

Nearly two hundred bloody caps spilled out at Marcus' feet. No one needed to count them. It wasn't even close to a tie. The Ranger folded his hands together and leaned forward. The speaker still stood at the front of the group and said, "Well, I think we can see the opinion of everyone here."

"And what exactly are you going to do about it?" Marcus asked. He stared at the man from behind his opaque helmet. He sat as still as a rock, an easy feat given the damage to his body. Everything was locked up with swelling.

Mr Boseman scowled. "I don't suppose you would kindly walk out the airlock yourself?"

"No."

"Then we are at quite the impasse. Everyone here will remember this though. Plenty of people aboard have political connections of one kind or another. You'll be a marked man on Scythia."

Marcus said, "That would be a real problem if I was planning to stay on Scythia."

"Next! Next we're voting on Mr Nebulae."

"Samaras," the captain said, his lips snarling. "And where is that mutant? Isn't he on trial as well?"

"He's to be brought here, after he and Miz Almada conjoin the ship AIs," Mr Boseman answered.

Charles scoffed. "You expect me to believe that? You're his stooge, aren't you? Took his place to speak on his behalf at the council. I'd call that lying."

Boseman scowled as a few others began piling the caps back up into the distribution pile. "I don't work for him anymore. I was cooperative because he promised results. He delivered death. His time will come too, don't worry. You've got yourself to care about."

Charles sat down beside Marcus and stared at his hands. "I don't suppose I could run away at this point? Lock myself in the bridge?"

A convulsion of black thought passed over the Ranger. "You wouldn't last long without an AutoSec at your door. Determined people can always find a way through a door. Hell, they could just move over to the *Phalanx of Starlight* and abandon you to your death."

Charles turned to face him. "Hard to think of a worse way to die than alone in the void."

I can think of plenty.

"You know, I never asked. Do you have a family somewhere?" Marcus asked.

"Estranged. Not even sure what planet they're on anymore. The kids used to keep in touch, but you know how that goes, don't you? Once you're two star hops away, correspondence doesn't really go both ways and the messages dry up."

The people shuffled back into a queue. It moved past them slower, each person deliberating more. He tried to listen to the clatter of caps within the buckets, but the bloody marks didn't sound any different. Marcus said, "At least you don't have to worry about what will become of them if you die."

"They'll inherit my money is what will happen. Or at least whatever the insurance company pays out. They'll be happy to see I'm dead. You know, Athens Station isn't even big enough to have a proper circle of friends once you're at my point in life. I should have stayed on one of the big planets like Red Cairo. Having money would have at least meant something on planetside. But no, I ended up on Athens Station. I can't even remember the last time I had fresh sushi. Like real fish sushi."

That got Marcus to turn away from the shuffle. "You're a sushi man?"

Charles grunted. "You know, there's an art to sushi that's lost in Link Reality. You need a properly trained sushi chef. The kind that when he pinches the rice ball, every grain ends up pointing in the same direction."

Marcus couldn't help but laugh. "I've lived for centuries and visited dozens of planets, but I've never met one that skilled."

"You just haven't looked in the right places. I can't imagine an active soldier like you has had the time to hire private investigative firms to do the groundwork on something like that, now have you?"

"Can't say that I have. No, I can't say that I have, Charles."

Silence dragged between them as more people walked by. Plenty among them glanced over at the current captain, but they all averted their gaze quickly. They chose to look at their feet and squeeze the caps into their fists.

Charles said, "They're going to kill me, aren't they?"

"I wouldn't be surprised. I can't do anything to stop them either."

"Isn't that just like you? I can think of dozens of chess

games we've had where you've played it cool straight through a losing situation."

"Felicity told you then? About what happened?" Marcus' mouth went dry and he couldn't work up any spit. Staring back at the people who had impotently sentenced him to death was easier than glancing at Charles.

"The broad strokes," Charles said. "That you saved her and the other one. I imagine you feel like you're on a knife edge right now."

"Yeah, and you put the Alliance on one side of me. If it were just me, I'd wait all the way until New Gibraltar showed up."

Charles shook his head. "Can't do that. Nobody but you would survive until then. Not enough food, even with the extra provisions on the *Phalanx of Starlight*. And even if there was, we'd have to weather this infection."

The thought occurred to him that if he was left behind on the *Demos*, perhaps he would survive until New Gibraltar arrived. But then, perhaps they wouldn't be able to rescue him, given the Alliance presence. Perhaps they would put a nuke into the ship the moment they saw he wasn't with the refugees aboard the *Phalanx of Starlight*. Hiding didn't give him any options he could act on.

"I don't suppose you can think up a solution for me here, can you? I'm suddenly feeling very alone and friendless," Charles said.

"Bonds made in haste are quick to break. The people who supported you were only doing it for their own benefit and they've jumped ship."

Charles laughed. "If only. If they were all on the *Phalanx*, maybe there wouldn't be enough of a quorum. I'd be able to rightfully call them a mob, a gang of office workers. Maybe that would shame them enough. Just who do they expect to put in charge of negotiating their fates with the Alliance anyways?"

The Ranger turned to him. "That's a good question."

"We'll hold another election, same as before," Mr Boseman said. He was near the deposit bin, leaning against one of the struts that had held an acceleration bed the day before. In the half-emptied state of the *Demos*, it was nothing more than a nominal, partitioning wall. "Ensign Lawrence is the logical choice. They went to get the other ship, risked their life for us, and didn't do anything wrong."

"Not you?" Marcus asked.

Boseman spat on the ground. "Not after this. You think I'm stupid?"

"We do have quite the history of regicide in this short span of time," Marcus commented. Most of them seemed to be at his own hand, one way or another.

Pontius' voice burst from the hall to their left. "Unhand me you imbeciles. Don't you realize you need me?"

"Like hell we do, mutant. You got us into this mess!" the man hauling him in by the arm said.

The moment the two of them rounded the corner, Marcus recognized the ruffian. Hadria's former second in command. "Mr Nozette," he said. "I suppose that means we're all here."

Pontius turned his sneer on the crowd as he was brought before them. "Unhand me," he ordered, ripping his arm out of Nozette's grasp. "And what are you all looking at? Me? Is that it? A man who simply did what was best for himself. Just like all of you."

"Hold on, Pontius," Boseman said. "We still have to count his fate."

The bucket of lots for Charles was brought out. A few delegates surrounded it and began taking caps out by the handful. They matched bloody with clean and discarded pairs under watching eyes.

"They're going to kill you. You and me both," Pontius said, turning the might of his intellect to bear upon the two of them.

Charles stared at his hands, rubbing them together. "Is there more to say? Or are you just in the habit of stating the obvious nowadays? I hear that's an early sign of dementia, given your age, you decrepit bastard."

"If we don't do something, yes."

"Do you have an idea?" Charles asked.

The scientist wetted his lips. "No. For once, I do not. I've been checkmated by irrationality. And I don't have the raw violence that this one has to keep myself safe."

Boseman cleared his throat, drawing eyes to himself. "There we have it. A margin of five for blood. Mr Samaras, we'll be taking you to the airlock."

The CEO stood up and nodded. "Perhaps I should have argued for more than a simple majority... If it's all the same to you, I would prefer being shot to being vented out of the ship." He turned to Marcus.

The weight of the pistol felt gargantuan. Two bullets remained in it. "You're just giving up?"

"Didn't Captain Regulus do the same?"

"He did. I can do that for you. Better than vacuum," Marcus said, and rose from his seat. The motion was deliberate, almost mechanical in its exactness. It masked his weakness.

Charles smiled. "You know, standing here, I find that my last worry is circling back to my first. My employees, they're still on the exo mine. They still need to be rescued. I wasn't able to do anything for them in the end. When you all get aboard the Alliance craft, please, do what you can for them?"

Marcus couldn't bring himself to trust the Alliance to do anything other than execute them and bring in their own staff, but he didn't give life to those words. He turned and took a step towards the hall.

"If you wouldn't mind," Boseman said, following after him with a stern face. "I think it only appropriate to witness this. Make sure it's done properly."

The thought of faking it had crossed his mind. "You don't trust me?"

"Would you trust a would-be warlord?"

"I don't trust anybody."

Felicity threw herself into the room, bursting from a door. "Stop! Stop. What are you– you people can't be serious!" She charged over, brushing her hair back from her face. "This man is... Charles is the one who negotiated your safety! What are you people doing? Have you no souls? Marcus, say something. Stop this!"

He couldn't tell her that he wasn't able to. Even if she knew how injured he was, he couldn't say it. "You mean I should stand up for the man who sold me off like cattle for slaughter? My sympathy is lacking."

Her gaze turned to Mr Boseman. "Under what authority do you do this under? The people here aren't even half the people aboard the ship!"

Boseman frowned. "If they didn't attend, then they abstained. Simple as that. We are here to hold this man accountable, and to not let him slip away into the legal murk with his wealth."

"Then you're vigilantes. Murderers!" she shouted back at him.

Boseman turned up his hands. "Extraordinary circumstances. Besides, the vote was anonymous."

"Not you though," she said, jabbing a finger at him. "You organized this and if you follow through with killing this man, then I will hunt you to the ends of the galaxy to see you behind bars."

Boseman snarled. "You're at our mercy too," he said, glancing back at the men behind him, at the women sorting the caps back into pairs.

"Is she?" Marcus asked, staring at the man.

Boseman flinched back. "O-our priority is the three of you, who's fighting got us into this disaster. Not your friends. Look, we're not psychopaths."

"No, you're not," Pontius said. "You're people worn thin from the stress of trying to survive. Look at you, the lot of you. You're trying to act civilized and yet you hardly know what to do in such extraordinary circumstances. You've regressed to distant memories of times past, all for lack of a government to tell you what to do. You think this is what self-organizing looks like? You think this will pass muster when the gaggle of warlords we call the Alliance takes custody of you?"

"The Alliance is just going to hand us over!" Boseman responded, turning his attention to the researcher without a moment's hesitation.

"Oh really?" Pontius said, drawing out the incredulity. There was no way for Pontius to know anything that Marcus and Charles didn't know as well: he was talking out of his ass. "You think they will just kindly give us a ship with an A-Mov engine? That, out of all the wreckages, we could even trust the one they give us?"

You say that like it's hard to confirm engine integrity. Boseman doesn't know that though, does he?

Marcus thought over who was left: Miz Almada, the two Ensigns, as well as Pontius Livius. The rest of the people aboard the *Demos* existed in the fuzzy realm of ignorance, one step removed from understanding the task. Even the technicians and engineers among them were little better than people who knew what plumbing was but were not themselves plumbers.

"Wouldn't that just be the ticket they needed? Oh those gallant fighters for the Alliance, they sacrificed their own resources to get us to safety, but would you look at that, an unforeseen accident happened and poof, we all died. It wouldn't even take malice on their part. Just apathy."

His words were a spell cast into the minds of the crowd, a

shift in their minds thrust upon them. He wedged it into the gap of fear created by Marcus for just a moment. Then, he leveraged the crack.

Boseman pushed back. The one most attuned to Pontius' tongue. "Don't listen to him. He's just manipulating you to save himself."

Pontius didn't flinch. "Oh, how silly of me. You were here, you dragged me here, for this play acting murder, yes? Well, why don't you all get back in your queue so it looks official, and when you get in there you have your say and all pat each other on the back that you're in agreement even if it's only by a few percentage points. The majority of people must be right in their actions, no?"

Charles slipped behind Marcus, making himself as small as possible in the site of the uncertain crowd. Some people did move to get in line, to resume their posts and distribute caps. Others didn't move. Some even turned their backs on the whole affair and left. As the crowd shrank and hung their heads, Pontius stepped up to them and glared into one person's eyes and then the next.

"Come on then, make it look professional or you'll never be able to live with yourselves afterwards, when you have to go on living for years knowing that you justified to yourself the murder of people just like yourself just because you had agreement. We all know that's how you determine right and proper action, that virtue means what most people say it does. What are you all waiting for?"

"You should leave," Marcus whispered to Charles. "Go

do something productive. Adjust our flight to the Alliance construct or something."

"You don't have to tell me twice," Charles said, and vanished into a hall with Felicity.

Boseman saw it happen at once, but the instant he opened his mouth, Marcus stepped up to him and filled his vision with the spark splattered mottle of his chest plate. "Think hard."

Pontius stepped past Boseman, bringing himself up to the line of lynching voters. "Aren't most of you religious? What would your priest say of this? Lynching two men for being the same sinful beings that all of you are. Can any of you say you are without sin? Nearly all of you that stand here now were in one of the riots, possibly all. More than fights, some of you went crazy. The Ranger here had to shoot a cult in the crib, and where does that leave you fear mongers? Orphaned in thought. So I say to you, with the power of three thousand years behind these words, if you want to judge me, if your indignation and fear is so great that you would give the Alliance– our enemy of some three hundred years– dominion over you, then first find one without sin to cast the first lot."

He had butchered the line, but it still mollified the crowd. He had assaulted their minds, saturated their thoughts with fire, and overwhelmed their defenses. He had made a miscalculation however.

Maria silently stepped forward. She dug her hands into the pile of caps and marched over to the voting booth. Everyone heard the cling and clang of deposited caps before she emerged and marched away. With that, the mental barrier that Pontius had been erecting between them and the vote was shattered. The line of people congealed together and flowed through the booth.

Pontius pursed his lips. "Shit."

36

The Grex Ovium

The Eighty-Second Day

Pontius' speech hadn't been entirely for naught. Nozette, Hadria's trouble maker, had proposed that any action be delayed until after entering A-Mov. Using Charles to get on the ship and using Pontius to fix the ship simply made too much sense, and so the compromise was born.

Two days later, after some difficulty maneuvering the ships, the *Demos* docked with the Alliance construct. The Svabian flagship, the core that the goliath of floating steel had been built around, was hardly recognizable by the time they arrived. The *Woab Hammer* still sat in the middle, but Marcus had seen lunar dockyards with less fingers of steel.

The *Demos* didn't dock directly with it, but with the *Grex Ovium* at the fringe of the tangle. From even before the ships intertwined, the Alliance had people moving within and drones moving without, encircling the two shuttles. A curt message was delivered to the bridge by Captain Atish Raven of the *Woab Hammer*. "All air and resources will have to be extracted from both ships in tandem with the egress of people. Once the oxygen has been extracted, physical resources will be distributed out appropriately. In the meantime, Ranger Levy is to return with the corpse of Ranger Maximus."

To try and sell the lie, they had mutilated Levy's face with the heat lance. The smell of burnt hair still clung to the corpse even days later, tainting the airlock. It was the best they could do. The heat-mangled manacles on Levy's corpse at least still pinned him to one wall. Without spin, everything floated.

Felicity looked at it from over his shoulder. "Do you think it will fool them?"

"Does it matter?" Marcus asked. "My fate wouldn't be so different from Levy's fate. The only assurance I get is that they don't kill me on the spot. As long as I'm alive, there's always hope. As long as I survive, a chance will come."

"I'm sorry that there's nothing we can do for you, after so long..."

"The Alliance put us in checkmate. This is just what has to be done. Always play to your outs, never give up. You should get out of here, out of sight when Raven shows up."

Felicity nodded. "I'm going to be with Father Publius. He's not doing well and can use all the help he can get to move around. I think Charles will be here soon."

The door slid open and slid shut behind her, leaving him alone in the airlock. He waited, turning over the name Alexis Levy in his head as he stared at the corpse of his friend.

Soon enough, Charles pulled himself through the door

and floated into the airlock beside him. "I hope your lying is good."

"My poker face is perfect," Marcus said, facing Charles with his opaque visor.

Charles laughed. "You know, I was thinking. I should beg asylum from Captain Raven and stay on the *Woab Hammer* with you. I can't imagine what they'll do to me, but I might escape lynching."

Marcus hesitated, the words in his mind but not out his mouth. Then the airlock cycled open with a gust of air to equalize pressure between the two ships.

Captain Atish Raven floated opposite them, flanked by two AutoSec units and another officer of her ship. She had on a thick uniform, the kind with embedded body armor and yet still passed for dress. The first thing Marcus noticed, however, was that she was augmented. An enormous appendage extended from the small of her back and had itself planted to one wall. At a thought, the mechanical tail twisted and she aligned her orientation with the two of them. The tip broke free and she drifted through the airlock, alighting with magnetic boots against the floor. "Welcome back, Dog." She spoke with her eyes unfocused, reading something fed to her by her neural implant. His transponder ID most likely.

Marcus didn't flinch. He put all of his effort into observation. He took in her height, her demeanor, the almost hidden scars across her cheeks: shrapnel and ember burns hidden by the scarcest makeup. Hair as black as space and eyes to match.

"Captain Raven. Nice to see you in person," Charles said, holding out a hand.

The two of them shook, but then her attention went to the corpse. "You killed him. I thought I told you to bring him back alive."

"He ambushed me with thermite. I didn't have a choice," Marcus said.

"No matter. You'll simply have to make it up later, Dog. There are dozens of other Rangers out there to capture. I came here for the exo mine, not for bonus rewards. Where are your restraints?"

"Damaged in the fight."

"And your gun?"

"Lost it fighting the AutoSec on the *Phalanx of Starlight*." Felicity would put it to better use than he could.

"Well then, I hope you enjoyed your little excursion here, this taste of freedom. Return to your holding cell," she said, jerking her head towards the crew member behind her.

Charles cleared his throat. "Captain, you were told about the viral outbreak aboard the *Demos*, weren't you?"

Her cold eyes flicked over to him. "I have no reason to be concerned about a mild illness. The *Woab Hammer*'s medical facilities are state of the art."

The CEO put on a smile. "Yes, I just merely wanted to bring to your consideration that you should consider how much exposure you bring to your own crew by bringing Ranger Levy back to your ship. Perhaps it would be wise to portion a place in one of the salvaged ships for a few weeks to let it all sanitize?"

"And who would be the one to bring his meals?"

Charles cleared his throat and let his cheeks color. "In

truth, I would volunteer. I have made some enemies in the last few weeks that I would rather not spend any more time with. I actually need to request asylum from you."

Captain Raven laughed. "For the CEO of The Nebulae Company? I'd be happy to discuss it over dinner. In the meantime..." She turned to her crew mate again. "Take Dog here to one of the personal rooms on the *Grex Ovium* and lock him in it.

"The *Grex*?" Marcus asked. That wouldn't get him away from the others. It would keep him with people who wanted him dead.

"Nothing else has air. Would you rather suffocate?" Captain Raven asked, and she gestured to one of the AutoSecs. "Bring the corpse back to the *Woab Hammer* for inspection."

He was at least glad he had replaced the transponder in Levy's armor. He didn't voice any of his concerns, he simply followed behind the crew mate and floated into the *Grex Ovium*. No one else had boarded it yet, giving the ship the same cemetery air as the *Phalanx of Starlight*. People from Red Cairo had fought aboard the ship in an attempt to rescue them. Nuclear heat had slagged part of the hull into a glossy carapace and a kinetic round and ruptured the core of the ship, venting the air out faster than the life support could replenish it. Hasty repairs had patched it all back together, and the dozen corpses had been dropped into Mimir's gravity well.

Marcus found himself locked in much the same room he had begun the journey on: a guest room for visiting officials to use, down a few corridors from the bridge. There he was locked in with an order to the ship AI. He was strong enough to force the door, but an AutoSec sat outside just in case. They imprisoned him for two days before Captain Raven ordered that he be moved to an acceleration pod on an intervening piece of salvage. It had once been a Camrian vessel. The Svabians had only collected the front half of it, where the nuclear missiles had been kept.

The people had migrated from the *Demos* by then, and dozens saw him. Shouts of "Demon" and "Killer" filled the corridors. The crew of the *Woab Hammer* had managed to procure another set of magnetic manacles and bound his arms before floating him across the ship, which brought jeers from those that noticed.

It wasn't until Nozette caught sight of him that anything particular happened. "They haven't shoved you out a fucking airlock yet, Maximus?"

That made the Svabian officer stop and turn, his brow pinched as he looked at the man. "And who exactly are you?" he asked, a question much more dangerous with a two-ton AutoSec behind him.

Nozette's sneer melted off his face. "Peter Nozette," he said, scratching his jaw and glancing at the murderous machine. "I lived aboard Athens Station until the Camrians blew it up. I was a... bar owner."

Marcus had to suppress his laugh.

The officer didn't flinch a muscle. "And you voted to kill a war asset? Who exactly died and made you king?"

"Kings don't vote. Earth is a... the captain died. He killed the captain!" Nozette sputtered out, swinging a finger at Marcus.

The Ranger turned his gaze to the Svabian. "After I killed the other Ranger, it was easier to assume his identity and lie to the passengers. I thought it would be less friction than telling them I work for the Alliance."

The officer's gaze flicked from Marcus' helmet, to the cuffs on his arms. "Doesn't matter either way, does it, Dog?"

"Wait, wait!" Father Publius shouted, before a coughing fit overcame him. The old priest bumped into a wall and began to twirl through the air as his body convulsed and blood splattered into his hands.

The Svabian reeled back. "I don't have time for this," he said, punching the button to open the next door.

"This man saved our lives. Please, I'm a priest. Might I merely have the time to thank him and pray with him?" the priest begged as the AutoSec shoved Marcus along.

"I'll pass it along to the captain," the Svabian said, and shut the door between them. The next room Marcus was put into was even smaller than the last, and without even the option of going to Link Reality. He hadn't taken the risk before, but the connection's mere existence had comforted him. He had to lay in darkness and wait. No company but his own memories.

Eventually, Charles brought him food for the night, and bad news. "I heard about what Nozette said. Felicity passed it along, though I would have overheard it from Captain Raven anyways. War ships sure are tiny, compared to shuttles, aren't they? Ranger... They're autopsying the corpse. They'll find the difference."

37

Play To Your Outs

The Eighty-Fourth Day

"So, this was your grand plan, Marcus Maximus? Butcher of the *Pharus* and demon of the battlefield?" Captain Atish asked. He had been brought to the bridge of the half-ship, so she could watch him from a proper chair while he stood with magnetic cuffs keeping his feet to the floor in front of her. Some of the engineering techs had welded new cuffs for him, to replace what had been destroyed on Levy's body. What they lacked in elegance, they made up for in bulk. The *Woab Hammer* had no shortage of scrap steel to work with.

"I'd be lying if I said it was working out well," he said, rustling his metal cuffs a bit. They were more attached to his armor than to his body, but it was the AutoSecs that kept him prisoner, regardless. He couldn't destroy another one.

The metal tail Atish had connected to her lashed out and clamped around his throat. Pincers dug into the polymer between shoulders and chin. When it squeezed, it nearly cut through the inner material. "I'm conflicted," she said. "On the one hand, you killed my Dog, and I like my dogs. But on the other hand, I had gotten my use out of him and now I have you in my clutches."

"Were you the one who captured Levy?" He didn't let his voice falter just because of pressure on his throat.

Captain Raven pursed her lips and unscrewed the cap from a bag of water. "No," she said, and drank. "Do I look like a regular force for the Alliance? I'm a marauding conqueror. After the politicians wrang him up all he was worth, they used me to dispose of him... though, I think they imagined he would survive longer and they could use him for something in the future."

"You can only keep someone coerced for so long," Marcus said.

She responded by tightening around his throat and tugging him up. He became stretched between the clasp of his boots to his chin, the strain of his suit tugging at his unhealed skin. "Very true. So tell me, what can I do to coerce you?"

Marcus laughed. "Not a damn thing."

The pressure around his throat vanished and she flicked him away before retracting her tail. "Do you feel like talking, Marcus? I believe I've already given you a taste of isolation. In truth, I find myself quite like the captains of old... unable to connect with my subordinates and with quite a dearth of conversation. My crew, they call me the Dragon. It puts a wall between me and them," she said, giving her tail a forlorn look as it coiled around one of her legs.

He resisted the urge to rub his neck. "I can't imagine

the two of us have much in common that we could actually discuss. I was a war asset of the classified variety. You're not going to get me to talk about any of that."

She rolled her eyes. "Please, we have months until New Gibraltar arrives and about as much time before the *Grex Ovium* can make it to Scythia and send a response. It will be boring. Why don't you tell me about what happened on the *Demos*? What did you do that made you so hated?"

In zero gravity, slumping shoulders isn't quite possible. Certainly not something that can be seen by someone else. He did feel the shift in his own tension though. "I killed Captain Regulus and unsealed the chaos."

"A mutineer as well as a war criminal. Why am I not surprised? Care to tell me why you did that?" she asked.

"Because he wouldn't cooperate with us. His subordinates that is. He tried to lock us out and leave us adrift. I suppose, looking back on things, we would have ended up in the same situation we are now: at your mercy. Still, I shot him to make Sergei Seachnall the captain instead. Standard chain of command."

One of her eyebrows arched up and she licked the water from her lips. "Shot him? With that slug thrower we found in your armor?"

He bristled, gritting his teeth. When the autopsy had come in, so had a very thorough search of him. They had only barely stopped before peeling his suit liner off of him and bleeding him to death. "Yes. With that gun."

"Two bullets were left. Who got the other three?"

"Sergei a few weeks later, after he shot another mutineer.

The fourth went into a civilian who had gone mad with religious fervor. The fifth nearly went into Mr Samaras' head, until you agreed to give him asylum."

"So you killed three people?"

"Yes."

"Any others?" When Marcus didn't answer, she ordered him to take his helmet off and he slowly complied. "How many others did you kill?"

"Hard to say. I didn't follow up on the fates of those I hurt in the riots. About fifty, I'd say. I made the mistake of stopping the mutiny against Sergei when he proved himself incompetent. Plenty of people never forgave me for that."

"Humans can be like that, can't they? Don't you think it's a bit remarkable? We just wrapped up– mostly anyways– a war over the precise boundaries of what constitutes a human. They wanted to draw the line at survivability on Earth, even if they would never see it in their lives. But humans, even the gold standard of gene heredity like you had aboard Athens Station– aboard the *Demos*– couldn't survive with one another."

Marcus sucked in breath and let it out through his nose. "Are you a misanthrope, Captain Raven?"

She twisted her lips into a smirk. "I prefer the term anti-humanist."

"Surely you realize Earth doesn't give a shit about what people make their babies look like. The only thing they cared about was control. Do you want to know the real reason they signed the peace accords?"

That gave her pause and she frowned. "And why is that?"

"Because they realized that the war had pushed you people– the Alliance– into the same hierarchies that Earth has. You made your own interstellar aristocracy like a mirror of Earth. They realized they could just assimilate you now, so they brought you into the fold. Sure, the face of things might change a bit, but nothing about the power will change. In the end, they'll still be in charge."

Captain Raven laughed. "I haven't heard anyone speak like that since this war started. Given what you've done aboard the *Demos*, you'd do the same thing to your old government, wouldn't you?"

Marcus' mouth opened but he couldn't find the words. He didn't know what to say, whether she was right or wrong. Finally, he grasped the one thing and gave it life. "I'd rather just be left alone. I'd rather go far away in time and space and not deal with it at all. That's why I came to Athens Station."

"And the war came to find you again. Very touching. I think you're too dangerous to be left alive."

"What?"

She rose, gliding from her seat to upright before him. "You've been hardened in this isolation," she said, taking a few steps closer. When the difference in their heights became obvious, she planted the tip of her tail and pushed herself up to be eye level with him. "Isn't it obvious? You came a deserter and became a mutineer. I'm a captain. I'm an enemy captain at that. One who is well aware of your track record. I guess I'll have to scrub the records. Do you have a preferred cause of death?"

"For the actual cause or the recorded cause?" he asked,

letting his gaze travel across her body. He didn't hide it in the slightest, nor did he hide the disgust.

"Recorded. I imagine the actual cause will have to be at the hands of the AutoSecs if I can't get you with asphyxiation."

"What makes you think I won't kill you right now then? If you're saying you're going to kill me."

She laughed. "Because I know how you Rangers think. You don't give up for as long as there is a chance at succeeding. If you kill me, the AutoSecs will kill you and you won't stand a chance. I saw the pictures of what you look like inside this suit. Like blood soup. Until I give that order, you have a chance of finding a solution, so you won't so much as lay a finger on me. Welcome to the *Woab Hammer*, Demon of the *Demos*." She turned and pushed herself towards the door out, flying through the air.

"If I'm a demon, what does that make you? The one who brought me aboard and chained me up?"

Her hand landed on the wall to stop herself and she smiled over her shoulder. "Didn't I tell you? I'm the dragon and I hoard something much more valuable than gold. I hoard people and fuel."

"Not much of a hoard if you're sending all the people off to Scythia."

"I took the only two worth taking. The rest are chaff. They can go. I much prefer the ship that didn't destroy itself. They'll make excellent resources for my newly conquered star system. Don't you think?"

The last of the survivors were still out there. The *Demos* was under her control. The *Chase* had been shot down. The

Theopone crashed. The *Phalanx of Starlight* suffocated. The *Blue Andalusian* was still untouched and hiding on the far side of the star. Captain Raven lingered at the door, taking her time before cycling it open. The words he had to say were like bile in his throat. They burned his tongue as they passed his lips. "You need someone to go get them, don't you."

She smiled. "Come now. I only send my dogs to fetch the things I want."

He tried for a moment to rip free of his arm bindings, but couldn't. "It would keep me alive though, wouldn't it? You said it yourself. Rangers do whatever it takes to accomplish their goal, even if it means working with someone like you."

"Excellent answer, Dog."

38

Regicide

The Eighty-Seventh Day

"Last meal and a priest. You'd think they could be more subtle, wouldn't you?" Father Publius asked as he pulled himself into a seat in the mess hall with Marcus and strapped himself to a chair.

The Ranger looked up from his meal in surprise. The Svabians at least knew how to feed a man properly. He had eaten over a kilo of meat and potatoes, quaffed weak beer till his head went light, and was actually looking forward to hours of isolation to sleep it all off. "This isn't my last meal. Or they told you something they haven't told me. How did you get in here?"

The priest's eyes glinted until he coughed and quickly covered his mouth with a rag. "Well, while I was on the new ship, they said they were killing you. There was much too much rejoicing. When they let me off to see to your rights,

Captain Raven said it was merely your last meal as a human instead of her hound. Still, here I am."

"Ah," Marcus said, and lowered his head to continue eating.

"Not very enthused about your new lot in life?"

"It's about what I deserve after how the *Demos* went down. And to save myself, I'm going to have to doom a whole lot more people," Marcus said.

The priest frowned and folded his hands on the table across from him. The lighting in the warship's galley was poor and cast deep shadows over his eyes when he leaned closer. "I know you're not particularly religious, Marcus. But I did want to speak to you about the riots."

His fork dropped from his hand, bouncing off the bowl and careening away. He could have grabbed it, but he just let it go.

"After Hadria's death, the incident in the mess hall, you see, I made it a point to speak to everyone who witnessed it. I got all of their stories and corroborations and did my best to console the survivors, like Maria. And the words I gave them aren't quite what I will give you. Marcus, you did everything I think you could have done. It's not your fault that you became their image of fear. The fault lies with Hadria's murderer, if anyone."

The Ranger met the priest's gaze and sighed. "The original mistake is still mine though. I shouldn't have sided with Sergei over Ray. I didn't properly evaluate the wisdom he had from his years of service. It all happened because of my choices."

Father Publius tried to smile, but there was a quiver in his lip. Another cough cleared the emotional tumult and he continued, "Ray had his share in the fault. But I know you weren't simply thinking of yourself when you took those actions. You need to remember that yourself. Besides, you can't atone for anything if you're dead. You've got plenty of time to make up for your mistakes."

Marcus scoffed. "I don't think you realize how many years of mistakes I have."

Father Publius nodded. "Oh, I suspect even in biological years, you're older than me, Marcus. But, as a proportion of your life, you might be younger than Miz Lenz."

Marcus gestured at the room. "Well, my life just became nasty, brutish, and short."

There was a fraction of a smirk on the priest's face. "Some time ago, you told me that you ask for forgiveness when you understand the consequences..."

Marcus hung his head. He jabbed his fork into a piece of meat and left it there. The juices ran like blood. "Are you offering to absolve me of the mutiny? I thought the sulfur of Hell was upon me."

The priest was smirking. "Well, that will be true until you repent and atone, don't you think? But, I don't see why that should trouble you so much. Of everyone here. Not just here, this ship, but this entire star system, I can think of no one with more capacity to atone in the worldly sense."

"My actions got hundreds of people killed."

"Then you have a lot of work to do."

"It's going to get worse too. The way I am now, my only choices are between piling on the mistakes, or dying."

"We all die someday."

Marcus lifted his head. "I might be old and a killer, but I'm still afraid to die."

"Then you'll have to find a third option. That's your specialty, right?"

The Ranger could only shake his head. "Isn't the Grex Ovium about to depart?"

The priest wetted his lips and glanced over his shoulder. Beyond the door he had come from was an AutoSec. "Yes, they've finished checking it over for faults and have gotten everything into working order. We should be able to make it to Scythia."

"They still going to kill the schemer?"

"Unfortunately."

"Shame it won't be my gun that kills him. An airlock is good enough though. I'm pretty sure he's the one who killed Hadria," he said, eyes unfocused and his mind imagining the mutant clawing at his throat in the vacuum of space.

"Do you have anything you'd like to pass along to people on the ship?" the priest asked.

Marcus stared at the remains of his meal for a while. "Just tell Felicity that I'm sorry. Sorry for what I said aboard the *Phalanx of Starlight*. It was dumb and thoughtless of me."

A smile appeared on the priest's face, the kind of grin a magician puts on as he reveals his trick. "Miz Lenz? You can tell her that yourself. She's taken asylum alongside her former employer here on the *Woab Hammer*."

Marcus blinked and watched the priest unfasten himself from the seat, after having only visited for a moment. "She's going to be here with me?"

"Indeed. You know, these warships really are a curious thing, don't you think? For all the weapons they have, almost everything is controlled by a shackled artificial intelligence. Only a few dozen souls and two machine brutes. They have to rely on cameras and automatic doors... Felicity said she'd be at one of the viewing windows, watching Mimir if you wanted to go and find her. Now, I've heard your confessions. We're different sects, so figure out your own prayers, but do them before an electric cross."

What the hell is an electric cross?

The priest shoved off to the door and said, "Now if you'll excuse me, I need to be escorted back to the Grex Ovium." He opened it up and waved at the AutoSec, which chased after him.

For a moment, Marcus, prisoner aboard the *Woab Hammer*, was unwatched and his restraints unactivated. Captain Raven had wanted to take him out of his suit, but her medical staff had simply laughed. They had likened it to taking the shell off a raw egg and expecting to not spill. A long series of choices and coincidences had left him almost free. There was only the threat of death, and that came from the AutoSecs.

Marcus slammed his boot into the table, launching himself in the opposite direction. There were only a handful of residential areas with oxygen in the whole construct, and he only knew of one viewing window: the meeting room for the captain's quarters.

Memories nearly four months old resurfaced: the day the two of them had met during the approach. The view out the window was horrid compared to the ice clouds that had once cloaked Mimir's core. It was a wretched ball of lightning and lava that boiled any ice that fell to it. The room itself was an ugly thing of Camrian aesthetics, built for their compressed frames and club fingers.

The entire room shuddered when the Grex Ovium detached from the construct. They must have barely given Father Publius time to close the door behind him before beginning their descent into the gravity well and firing up their A-Mov engine. With their separation, it became a near certainty that he would never see them again, be it through distance or time, the fate of the *Demos* went on without him and without those aboard the *Woab Hammer*.

Felicity held herself at the wall, one hand to the enormous observation window that gazed out to the ruined planet. She had on new clothes, a sleek fashion from the Svabians that looked far more fitting on her, without the body armor Atish clad herself with. The sight he took in, silhouetted by the window, was the most enticing thing he had seen in years.

Lost for words, he walked over step by step, peeling off pieces of his armor to slip the restraints. The inner liner tore off with them, stripping skin and scab and leaving him limbs raw and bleeding. The touch of air burned, but it didn't kill.

"You know," she said, facing out the window for the first time at a Mimir she had never seen before in her life. "When we first met, you told me about the kinds of problems that you could deal with and the kinds you couldn't. So I thought I should help in some way."

"I owe you multiple apologies," he said, saying each word slowly as his eyes soaked in what he was looking at. It made his hands tremble and his heart pound. It dried out his mouth and intoxicated him with ideas.

Felicity laughed. "It took four months for me to see what you look like? Marcus, I know you're old, but isn't that a little too conservative?"

He grinned and held up his hands. They hurt where the mag-lock restaurants had been. His knuckles had been split to the bone after fighting on the *Phalanx of Starlight*, but his palms still looked good. He could still ball them into fists, and he could still grab on. "I'll have to make it up to you."

She smiled over her shoulder at him. "I think you owe me more than mere apologies." Then she kicked over what he had been staring at.

He had been ordered to pray before an electric cross, and he finally understood what Father Publius had meant. Marcus wouldn't have called it an electric cross though. The magazine only stuck out from the bottom, an incomplete cruciform at best. Marcus would have called it a railgun able to give him a fighting chance against the AutoSecs.

The weapon Levy had brought with him to the *Demos* flew into Marcus' hands. He had no idea how Felicity had smuggled it over, but it was loaded, charged, and ready for action. His hands trembled in pain and anticipation as he held it. "I suppose this is the kind of problem I'm an expert at," he said, and loaded a slug into the chamber.

Epilogue

Halfway between the ecliptic plane and the Fuls-Hades-1, an object slightly smaller than a coffin turned on a distress beacon. Amid the radioactive debris of the Scythian craft that had brought it, it pinged out radio waves to ask why it had been forgotten.

James likes to think about worlds that don't exist. Growing up on a diet of video games, anime, and the internet, ending up as an engineer was accidental. At least it helps write about computer systems and robots. The covid pandemic re-ignited his childhood dream of being an author, dating back to when he was a child sitting on his grandfather's knee making up stories. Now, he has a head full of stories he wants to tell, and the freedom to do so.

Check the website for the latest releases. Jameskrake.com

Government surveillance is a wonderful thing, isn't it? If someone tries to kill you in your own apartment, police and EMS will get dispatched to help right away. They can even fly in a hunter-killer drone to take the guy out. So... why didn't that happen? Why did the city AI not even know there was a corpse rotting in this apartment next to a half finished VR game?

Detective Blackstone is the man for the job, because, well, it's this or get in another fight with his wife as she languishes in a not-quite-successful streaming career. The only real question is, what's worse? The half-employed scum at the bottom of the city, itching for their next drug high? Or the half-useful elites wallowing in their own corruption?

Faceless
BASTION/Blackstone Book I

2140/09/03

Elliot trudged onward, in a world lit by advertisements and cigarettes. He descended rattling stairs and slogged through splashes of mud with one eye on his WPS map. Navigation to the stiff had failed, again. It was updating and buffering and apologizing for its failure to function, while he skirted neon pools and tripped over drip buckets.

Should have trusted my gut.

His nose wrinkled when he recognized the train station he passed underneath. He had known it was closer. He had known that, and still listened to the misguidance of his WPS map.

Rain pounded on the glass awnings overhead, the drizzle of static like a dying speaker. Rain never fell on the ground in Bastion. Whether it was bridges, signs, power cables or train lines, something hung overhead, covering the ground with unchecked growth.

Elliot jabbed his thumb on the map to no avail. The program apologized for low bandwidth. "EVE, come on. First you can't talk to me, now you can't even navigate me?"

He glanced up, to the strata of city above where air could still circulate. A trickle of data flowed down, alongside the rain. Water gushed from cracks and gutters between the sky-scrapers, carrying the echoes of the city.

While he was staring in the direction of his own apartment, his phone chimed and glowed blue. It had triangulated with all the wireless routers. The light colored his face with the triumphant order, "Turn left."

Elliot was faced with a huge sheet of corrugated steel, fused into place with construction foam. It rattled like paper with the merest gust of wind from the storm. Ripped from a life as a security shutter, someone had given it new life to cordon off the alley into a shanty. Grime and paint sealed the segments shut. Someone had come by to add some beauty. They had graffitied onto it a woman blowing off her own head with a cellphone-turned-pistol. The artist's signature took the place of the woman's face.

After waiting all day, I at least hope they won't mind another fifteen minutes.

Elliot pressed the button on his phone to report the obstruction and waited until a new route was presented. "Go forward, then turn left," it said. That brought him to a better maintained passage. Calling it a road would have been over-stating it, but the path essentially led into a shopping mall through the bottom floor of a tower. The floor was dry and the shelves full. The gate, however, was locked shut before him and manned by a computer.

"Welcome to Romulus Shopping Center Seven," the digi-tal mascot announced. The primary arms manufacturer in

Bastion currently had a cartoon girl with dog ears and a fluffy tail as their representative. The mascot smiled and saluted. She said, "This area is private property of the Romulus Corporation, and we'd be happy to let you visit. For record keeping purposes please-"

Elliot stuffed his badge up to the camera. The computer stuttered as it skipped scripts. "Welcome officer. Is there anything I can assist you with today?"

"Just passing through. I've got a case on the other side," he said, and shoved through the turnstile gate. The mall didn't sell guns, despite the landlord. People from the apartments above passed between stalls of food and drinks, clothes and neural uplinks. They heard the wet slap of his boots as he marched through, and stared at him. Some merely gawked, others ducked behind walls or slipped out doors. More than one snapped pictures of him before he could get out the other side of the mall. None of them were happy to see him, his uniform.

His WPS led him out from the corporate protection and back into the wet slum. He found a utility staircase with the door broken down so anyone could use it, and ascended to the third floor. "You have arrived," it said whence he stood outside Apartment 314. The door yielded to him, unlocked. Rot seeped through the doorway.

"Well, I'll be damned. A cop actually showed up," an older woman said. She had black hair streaked with grey pulled into a bun. The coat she wore had once been tailored to her, but clearly her waist wasn't so slim as it had been.

Must be the landlady.

"Did I get here before the compost crew?" he asked.

She shrugged and dug through a coat pocket. Out came a cigarette, which she lit and puffed on. "They're running late too. I guess I should call them off. Didn't think you'd actually show up... You never have before." She frowned and waved her hand through the smoke.

Always nice to see people happy to see me...

"Well, here I am," he said, and flashed his badge: E11107. "Detective Blackstone, Military Police. You can call me Elliot. Please keep the smoke outside."

She squinted at him. "Why? You actually want to smell that filth? Just walking near it makes my nose close up. It's giving me wrinkles is what it's doing. I'd sue him for medical expenses if I could."

Well, isn't that a charming personality.

Elliot grimaced. "You never know, a good nose might help find something."

"Is it just you, then? No partner? They deigned to send one of you down here, but not a pair?" she asked, eyeing him as he reached for the door again.

No way Cinder would put two people on this case.

He sighed. "It's just me tonight," he said, and opened the door.

Now then, what was the cause? Money? Love? Hate? Where's the betting money tonight?

Calling it an apartment was only correct in the literal sense. The bed, down at the moment and covered in sweat-stained sheets, folded into the wall. Its central position cut the room in half. Beside Elliot and the door sat a microwave on top of a mini-fridge. Beyond was the room's only seat; the toilet. The John Doe laid across the floor in the middle, filling the air with eye-watering decay.

At first, he thought the buzzing was some off-kilter cooling fan, but as his eyes adjusted to the gloom, he saw the flies swarming in the air. The insects orbited the gas-bloated body, diving in to bite at the soft bits of flesh. They—and the maggots—had eaten the face off.

How am I supposed to find a cause of death like this?

Elliot pulled a few things out of his jacket. First, he powered on a pocket-drone. The little quad copter lifted into the air and began streaming omni-directional video back to the office servers. It stuttered every few moments; when one of the blades cut a fly from the air. Then, he pulled a nitrile glove on.

He stepped into the black filth dripping out of the corpse, and folded the bed back into the wall so he could inspect the body better. The face was unidentifiable; he had no hope that EVE would be able to piece it together after the maggots had feasted. He didn't handle the body too much, lest the skin tear and the filth erupt. He did, however, run his fingers across the back of the head. His fingers found no sign of a neural implant.

No sensory log then...

Quelling his rolling stomach, he checked the corpse's pockets. He found pre-filled credit chips, but no wallet. The man didn't even have a phone, just a fitness tracker watch.

Who would steal a phone but not money?

The detective grumbled and stood up. The computer desk

—what had been improvised as one—was beside the toilet, so he had to step over the bloated body. Empty energy drink cans clattered from the sweep of his step. The aluminum debris was the only sign of a struggle.

The John Doe's computer was still on, the little fan fighting dust so thick it looked like moss. No webcam peered back at him for EVE to break into. Elliot took a seat on the toilet and invaded the man's privacy. No social media was pulled up, nor an email account. There were no online games, just some old school stand-alones. The one thing on the computer was a 3D rendering program with the message, "Rendering Complete."

Talk about a privacy freak... Was he trying to make my life hard?

Elliot phoned into the office and got through to his boss. "I'm at the 314 death. I'm going to need a cleanup crew down here to get the body in for DNA testing and a cause of death."

Chief Alissa Cinder was only a year older than him, and he was reminded of the disparity whenever he heard her voice. "Can't you just take some hair and dump the body in compost? This is a waste of fucking time. Nobody cares about a John Doe down on the ground." She still swore like she was overseas.

Elliot meandered his gaze away from the computer and paraphernalia, back to the ballooning corpse. "At least send a doctor to give an official opinion on cause of death."

"What? You can't see one? Is anything stolen?"

"Money is still here, his computer wasn't even touched.

The thing's been idling for…" He looked at the state of the corpse again. "About a week, I'd say. Seems that he kicked the bucket right as he finished his new VR avatar or something."

"Hold on, I'm getting the feed," Alissa said, and a moment later he heard her gagging. "Blackstone, get the hell out of there. This is a waste of resources."

The detective scratched his chin. Taped to the wall hung an eight terabyte hard drive hooked up to the computer. The John Doe had written on it with a marker, [The Faceless Well]. Elliot pulled up the file explorer to check it. The computer's partitions had just been reset; the bare minimum for the operating system and rendering program on the first drive, enormous modeling outputs in the rest of the space. The drive labeled [The Faceless Well] didn't open; encrypted shut.

Shit Mr. Doe, if you were going to be this greedy, why didn't you get a better computer?

"Come on, Boss. Something's weird here. If he died a week ago, why weren't there any EMS alerts? Why did it take until the landlady called it in a week later?"

"Submit a bug report to EVE and get out of there."

He shook his head. "Come on boss, it's not like I'm getting paid time and a half here or something." At the same time, he tried accessing the encrypted drive. An executable ran when he booted it, and an error popped up that no VR system was connected.

Must be a game.

"Look, Blackstone, the John Doe overdosed on energy drinks, had a heart attack and died because he lived alone. End of story. I've got a hundred other things you could be doing that would be more beneficial for the department than this. Nobody cares about some delinquent renter."

The landlady does, I'm sure. More than she cares about me anyways.

"Hey, Cinder, these people down here don't see a cop but once in a blue moon. What are they going to think if the one time they do, the case just gets written off and ignored?"

She didn't respond for a while, but eventually she sighed and relented. "Fine, I'll request an EMT assessment and some DNA testing; but, the body is getting composted, not taken to a hospital. Finish up and get out of there before you get sick. And get me a report on why EVE didn't get him an ambulance in time. They probably broke the cameras or something."

"Understood," he said, and ended the call. He reached down and pressed the control button on the John Doe's watch. It booted up and showed a flatline, zero beats per minute.

EVE should have been able to see that, no cameras neces-sary... Well then, for me it's back to motive.

The drone powered off and he put it away. He stuffed his phone back in his pocket too, and took the hard drive for good measure. Closing the door behind him stymied the outflow of the smell, but his clothes had absorbed it. "So who was the guy?" he asked as he walked over to the landlady.

She crossed her arms and shrugged. "I don't remember. I own a hundred of these apartments and if I tried to keep track of every burnout that misses his rent, I'd have no time for myself."

The apartment block grew around the base of the tower, like a thick coating applied to the bottom twenty floors. The rest of the tower's eighty floors reached up to the sky from the middle of it, beyond the reach of those below. The bridges and railings were some of the thinnest and most rusted pieces of construction he had ever seen. "Then how do you keep track of them?"

"Automatically," she answered with a flick of her hand. "They pay rent to keep me from putting a hit out on their credit rating. Works for people who care about that sort of thing. Those that don't, they don't stay here long."

Elliot hooked a thumb over his shoulder. "So pull up your system and tell me who the guy was."

She suddenly found her fingernails interesting. "That one, he pre-paid with a credit chip. He wasn't in the system."

"Right... so you weren't coming after him for rent, therefore you have no idea who he was?"

"I knew him, when he moved in a few months ago. He didn't cause problems and didn't leave much, so I forgot. Is that a crime?"

"No, I suppose it's not," he answered. "So he didn't get visitors? I can't imagine he entertained anyone in a room of that size. Looked to me like he was some kind of game designer?"

The landlady crossed her arms again and pursed her lips. "For someone with a ring on their finger, I figured you would know better than to think women ever get brought back here. The people here? Their only intimacy is digital, and pay by the minute."

Elliot squeezed his hand into a ball and covered his wedding band with his thumb. He pressed on the metal ring till his knuckle cracked. "It's always worth asking the question."

She scoffed and sucked on her cigarette. "Don't act like I'm going to be offended. I know what service I'm providing and to who I offer it to. The lowest scum in the city, the biggest rejects and losers. The kind of people who die and no one notices for a week. But, this one only paid to the end of last month. That room ain't worth much, but it's still my property to rent out, so... Officer, when is the filth getting cleaned up so I can get a new renter?"

A sexual pauper, but not a debtor. I guess that leaves hatred as a cause.

Elliot pulled his phone out and checked the time; quarter to midnight. "They'll be here in the morning. Thank you for your cooperation. If you can think of anything useful, you can access the web portal at any time," he said and brushed past her to head back down the steps.

He returned to the street, to where dust had turned to dirt and little weeds eked out a living between vending machines and broken signs. The floor of Bastion was concrete striped with steel— a skin over top the infrastructure— and the rain churned the dirt into mud. Plenty of the refuse would wash away to the river and vanish from the city. Some of it would find safe harbor in the stores that did the same for the people.

As with anywhere in Bastion, he only had to turn his head

up and look to find the cameras watching him. Three of them stared back at him blind. Paint covered one lens, another had been snapped off at the stem, and the last had dirty laundry dangling from the balcony above. EVE couldn't see a thing.

The stores and corporations like Romulus had their own cameras though, and they were harder to deface. Elliot began his investigation the hard way.

www.ingramcontent.com/pod-product-compliance
Lightning Source LLC
Chambersburg PA
CBHW071938210726
48293CB00001BA/207